CHANGE MY LIFE

KNOX COUNTY
BOOK 3

RACHAEL OGLE

Change My Life © 2023 by Rachael Ogle

All rights reserved.

ISBN: 979-8-9919576-7-0 (paperback)

CONTENTS

Author's Note   vii

Chapter 1   1
Ophelia

The Confessions of Ivy Sinn   9

Chapter 2   12
Jess

Chapter 3   25
Ophelia

Chapter 4   35
Ophelia

Chapter 5   44
Jess

The Confessions of Ivy Sinn   53

Chapter 6   55
Jess

Chapter 7   65
Ophelia

Chapter 8   75
Jess

Chapter 9   84
Jess

Chapter 10   92
Ophelia

Chapter 11   102
Jess

The Confessions of Ivy Sinn   109

Chapter 12   111
Ophelia

Chapter 13   119
Jess

Chapter 14   127
Jess

Chapter 15   134
Ophelia

Chapter 16   144
Jess

Chapter 17   150
Jess

Chapter 18   160
Ophelia

Chapter 19   173
Jess

Chapter 20   181
Ophelia

Chapter 21   192
Jess

Chapter 22   201
Ophelia

Chapter 23   212
Ophelia

Chapter 24   224
Jess

Chapter 25   235
Ophelia

Chapter 26   244
Jess

The Confessions of Ivy Sinn   247

Chapter 27   251
Jess

Chapter 28   254
Ophelia

Chapter 29   262
Jess

Chapter 30   269
Ophelia

Chapter 31   285
Ophelia

Chapter 32   294
Jess

Chapter 33   304
Ophelia
Epilogue   311

Also by Rachael Ogle   317
About the Author   319

AUTHOR'S NOTE

Dear Reader,

As always, I strive to be transparent when disclosing my content and trigger warnings.

YOUR MENTAL HEALTH MATTERS!

And I'll be honest, when I started this book, although I knew there would be elements of **religious trauma**, I don't think I realized until I was going through the edits how cathartic this book was for me in working through my own trauma. So, Ophelia's evangelical religious trauma plays a huge role in this book; as does purity culture.

There are also themes dealing with the realities that families—and the children who grow up in extreme purity culture and a religious patriarchal upbringing—sometimes encounter.

Some of the things included within these pages are **forced birth** (not of MC, historical, and off-page), **postpartum depression** (not MC), **body shaming**, **self-loathing**, **traumatic childbirth and miscarriage/stillbirth** (not of MC, historical, and off-page), **homophobia/bi-**

phobia (not MC), and **death of a parent** (off-page, historical).

Take care of yourself. No book is worth risking your mental health; even mine.

Much love,

Rach

CHAPTER ONE

OPHELIA

I don't know much about my new roommate, Jess. Well, except for the fact that he has a beautiful dick. I mean, from what I can remember when I was fifteen. And maybe it really wasn't beautiful. He was far away and had a girl's head in his lap at the time, after all. But the few instances she came up for air, I got a glimpse.

And in hind site, I realize the fact that I was watching a couple engage in oral sex for more than just the initial "oh my God, some girl giving a guy head in the park where I run every day" would probably land me firmly in the peeping Thomasina category. But in my defense, they were in public. Legally, there is no expectation of privacy in a public setting. So, really, who were the creepers in this situation?

But back to the beautiful dick. Never mind that it was the first one I'd ever seen outside of an outdated science textbook we had at home. Let's also not dwell on the fact that I was firmly ensconced in extreme purity culture at the time. And no, I have no trauma at all from being told my entire life that sex is sinful and dirty outside of the confines of marriage, but that I would be expected to turn into a wanton goddess on my wedding night to satisfy my husband. None, whatsoever.

Having seen Jess Tate—although back then, I didn't know his name, of course—receiving a blowjob in the park, it wasn't the act itself that fascinated me. To be sure, I was plenty fascinated and the feelings watching the act elicited were what I now recognize as arousal, as well as confusion. But I'd always been told that for women, sex was a "duty" and something to be endured, but the girl with Jess sure seemed to be enjoying herself. It was more the way this hot guy looked at her, with something like appreciation and affection and maybe even love that struck my naïve heart.

If sex was dirty and sinful, why did his face look like that? Why did they look like they were both enjoying it so much? And were all penises that nice looking? I now know this is very much not the case. In fact, I know a lot of things now that would make fifteen-year-old me faint dead away if she could only see what thirty-year-old me gets up to most days.

I certainly didn't plan on becoming Jess's roommate; it was a total fluke. I didn't even know Jess was Park Blowjob Guy when I saw the flyer for the room to rent on the board at work. But student loans aren't gonna pay themselves; especially when you get a degree that you don't even end up using because you decide a year into teaching that you absolutely hate it and it's much too people-y for you to do for the rest of your adult life. So, instead, you get a job in the records office of a hospital where you're making barely above minimum wage, but you are almost entirely alone.

It's paradise.

My parents are so proud of all of my life choices. At least, that's what the parents in my mind say. In real life, my parents don't say anything. Not for nine years. And lord help me if they ever find out about *the other thing*. Brimstone and hellfire would probably rain from the sky and I'd be burned at the stake or publicly flogged or something equally antiquated and primitive.

But more on that later.

Working in the records room is a nine-to-five job, and I hardly see other hospital staff members. Usually, I even take my lunch alone. I walk the same route every day from the records room to the cafeteria to eat my ham and Swiss with mayo on whole wheat, an apple, and carrots with ranch. I sit at the same table and don't talk to anyone. I am invisible.

But a few weeks ago, I noticed a flyer on the bulletin board. It was bright orange and had tabs at the bottom with a phone number and a note saying "calls only". I almost thought it was some sort of joke, simply because I hadn't seen a flyer like this since college. In this current day, who advertises for a roommate on a flyer? Did this J. Tate person not know that stalkers and serial killers exist?

I read it and noticed the neighborhood listed was only ten minutes from the hospital—a shit-ton closer than my current apartment and about the same price for rent. J. Tate's flyer said they were open to a roommate of any gender, they were pet and LGBTQ+ friendly, smokers need not apply, and bonus points if the applicant worked at the hospital.

Knowing my lease on my current apartment was about to be up, I hoped it was some sort of sign and I immediately called the number, a deep, masculine voice answering on the third ring. "Hello?" He sounded like I'd woken him up and I immediately felt bad, but it was after noon, so plenty late to conduct business.

I cleared my throat before speaking. "Yes, I'm calling about the flyer. The room to rent; is it still available?"

J. Tate cleared his own throat. "Oh. Yeah. Wow, that was

fast. I just put that up this morning. Do you work at the hospital?"

"Yes. In records. Is that a problem?"

"No. Would it just be you? Do you have pets or a spouse or anything?"

"No, just me. And do pets rank higher than spouses?"

He huffed a laugh. "Sometimes, I think. Can I get your name?"

"Oh. Right. Ophelia. Ophelia Danvers."

"Okay, Ophelia. I'm assuming you'll want to come look at the house and room and stuff before you commit. I have to work tonight, but I'm free about five if you can come today."

"Sure. I get off at five, so it might be a few minutes after. Is that alright?"

I really hoped it wouldn't be a deal breaker.

"That's fine. I can text you the address. Is this a good number?"

"Yeah. That'd be great. And what was your name? On the flyer it just says J. Tate."

"It's Jess."

"And you also work at the hospital?"

He yawned, reminding me I'd woken him up and I vow to wrap the call up so he can return to his sleep. "Yeah. I'm a surgical tech."

"Okay. Well, I'll see you a little after five."

And I'd shown up, only to be greeted by Park Blowjob Guy.

Obviously, he had no clue who I was, but as seeing him and the girl that day was my sexual awakening, so to speak, I've never forgotten his face or what it looked like when he got off. Not even fifteen years later.

Luckily, my poker face is solid, and I reminded myself that I'm a grown-ass woman and Jess is not the guy from the park. No, apparently we work together and possibly have for years.

And who knows, maybe Jess's penis isn't still beautiful all these years later, but he sure is. Although taller—from what I could surmise with him in a sitting position—and more filled out than he was at about twenty, he's much the same as he was fifteen years ago. His hair is still thick, and he still wears it stylishly messy, and other than the beginnings of gray starting to creep in at the temples, his dark brown hair is still exactly the way I remember. And now that I'm not a hundred feet away, transfixed by the sight of him receiving a blow job, I can appreciate his chiseled jaw, full lips, and green eyes that have a ring of gold around the pupil.

He showed me around the small colonial in a nice neighborhood with a fenced-in backyard and top-of-the-line kitchen appliances and a newly remodeled bathroom. "Rent includes utilities, too. My previous roommate and I always split the utilities, but it was pretty much the same every month, so I just averaged what those are and worked it in."

"Oh, okay. And it's just you?"

"Yeah. My girlfriend has her own place and travels a lot for work, but she's here some. I mostly work nights, but occasionally pick up other shifts, so my schedule can be sorta wonky. And I'm gonna assume if you work at the hospital, your background is clean."

I nodded. "Yeah. I don't do drugs or drink much, either. I can pay first and last month's rent and can provide references from some of my colleagues."

"Okay. And you don't have an issue with having a male roommate? Some women do."

I shake my head. "No. I'm assuming if you work at the hospital, your background is clean?"

He smiled and God, it was a great smile and made something in my belly clench to see it. I was immediately reminded of the way he looked at the girl and the smile he gave her.

"Touché. Yeah, clean background. I also don't do drugs and I'm too tired to drink more than half a beer most of the time. If you want, I can give you the number of my last roommate. She's a good friend, but she wouldn't lie about me being easy to live with. She'd probably tell you I keep odd hours and she went days without seeing me. Do you have any questions?"

"My current lease isn't up for a few more weeks. Would you be able to hold the room?"

"Sure. That's no problem. Do you have any food allergies I should be aware of or anything like that?"

I shake my head. "No. You?"

"No. Also, I don't have issues with you bringing guys or girls or whomever home. I just ask that you keep the noise level respectful. This is a pretty quiet neighborhood. The HOA tends to get a little pissy about raucous parties."

"No worries there."

"Okay. Well, I'll email you the paperwork and if you can get that filled out, we'll be good to go."

And somehow, a month later, I'm settled into my room at Park Blowjob Guy's house. Every time I see him in passing—which is sporadic at best with the hours he keeps—I remind myself his name is not, in fact, Park Blowjob Guy. His name is Jess. When he's around, I mentally chant it, lest my living situation get real awkward real quick.

If I see him, it's only as I'm heading out the door to the hospital in the mornings when he's coming home or as he's leaving just as I'm returning. It is the epitome of ships passing in the night, but I don't mind. As it's well established, Ophelia likes her solitude. And him being gone so much allows me ample free time for *the other thing*.

The other thing, AKA, *The Confessions of Ivy Sinn*, is my outlet. And "Ivy" has hundreds of monthly subscribers who like to listen to her get herself off and share her stories. I thought for sure, by now, it would have fizzled, but it hasn't. So every week, like an actual job, I upload content.

Tonight is no exception. As is my custom on Friday nights, I setup my equipment next to the bed—a decent quality external mic hooked into my laptop along with lube and my vibrator—before settling into a long bath with a couple of glasses of wine.

Once I'm fully relaxed, I climb from the tub and head to my room, dressed only in a towel since I'm home alone. I hit the record button before dropping the towel and lying on the bed. And as I begin every session, I simply let my hands skim over my body and pretend there is someone else with me in the room, watching in the corner—because exhibitionism is apparently one of my kinks—and talk to the unknown person about the fantasy I envision.

THE CONFESSIONS OF IVY SINN
EPISODE 72: THE DAM BREAKS

I thought about you at work today. I wondered if today would be the day you actually did more than simply watch me from across the office. I wondered if today would be the day you'd come up behind me and, without even speaking, would push me down on my desk and pull up my skirt. Did you know I've stopped wearing panties to work?

My nipples are so hard; would you lick them? Take the ache away?

I stopped wearing panties in the hopes that when you push my skirt up, you'll remind me what a dirty girl I am for being in public with no underwear.

I'm also not wearing any now. I'm lying in bed, and God, I'm pressing my thighs together. I wish you were here to touch me. I wish you were here to just barely touch my clit; to tease me.

Would you spank me for tempting you at work? Would I be forced to wear your handprint for the rest of the day like a badge of honor? Or would you have to do more than simply look and touch?

I had to sneak away and touch myself during my morning

break, just like I'm doing now. Imagining you so overcome with the need for me, you wouldn't care who might walk in at any moment. I'm so wet just thinking about it.

While I was bent over, would run your hand between my legs so you could feel how wet I am? Would it make you hard to know exactly how soaked I am for you? Fuck, my pussy is throbbing. Can I touch it? Would you like that? Would you give me permission, or deny me? Something tells me you'd want to see for yourself.

And because you're wearing that tie I like—the one with the stripes—and because I couldn't stop touching myself, you'd have to take it off and tie my hands behind my back so I'd be a good girl.

Would you touch me? Or, would you just need to pull out that fat cock of yours and finally fuck me? I mean, you've been eye-fucking me for months, so something tells me we're both more than ready, right?

I have to touch it. Jesus, it's aching. I need it so bad. Can you hear these moans that are just for you? I bet you'd have to cover my mouth to keep me from alerting everyone in the office.

I've wanted it for so long; to finally have you inside me. To watch you finally lose control and take what's yours. Fuck, you'd probably stretch and fill me so good, I'd scream. And don't worry, I can take it. You don't have to be gentle with me.

You can even pull my hair. I bet you've been dying to see what it looks like down. Would finally watching that final bit of my professional persona fall away be the thing that pushes you over? Or would you also need to see my mascara running down my cheeks and my lipstick smeared to really feel as though I was truly well fucked?

Oh, Jesus. I'm so close already. Are you loud during sex? I hope you are. I hope you'd tell me I'm being good for you. I want to be good for you. I promise, I can be so good for you. Fuck. Oh, God.

I need you to get there. Please, I want you to fill me up. I want to be forced to feel your cum leaking out of me for hours. Shit. I'm gonna come. Do you want to hear it? Will you come with me?

Oh, Fuck. Fuck. Fuck. Fuck. Yes. That's it. Please, I want you to come with me. I'm coming. Shit.

Thank you for hearing my confession.

CHAPTER TWO

JESS

Being a landlord wasn't originally in the cards for me. And in truth, it's not something I *have* to do. But until Brooklyn finally agrees to move in with me or we get married, having the second source of income is nice. And having lived with Josie, I discovered I enjoy having a roommate. She was a great one and I can only hope Ophelia will be, too.

In the week since she moved in, I've only seen her for a few minutes at a time. She doesn't eat my food, and she picks up after herself, so honestly, it feels like she's not even there.

And although we've worked together for who knows how long, I've never seen her around the hospital. Of course, I'm firmly ensconced on the surgical floor overnight while she's in the records department during the day, so it's no wonder we'd never met before the day she came to look at the house.

I'd only put the flyer up that morning as I was leaving the hospital, so the fact that I got a call so quickly was kind of surprising. And yeah, I could've posted something on social media about the room like I'd done when Josie eventually became my roommate, but I'm really not a fan of social media in general and try to limit my exposure as much as possible, with the exception of Brooklyn's Instagram posts. And I figured only really serious people would call since who actually uses a phone for calls these days?

When Ophelia showed up, I was struck by how different she looked versus how she sounded on the phone. Not gonna lie; she's got this sexy voice that had me picturing a leggy, platinum blonde with big tits and an ass that wouldn't quit. The woman who showed up was almost the opposite. Not that it matters. I'm not a cheater and I love Brooklyn, so a cursory glance is all I gave her. Even so, the reality of this woman who looks as though she'd be a kindergarten teacher or librarian was not who I would've pictured.

And while cute in a girl-next-door kind of way, with her long, dirty blonde hair pulled up in a sleek high ponytail, black dress slacks, light blue button-down shirt, and red cardigan complete with a set of pearls, she reminded me of my grandmother. Paired with the fact she wore no makeup to accent her big blue eyes or jewelry other than the simple pearl necklace and a brooch—an honest-to-God brooch—she was entirely unadorned. Even her shoes were boring, basic flats. Other than her height, which is around five-foot-five, it's hard to determine what kind of figure she has. The clothes she wears do her no favors, and although she's not large by any stretch of the imagination, she's also not rail thin or lacking curves.

Although I know she's thirty based on the copy of her driver's license and the information on her lease agreement, she looks to be a lot younger, more like early twenties.

She also didn't come with a lot of stuff. When the movers brought her things, it took them all of thirty minutes to unload her simple black wrought iron bed and mattress and box springs, a dresser and two nightstands and lamps, one small bookshelf and a desk and chair. As far as I could tell, she had one box of books, four boxes of clothes and linens, and a single large black plastic tote. She didn't even bring a TV.

She has little in the way of hair tools and toiletries. Having lived with Josie, I'm used to having a woman's things spread out over every surface like some sort of creeping vine, eventually crowding out all things *not theirs*. But again, aside from a single bottle of two-in-one shampoo and conditioner, a basic bottle of body wash, and a razor, she has nothing else in the shower.

Not that I've snooped; I don't do that. But she has a whole empty cabinet to fill with her things in the bathroom and other than four towels, four washcloths, a jar of facial moisturizer, tube of body lotion, a stick of deodorant, a toothbrush, toothpaste, and a box of tampons, she has nothing else.

Even her food tastes are basic. A loaf of whole wheat bread, package of both deli Swiss cheese and ham, mayo, half-gallon of milk, box of decaf tea bags, a jar of honey, bag of apples, a package of baby carrots, a bottle of ranch dressing, several frozen dinners, one bottle of wine, and a pint of chocolate ice cream, her kitchen cabinets are bare.

Maybe she doesn't cook?

By comparison, I'm a cluttered, glutenous, clotheshorse.

Although I work a ton—mainly by choice—I haven't picked up any additional shifts this week since Brooklyn is coming in for the weekend. So, when I'm still up this Saturday morning as Ophelia comes into the kitchen, she seems surprised to see me. "Oh, you're still up?"

I nod and sip my coffee. "Yeah. I'm off tonight and tomorrow, so I'm catching up on paying some bills. There's coffee made if you're interested."

She crosses to the stove where her kettle sits and fills it with water at the sink. "No thanks. Just tea for me."

I take in what she's wearing, as it's different from anything I've seen her wear thus far, and realize she must run or work out, unless she regularly wears baggy sweats and a hoodie with sneakers and bluetooth earbuds to run errands.

"Sure. Are you settling in okay?"

She offers me a warm smile. "Yeah. This is such a quiet neighborhood. I think I'm sleeping better than I have in years. My last building was really loud; lots of college kids coming and going at all hours."

I notice the hoodie she wears is most likely from a college and judging by how it's beginning to fray at the cuffs, it's well-loved. "Is that where you went to college? UNCW? Where is that?"

She looks down at her chest, as if needing the refresher, and nods. "Yeah, University of North Carolina Wilmington."

"Is that where you're from?"

She huffs a laugh, just as the kettle begins to whistle and she pulls it off the burner and turns off the eye, pouring boiling water into her waiting mug. "No. I'm from here."

"So, why did you go there for school? I've never heard of it."

"I like Wilmington and Wrightsville Beach. We went there a lot on family vacations because we have some family there and the tuition wasn't killer."

I nod. "Understandable. Where did you go to high school? Here?"

She shakes her head and wraps the string of the tea bag around her index finger and dunks it in and out of her cup. "I was homeschooled."

"Did you like it?"

"No." When she doesn't elaborate and simply drizzles some honey into her mug after dropping the tea bag into the trash, I nod. After a beat she asks, "I'm going to the store later; do you need anything?"

I shake my head. "No, thanks. Brooklyn's coming in, so

we're going to go out for supper and then have a chill night at home. So, if you're here, you'll get to meet her."

"Sounds good." She quickly downs her tea, which must still be near boiling, and washes her mug at the sink and places it back in the cabinet. "See you later," she tosses over her shoulder as she heads out the door. Through the window, I see her put her earbuds in as she steps off the porch before tapping her phone screen and stuffing it in the pocket of her sweats and taking off at a jog down the driveway.

Turning my attention back to my computer screen, I finish paying the light and water bills and check the movie times for the movie Brooklyn and I have been discussing going to see. Taking a quick screenshot of the times, I send it to her so we can best decide on our plans.

Not ten seconds after I send it off, my phone rings and Brooklyn's name flashes on the screen and I smile. "Well, hey," I say, answering the call.

"Hey, yourself. Do you have a preference? I'm probably not going to get in until around seven, so I didn't know if you wanted to go eat first or see the movie."

"Well, first of all, I think we both know you'll be naked for at least a little while after you get here, per usual. Secondly, I will need to replenish my energy stores, so I vote eat. Third, I'm a night owl these past few years, so we can do the ten o'clock showing if we really wanted."

"You might be able to, but I'm an early bird and I've been up since four already."

"Damn, babe."

She sighs. "Yeah. Tell me about it. Would you care if we skipped the movie, actually? I'd love to just chill. And do you just want to come to my place so your roommate doesn't hear your filthy mouth?"

"We can do that. Want to swing by and pick me up on your way home from the airport?"

"Sure. Speaking of roommates, how's the new one working out?"

"She's great. Most of the time, I don't even notice her. She's so quiet and barely takes up any space."

"She doesn't go out or anything; have a boyfriend?"

I scrub my hand down my face, exhaustion settling in from working last night. I yawn. "Not sure. She's only been here a week, and she works Monday to Friday, so for all I know, she goes clubbing. But I doubt it."

"Why?"

I snort a laugh. "Because she lives like a nun. She barely has any possessions. She doesn't even drink coffee. When she came to see the house, she said she doesn't drink much, but I've not seen her drink anything and other than one bottle of wine, she doesn't keep any booze in the house."

"Well, maybe the next weekend you're off and I'm back in town, we can all go out; see if she's any fun."

"She's not Josie, that's for sure."

Brooklyn chuckles. "Just because she's not Josie doesn't mean she won't be a good roommate."

"Oh, I know. And I think Ophelia will be fine. Like I said, it's just the first week. Maybe she just needs to settle in a little more before she opens up."

As I'm standing at the kitchen sink, drinking a glass of water and waiting for Brooklyn, Ophelia comes into the living room in flannel pajamas, her hair up in a messy bun, e-reader tucked under her arm. She curls up on one end of the couch and pulls one knee up. "So, I guess no big plans for tonight?"

She smiles and waves the e-reader. "Only with my current book boyfriend."

"I see. Well, I'm staying at Brooklyn's tonight, so I hope you and your fictional man have a good night."

She nods. "And I hope you and Brooklyn have a good visit. How often do you get to see her?"

I sigh. "Not as often as I'd like. She's a travel blogger for an online magazine, so she's all over the place."

"Wow, that sounds glamourous."

"If you like living out of a suitcase, it probably is. She seems to like it. Thank God for FaceTime, am I right?"

"I'm sure."

The front door opens and both our heads snap in that direction and my smile widens when Brooklyn comes into view. Her hair, currently a shade just this side of navy, is pulled up into Princess Leia-style space buns and her brown eyes are accented with her signature winged liner, her lips their usual crimson. She wears her typical uniform of jeans and a band tee that's been artfully distressed to the point you'd wonder if she bought it that way. She slips off her Vans and makes her way over to me, throwing her arms around my shoulders.

I pull her into my arms, feeling like the other half of me is finally back, and bury my face in her neck. When she pulls back, I take her face in my hands. "Good to see you outside of the Matrix."

Brooklyn grins. "You, too. Are you ready?"

"Sure. I've gotta grab my bag from my room." I gesture toward the living room to make the introductions. "Also, this is Ophelia, my roommate. Ophelia, this is Brooklyn."

The two women shake hands, exchanging warm smiles. I jog back to my bedroom to grab my bag and when I return, Ophelia gives me a friendly nod. "Y'all have fun. Nice to meet you, Brooklyn."

"You, too, Ophelia. Maybe next time I'm in town, we can all go out or something."

Ophelia nods. "Maybe." I wave to my roommate as Brooklyn tugs me out the front door and toward her Audi.

After I drop my bag into the backseat and shut my door, I notice Brooklyn's expression is contemplative. "What is it, babe?"

She shakes her head as she starts the car. "Something about Ophelia is familiar."

"You don't think you've met before, have you? Maybe on one of your trips?"

"No. I'm not sure what it is, but I know we haven't met before. Maybe she just has one of those faces."

I huff a laugh. "Maybe she's like Ford and is a secret celebrity."

"Could be."

"Speaking of Josie and Ford, they're coming over for supper tomorrow night."

Her face brightens. "Are they bringing Gouda?"

"Of course. She knows that's the price for supper."

By mutual agreement, Brooklyn and I head straight to her apartment and make it two steps in the door before our mouths collide in a hungry kiss. As the apartment is a studio, it's only about twenty more steps until we're on the bed and she pulls me down with her. I toe my shoes off as she tugs my shirt up and over my head to toss in the floor before bringing her mouth back to mine.

For what seems like hours but is probably two minutes, we're all hands stripping one another naked between frantic kisses. "God, I've missed you. Is this pussy needy, baby?" I ask, slipping my fingers between her thighs and teasing under the crotch her panties before dragging them down her legs and dropping them on the floor.

"Yeah. Fuck. I can't wait." She rolls onto her stomach and pushes up onto her hands and knees.

I huff a laugh and jump off the bed to jog over to my bag to retrieve a condom. I rip the foil with my teeth and roll the latex down over my cock. "Someone's anxious tonight," I remark and deliver a swift smack to her ass as I climb up behind her. Brooklyn sighs and I watch as my handprint blooms on her cheek, primal satisfaction swelling in my chest.

Gripping my cock, I slide it up and down her pussy, teasing her clit with the tip. "Jess, if you don't hurry up and fuck me, I'm gonna die."

I slam myself to the hilt and she gasps. "That what you want, Brooklyn? You want this fat cock to fill you up?" I grip the back of her neck and push down, and Brooklyn instantly drops her chest to the mattress.

"Yes, fuck, Jess. Just like that."

I slide my hands down her back to grip her hips and dig my fingers in as I set a brutal pace. "I know. I know exactly what you need, don't I?"

"Yes. God, I'm gonna come."

I smack her ass again and she moans. "Come on my cock, Brooklyn. Fuck, I wanna feel it. Jesus, you're so tight." I reach around and work her clit and seconds later, she screams, her pussy clenching so tightly I grunt, unable to hold back my own release as I follow her over the edge.

I drop kisses onto her shoulder blade as our breathing returns to normal and she turns her face to capture my mouth in a deep kiss. Pulling out, I give her one last smack on the opposite ass cheek and rise to dispose of the condom.

When I return from the bathroom, she's already slipped

her panties and tee shirt back on and she's leaning against the headboard, scrolling through her phone. I pull my underwear back on and sit next to her. "Are you ordering food?"

She doesn't look at me. "No, answering an email about next week's assignment." Annoyed, I pull her phone out of her hand and lay it on the nightstand. She scoffs in protest. "What the hell, Jess?"

"I haven't seen you in almost a month and you can barely stop working long enough to have a quick fuck, let alone spend actual time with me." She picks her phone back up and I snatch it out of her hand again. "No, Brooklyn. Just for tonight. Put it away. Please."

Her nostrils flare in indignation. "Fine. Let me finish that email and I will."

I reluctantly hand her phone back over and order a pizza while she finishes working. True to her word, she doesn't pick her phone back up for the rest of the evening and as we sit on the couch eating our sausage and mushroom pie and watching TV, I nudge her knee with mine. "I'm glad you're home. I've missed you."

"I've missed you, too," Brooklyn says with a soft smile.

"When are you finally gonna make an honest man out of me?"

She huffs a laugh. "What, you pregnant or something?"

I roll my eyes. "Brooklyn. Seriously, you said before you left for this last trip when you got home we'd talk about you scaling back and looking for work closer to home."

She drops her half-eaten slice onto her plate. "No, that's what you said. I already told you; I'm not planning on quitting my job. You know how much I love it."

"So, what's going to happen when we get married or have kids? You're still going to be traipsing around the country writing about all the sights while I'm keeping the home fires burning?"

Her eyes go wide as she turns her body toward mine. "Who said anything about kids? I'm not having kids."

I blink rapidly. "This is the first I'm hearing about it. We've talked about having kids forever."

She sighs. "No, again, that's you. *You're* the one who's talked about having kids. I've been markedly silent about the topic. I figured you would've taken the hint. I have an IUD and we still wear condoms. There's, like, no room for error with that."

"So, now you're saying you never want kids? You're never gonna want to stay put?"

"No, I don't want kids. I'd be happy to maybe get a dog, but even then we couldn't travel like we'd want to."

"I don't give a shit to travel."

"Well, I do. I was a travel blogger when we got together. I don't know why you thought us being in a relationship would magically change things."

"It's been three years, Brooklyn," I argue.

"And?"

"And if we're not working toward a future together, then what the hell are we doing? Are you ever gonna want to get married?"

Her brows draw down in aggravation. "It's a fucking piece of paper, Jess. What's it matter?"

"It matters to me. It's a commitment."

"I am committed to you. Why are you pushing this all of a sudden?"

"I've been bringing up us getting married regularly for the last year. I've not been subtle. I thought when you got back this time, we would have a serious conversation."

"Well, I'm not ready, Jess. My career is just getting to

where I can start to call the shots. I have job offers coming in from bigger outlets. You can't expect me to give that up. Not when you can get a job anywhere."

"Yeah, I can, but my job still requires I be based out of *somewhere*, Brooklyn. Are you ever gonna be ready to get married or, at the very least, settle down? I need you to be in the same city as me more than once a month."

Her eyes narrow and she stands. "Why, just so you can get your dick wet? We talk all the time. We text. We FaceTime. That is a relationship."

I toss my plate onto the coffee table and stand, too. "No, not just so we can fuck. Jesus. I love you, Brooklyn. I'm ready to build a future with you. I want to have kids with you. Are those things you're never gonna want?"

She sighs and looks up at the ceiling, pieces of her space buns falling loose around her ears. "I don't know. And actually, I've been thinking about accepting one of the other job offers."

My stomach drops, but she doesn't stop talking. "They're based out of Asheville. They're a startup with a shit-ton of capital from this tech-guru genius looking to add an additional income stream to his portfolio. I've gained quite the following over the past couple of years and he likes my take on the locations I visit. He likes how I always seem to tap into the places only locals know about. They're offering to triple my current salary."

I swallow, hurt and anger settling into my chest. "You've already interviewed, haven't you?"

She nods and folds her arms across her chest. "Yeah. The job is mine if I want it."

Tears burn my eyes. "What did you think would happen, Brooklyn? I'd bust a quick nut and roll over and be happy you want to move four hours away? Especially if you're never fucking gonna be there? It would be one thing if you were going to stay put, but you won't. Why the fuck would I pick up my entire life if you won't be there to share it with me?"

"I'm not asking you to go. I can still come and see you exactly like I do now."

"What's the point?"

"I love you, Jess."

"If you loved me, you'd take what I want into consideration."

Her eyes turn flinty. "And if you loved me, you wouldn't expect me to change the things you loved about me when we got together. You loved that I was worldly and traveled. You loved that I was adventurous."

"Yeah, I did," I agree, "but I also loved that you still seemed like you cared enough to consider my feelings in your decision making. You tell me you've been offered a job when you didn't even bother to tell me about the fucking interview."

"I'm telling you now."

I scoff. "I know. After you've already practically accepted the fucking job. I can see it all over you. You're going to take it. But know if you do, we're done. I thought we were building something. I thought you wanted the same things as me. I want a family. I want to get married. I've never kept those things a secret from you. Did you think your pussy would be so good it'd make me forget?"

"Fuck you, Jess. If you want to stay in your small, dead-end life, you go right ahead. You want to find someone to pop out a bunch of babies to satisfy some primal need you have, that's fine. If you want to throw away three years for the chance at some fucking antiquated way of life, have at it."

I walk over to my jeans and pull them on, followed by my shirt, socks and shoes. I give Brooklyn one last look before I head out the door. "I hope you come to your senses, Brooklyn. I don't want to throw this away. I want to make it permanent."

CHAPTER THREE

OPHELIA

The front door crashes open and then slams, followed by Jess's bedroom door. I'm at my desk editing my upload for this week when loud, angry music begins to stream through the walls. I debate whether I should go check on him, especially considering what he said about the HOA and noise levels, but I think better of it.

I put away my equipment, making sure to clear off my laptop screen after saving my edit. Sliding off my blue light glasses, I lay them on my desk and rise from my chair. I open my bedroom door and stick my head out and hear what sounds like someone throwing things. For a brief moment, I wonder if Jess has any enemies who might come into the house and jack up his room, but I know I locked the front door after he left, so it has to be him. Even so, I'm more than a bit nervous as I step toward his bedroom door.

Raising my hand to knock, I steel myself. I hate confrontation. I hate showy emotions. I don't know how to comfort people when they're having a hard time. The only advice I ever received growing up when I was struggling with something was, *have you prayed about it?* Having that be your only means of coping leaves one emotionally stunted and unable to empathize.

But I have to live here. With Jess. And something must've happened with Brooklyn for him to be home so soon. He seems like a nice guy, and I don't want to be unfriendly to him since I'm going to be living here for the foreseeable future and if we don't talk, won't that be weird?

Blowing out a breath, I draw my hand back to knock and the door flies open, startling us both. His face is awash in anguish and something in my stomach twists seeing it. Jess's eyes dart to my hand, still poised in midair, and I drop it, embarrassed. "Are you okay?"

"No. I've gotta go."

I hurriedly step back out of his way and can't help but notice he's changed out of his earlier jeans and tee shirt into gym clothes and sneakers. He walks out the front door, letting it slam behind him, not bothering to say goodbye.

His bedroom door is open and despite my best efforts to the contrary, I can't help but glance in. Judging by the rest of the house, Jess is a borderline neat freak. His room currently doesn't reflect that. At all.

Music still blares from a bluetooth speaker on the dresser, so I reach to turn it off as I step into the room. The mattress is halfway off the box springs and the blankets have been ripped off and are currently in a pile over by the window. All the books and DVDs on his bookshelf are on the floor. Several framed photos, mostly of him and Brooklyn, are smashed on the floor next to the bed. Thankfully, the glass in the frames seems to only be cracked, not shattered, so I won't need to worry about Jess stepping on stray shards.

And maybe it's because although I can't comfort him like a normal person, I can clean up a mess. He's obviously been through something and when he comes home, he might just want to go to bed. I can make sure he can do that without having to wait.

An hour later, everything is put right, except the framed photos, which I put into a box and set on his dresser. Satisfied with the completion of my task, I head to the bathroom to brush my teeth before turning in for the night.

I'm jarred awake by a loud thudding sound coming from the living room. It hits me that I have no way of protecting myself in this house, but I'll be damned if I lie in this bed and wait to be murdered. I grab my umbrella from beside the dresser and open the door to see a woman in her mid-thirties with brown hair coming down the hallway. I scream and draw back the umbrella, poised to strike, and she holds up her hands.

"Wait. Are you Ophelia?" I pause, unsure if it's a good thing or bad that the woman knows my name. Seeing my hesitation, she continues to hold her hands up defensively. "I'm Josie, Jess's old roommate."

She points to the living room, where a giant of a man stands beside the couch where Jess is currently passed out. "We're just bringing Jess home. He said he trashed his room; I was just going to straighten it up before we put him in bed."

I nod, understanding dawning as I lower the umbrella. "I cleaned it up already. He seemed really upset, so I thought I could help out. Is he okay?"

Josie frowns. "Not right now. Hopefully, someday." She hollers over her shoulder. "Ford, you can go ahead and bring him back here. Ophelia's a better roommate than I was." She gives me a friendly smile and a wink.

The giant—Ford—scoops Jess off the sofa as though he

weighs nothing and carries him over his shoulder like a sack of flour. Seeing my wide eyes at this show of strength, Josie laughs. "Yeah, he's pretty strong. Comes in handy sometimes."

"Shut it, Freckles. Jess is drooling all over my back. I'm gonna remember this for the future. I can't believe he drank all my booze and interrupted our date night. One of the only fucking days I have off for two weeks and Jess had to crash it. He's so gonna pay for this."

"Give him a break, Viking. He had a bad day." As Ford passes us, she turns back to me. "So, how are you settling in? You know, minus the theatrics."

"Fine. We don't really see each other much."

She nods. "Yeah, you get used to that. Jess is a bit of a workaholic."

Ford steps out of Jess's room and toward Josie. "He should be good. You think we need to stay?"

"Jess is a big boy. He'll wake up and remember why he shouldn't be drinking Pap's fully leaded shine."

I pipe up. "I can check on him."

She smiles. "All right. Don't worry, he's not a handsy drunk. Just a contemplative one."

I nod, unsure how to respond.

"Come on, Freckles. Nice to meet you, Ophelia. Hopefully, it'll be under better circumstances next time."

"So antsy. Damn." Josie gives me one last smile. "My number is on the fridge if you need us to come hose him down if he gets sick." She chuckles. "Ain't nothing I haven't seen before."

Heat creeps into my face at the thought of Jess needing someone to help him shower, and I nod quickly. "Okay."

"Josie, you were in high school. That was almost twenty years ago. I'm not one to kick a man while he's down, but if you're telling me you've seen Jess naked since then, I will have to murder him in his sleep. And I'm too pretty for prison."

Josie rolls her eyes and shoves Ford in the direction of the front door. "So possessive. You're the only one I see naked now. That's the important thing. And you are not too pretty for prison, you are just the right kind of pretty to be somebody's bitch," she says with a laugh. Just before they're out the door, she looks back at me. "See you, Ophelia. Sorry to wake you up."

"No problem," I call after them as the door shuts. Walking over to ensure it's locked before returning to my room, I leave the door open so I can hear Jess in case he gets sick, but I'm not sure I'd hear it from all the way in here. Knowing I probably wouldn't be able to live with myself if Jess died in his sleep by choking on his vomit—which, as a kid I was always warned was one of the side effects of drinking, and not that my experience with alcohol is so vast, but I've never seen or heard firsthand of it ever happening. Still, I drag my comforter and pillow off my bed and lie down in the hallway, right outside Jess's room, since I don't know him well enough to simply crash in his room.

And for the second time, I'm jarred awake by a thud. This one following pain in my back and butt and a loud, "What the fuck?" from the floor in front of me. I peek out from under my covers and Jess is sprawled out, face down. He slowly climbs to his feet and looks at me. "Why the fuck are you on the floor?"

I stand and rub my butt, where his sneaker-clad shoe collided with my body. "I was afraid you'd get sick and I wouldn't hear you throw up and then you'd choke on your own vomit and I'd be charged with negligent homicide."

Jess rubs his face. "Jesus, that was way too many words for how drunk I still am." He stumbles toward the bathroom and tugs his shirt off before he's in the room. And I'd be lying if I said I didn't look at the plains and ridges of his muscled back as he rounded the corner. I so looked.

I head back to my room and remake my bed and stretch, knowing I will pay for sleeping on the floor. I dress in my sweats and hoodie and walk out the door to take care of my morning jog.

An hour later, I'm pouring sweat in the late March sun and hoping Jess didn't fall asleep in the shower and use up all the hot water. I step back into the house and am halfway to my room when I hear my name. I turn to see Jess sitting at the kitchen table with a cup of coffee, looking a lot better than he did last night when he stormed out.

He sighs. "Sorry about last night. I didn't have a good night, but I'm sorry if I scared you or anything. And I appreciate you sleeping on the floor, but you didn't have to do that."

I close the distance between us until I'm standing on the other side of the table. "No problem. I figured something had happened."

He nods and looks down into his mug. "Yeah. And Josie said you cleaned up my room. You also didn't have to do that, either, but thanks."

I shrug. "I'm no good at pep talks, but I can make sure you can fall into bed and don't choke on your own puke. That I can do."

Jess gives me a sad smile. "Well, thanks."

"No problem." I turn to walk away and he calls after me again and I pivot to give him my attention.

"Do you eat normal food?"

I frown, caught off guard by his question. "Excuse me?"

"Stuff besides frozen dinners and sandwiches. Do you eat anything else?"

I nod. "I eat a lot of stuff. Why?"

"I was gonna make some breakfast, but if you have any specific dietary restrictions, I didn't want to offend you or anything. I need some grease and it pains me to open an entire pack of bacon and not cook all of it. Would you eat if I cook?"

"Sure. Just let me know how much I owe you for my portion."

He blinks, his brows drawing down in confusion. "You don't have to pay for anything. It's already paid for. I'd probably end up making the same amount just for me. Anytime I cook, I always make way more than I can eat on my own. You're welcome to anything I make. If I'm saving leftovers specifically for work or something, I'll label it. Otherwise, consider it fair game."

My cheeks heat in embarrassment. Sometimes I forget it's not normal to divide meal costs up like that all the time. "Oh, okay. Do I have time to take a shower?"

"Sure. How do you like your eggs?"

"Over medium." But even to my ears, it doesn't sound like a statement.

He lifts one brow in amusement. "Is that a question?"

I narrow my eyes. "Not a question. Over medium. You know, I would assume you'd be more grumpy, considering how wasted you were last night."

He grins. "Oh, I am, but I figure I already kicked you in the ass, so that was more of my attitude than you deserved to begin with."

I huff a laugh. "I think I'll be okay. I've got plenty of padding."

By the time I've showered and dressed in my usual weekend outfit of jeans and a tee shirt, I towel dry and braid my hair down my back and brush my teeth, the house is filling with smells of smoked meat and the sound of sweeping orchestral music. For a moment, I think I must be hearing things, but when I walk into the kitchen, Jess is standing at the sink, his hands braced on the edge, his head hung and eyes closed.

And it's no wonder. The music is emotional and sad and it's hard not to feel something listening to it. Attempting to be as quiet as possible so as to not disturb him, I lift the kettle on the stove to ensure I still have water in it. When I turn the knob on the burner and the ignition clicks, Jess inhales a breath behind me. "Sorry. I didn't mean to disturb you."

He clears his throat. "You're fine. The bacon will be done in a few minutes and I'll start the eggs."

"What music is this? Can I ask?"

He huffs a laugh. "Well, it's playing loud enough for the whole house to hear, so sure. It's the soundtrack to *Schindler's List.*"

I blink. "Damn. That's bleak."

He gives me a sad smile and proceeds to set a skillet on a burner and turn it on, just before pulling a pan of bacon out of the oven and setting it to the side. He takes a moment to fish the meat out of the pan and lay it on several layers of paper towel already lying on a plate. "Sometimes, bleak is necessary."

I'm about to ask him if he wants to talk about whatever happened yesterday, but the kettle begins to whistle and I shut off the burner instead. I pour the boiling water over my prepared teabag and drizzle in some honey.

"Is it the caffeine you don't like or the coffee itself?"

I snap my head in Jess's direction, where he still stands at the stove, cracking eggs into the preheated skillet, and give him a half-shrug as I dunk my tea. "My parents never drank coffee, and we never went out to eat or anything growing up, so I didn't actually know anything about it until college. Let's just say the college cafeteria version of coffee isn't exactly... palatable. And anytime I've tried it since then, I always have to add so much cream and sugar, it might as well be dessert."

"Gotcha." He dumps the eggs onto two plates, along with a few pieces of bacon each and some buttered toast he's already prepared. "Breakfast is served."

We take our plates over to the table and sit and, as I don't normally eat with anyone anymore, it's a bit strange. Jess tucks into his food hungrily in between sips of coffee. "So, do you jog a lot?" he asks after swallowing a bite of toast.

I nod. "Almost every day."

"Did you do any kind of track or anything in college?"

"No. I just enjoy running. I've done it since I was about fourteen, I guess. Do you work out?"

He swallows another bite of food. "Yeah. Josie's brother works at a gym. I go there. Do you have a boyfriend?"

"Didn't you already ask me that before I moved in?"

"No, I think I asked if you had pets or a spouse, and you asked me if pets ranked higher than spouses."

"Oh, right. No, no boyfriend." I don't ask him if he has a girlfriend since either I've met Brooklyn and she still is his or she's not and I don't want to make things awkward. "Do you like being a surgical tech?"

Jess gives me a genuine smile. "I love it. I enjoy prepping the instruments and the room and sometimes I get to watch or take part in surgeries, so that's pretty cool. Do you like working in the records department?"

"Yeah. I'm not much of a people person, so the solitude is nice."

"What did you study in college?"

It hits me that this is probably the longest conversation I've had with someone in several years, and I'm not sure how I should feel about that. I mean, Jess is easy to talk to and I'm not feeling the need to scamper away, so that's a good sign, right?

"Education. I wanted to be a teacher. Turns out, I don't like kids. Well, actually, it's not that I don't like kids. I'm sure I'll like my kids just fine someday. The ones I raise. I liked my siblings just fine and pretty much helped raise them, so I guess it's just other people's kids I don't like."

He nods, considering. "How many siblings do you have?"

I sigh. "Nine."

He blinks, his mouth falling open. "I'm sorry, did you say *nine*? As in, you are one of *ten*?"

"Yeah."

"Wow. Your parents were busy."

"It would seem so," I agree.

"And where do you fall in the lineup?"

"I'm the oldest."

"Are you close with your siblings?"

That is such a loaded question, I wouldn't even know how to begin to answer it. The easiest answer I can give is, "I haven't seen them in a while."

Sipping his coffee, he nods. "Do they still live here?"

"I'm not sure," I admit.

His brows draw down in confusion. "When was the last time you spoke with them?"

I blow out a breath and sip my tea to stall and he examines my face. "Sorry, it's none of my business."

I shake my head. "No, it's fine. It's complicated." Heat creeps into my cheeks, thinking about the last ten years and what my life's been like since then.

Jess gives me a friendly smile. "Like I said. None of my business."

"I don't have friends," I blurt out.

CHAPTER FOUR

OPHELIA

He looks utterly confused and starts to say something and I press forward before I lose my nerve. Because it's been so long since I actually had a real conversation, I might as well make the most of it. For all I know, Jess may think I'm a total weirdo by the end of this one and avoid me for the rest of my time here.

"I grew up super religious. Extreme to the point of having church in our house; not even at a proper church. We were homeschooled and the only acceptable reading that wasn't the Bible was Shakespeare. In fact, my siblings and I are all named after characters from Shakespeare. Me, Juliet, Angelo, Marina, Viola, Bianca, Duncan, Edgar, Lavinia, and Ajax. And I guess it's possible I have more, but they were the last I knew. I raised most of my siblings and helped school them. Thus the reason I thought I wanted to be a teacher. My parents were against establishment education, so they sure as hell didn't want me going to college. In reality, I didn't know it was even an option because we were so sheltered. And because we didn't have a TV or radio or internet growing up, I knew nothing about popular culture or fashion—honestly, I still don't—or really

anything an eighteen-year-old girl should know." I glance up at
him. "Nothing."

Well, except what your dick looked like.

"So, how did you go to college?"

"When I was twenty, we went to visit our family in
Wilmington. My cousin, Rosalind, who's the same age as me,
was allowed to get a job. We would always spend time
together whenever we'd visit and she even had a car; her
parents weren't as extreme as mine. They were still super
religious, but she was allowed to work outside the home. I
wasn't. We lived on a farm and sold produce and meat and
basically only consumed what we produced, with certain
exceptions.

"Anyway, Rosalind had gotten a job at this bakery a lot of
college kids frequented. She started picking up all kinds of
'worldly' knowledge; including stuff about college. Rosalind is
beautiful. She's tall and has these great curves and pretty
blonde hair. So, of course, she drew the attention of boys and
she had a secret boyfriend that summer.

"And that summer, we talked, and she told me all the stuff
her boyfriend told her about college and everything kids our
age should've already known. That summer was sort of the
summer I grew up. God, I was so naïve. Rosalind and I snuck
out every night. I drank for the first time, kissed a guy for the
first time; even drove a car. All basic rites of passage for most
kids, right?

"By the time I went home a few weeks later, I was a
completely different person. I realized how closed-off my world
was and I demanded that my parents let me go to college and
get a car and all the things I'd experienced in North Carolina.
They refused and said my place was on the farm and if I left, I
couldn't come back."

"Was your family amish?"

I shake my head. "No. Just evangelical times about a thousand."

"I'm guessing you left, obviously."

"Not at first. I mean, where was I going to go? I had no real formal education, no money, no place to stay. And there were my siblings to consider. The youngest, Ajax, was barely five and I felt like he was mine because I'd practically raised him. I know now that after he was born, my mother had severe postpartum depression and couldn't take care of him. And because my parents also didn't believe in prescription medicine or anything like that, she didn't get any help.

"It was the hardest decision of my life. But by the following summer, Rosalind had moved in with her boyfriend and she said I could live with them and get a job and if I wanted to get my GED and apply to school, they'd help me. Plus, my parents had started talking about me getting married; which I had no desire to do then. So, I took that as my cue to leave."

"And you haven't seen your family since then?"

I shake my head. "I haven't spoken to them in nine years."

"Wow. That's a wild story."

"I know. And I didn't mean to dump all that on you. Like I said, I don't have any friends, and it's been a really long time since I had an actual conversation with another person about more than just medical records or small talk. And I don't say that so you'll feel bad for me or anything. I have trouble talking to people because, for the most part, I can't relate to things and I don't understand a lot of movie references and music and things. I mean, it's a lot better than it used to be, but with work, I don't have a lot of time to cram pop culture, so I miss a lot. My upbringing was worlds apart from most others and people would most likely look at me like I have three heads. So I usually don't share."

I blow out a breath, embarrassment washing over me from

emotionally vomiting all over him. "And I'm sorry I just put all that out there because, replaying it back in my mind, I probably shared too much and you could think I'm some weirdo. I probably am, so you wouldn't be wrong if that's your assumption."

Jess is quiet for a long moment, absorbing everything I've said. "Well, you have a friend now, Ophelia," he says gently, "and you can talk away. I'm happy to listen."

I wait to be hit with some sense that anything he's said was disingenuous, but I only feel sincerity from his words and I nod, relieved and give him a grateful smile. "I appreciate it."

He looks thoughtful for a minute and scratches his chin. "Can I ask you something? You know, since we're friends and all."

I chuckle. "Sure."

"You really didn't kiss a guy till you were twenty?"

I shake my head. "Nope."

"Wow. Did you have boyfriends in college and stuff?"

I nod. "Yeah." He opens and closes his mouth and seems unsure how to proceed; as if he wants to say something, but is afraid of what I'll think. I lift a brow. "I'm not a virgin, if that's what you're really trying to ask."

He huffs a laugh. "No. I mean, good. I mean, shit. Sorry." He blows out a breath, obviously flustered, and I want to laugh. "I mean, I was curious while you were telling your story about how sheltered you were. And honestly, I've been curious since we met, with how minimalist you are, if that was for a specific reason or something."

I shrug. "I didn't grow up with much of my own; nothing, really. So, I can live without a lot. I read a ton, so a fair bit of my money goes to that. I joined a book club in college and they opened my eyes to romance books—which are my main genre."

"I bet that was quite a jump from Shakespeare to smut."

I snort a laugh. "You have no idea. The first book we read was 50 *Shades.*"

Jess chokes on his coffee. "Jesus. They threw you in the deep end, didn't they?"

"Yeah. Now, it's considered pretty tame compared to a lot of the other stuff I read, but at the time, I was...overwhelmed. Mostly in a good way," I say with a laugh.

"Man. Remind me to call my mom and thank her for my raising. I had a curfew until college, but my parents were pretty lenient. I can't imagine." He examines my clothes and I feel the need to sit up straighter. "Is that why you dress the way you do? And I'm not trying to be negative, but do you like the way you dress?"

I shrug. "I wore long skirts and baggy tops my whole life. I only had one haircut until I moved out of my parents' house. Honestly, this is pretty risqué compared to what I used to wear. And Rosalind tried to help me, but I never had a lot of money to spend on clothes or makeup, so I tried to do the best I could."

Sighing, I run my hand down my braid. "My entire life, it was pounded in my head that my body should be covered so I wouldn't tempt men to sin. So, extreme modesty is typically my default. I can only work on one trauma at a time, and breaking free of purity culture was a lot more important to me. Because, duh, sex."

Jess laughs. "Okay. I get that. Definitely." He eyes me again, his gaze scanning my entire body, and I'm not sure whether to cringe or preen. "If you wanted to change up the way you look, I bet Josie could help you. I mean, if you want it. Not that you need it—you look just fine the way you are—but you said earlier you still struggle with fashion. If you wanted help, Josie could help you. If I know her, she'd demand to get to take you shopping."

I shake my head. "I couldn't ask her to do that."

He rolls his eyes. "Oh, please. She'll probably make you. She's pretty convincing. I know she's going with Ford for his next road trip, but I'm sure once she gets back, she'd be all for it." He pops a final bite of toast in his mouth. "Which reminds me. Do you have issues with dogs?" Confused, I shake my head, and he continues. "Josie asked if we could watch her dog, Gouda, while she's on the road with Ford for a few days. I should've mentioned it earlier."

"That's fine. I like dogs. Can I ask you something? You know, since we're friends and all." His smile falters a bit, sensing what I'm going to ask, but he nods. "Did you and Brooklyn get into a fight?"

He looks down into his empty mug. "We broke up, actually."

I blink, trying to comprehend what he's just said. "What? Y'all looked so happy yesterday."

"She told me last night she doesn't think she'll ever want to get married or even settle in one place. She doesn't want kids."

"But you do," I supply.

"Yeah. And it would be different if she was like Josie and was choosing not to have kids of her own for health reasons. Brooklyn just doesn't want to be tied down by anything. Me, included, I guess. She'd been offered a job out of Asheville and didn't even tell me she'd already interviewed."

"Jess, I'm so sorry. How long were y'all together?"

"Three years. And again, I'm sorry if I scared you last night when I left."

"It was understandable. I'm sorry I can't empathize with you."

He gives me a small smile. "It's alright. I can't much empathize with you, either."

"What a pair we make," I say with a chuckle. "The homely,

religiously traumatized, emotionally stunted, recluse, and the heartbroken, wannabe family man."

"Here, here," he replies and raises his empty mug in a mock-toast.

The music coming out of the speaker changes, and while still orchestral, it has a completely different feeling. It's lively and hopeful. I listen for a moment before asking, "What's this music from?"

For a brief moment, he must think I'm joking, but then he blinks and says, "*Star Wars*." When my expression stays blank, his mouth falls open before he closes it again. "Seriously? In the nine years since you...escaped, you've never seen *Star Wars*?"

"What, is that some kind of movie or something?" He looks wounded by my question, and I can no longer keep up the ruse. "Yes, I know about *Star Wars*," I say, laughing. "I watched it during that summer I became an actual person."

He heaves a sigh of relief. "Oh, thank God. I thought we were gonna have to have a marathon." He's struck with a thought. "Your story; it's kinda like you left the Matrix."

I frown. "You said something like that yesterday when Brooklyn was here. Now that, I don't understand the reference for."

"You will. You need pop culture? I can hook you up. It'll be like when Neo learns kung fu."

———

Later in the afternoon, Josie and Ford drop off the adorable ball of yellow fluff that is Gouda and I'm immediately in love. We had a lot of animals on the farm, even some dogs and cats, but they were all livestock guardian dogs or herding dogs or mousers, so none of them were actually pets. And Gouda is so sweet and affectionate, I'm addicted the moment she looks up at me with her chocolate eyes.

True to his word, Jess introduces me to *The Matrix* and we've just gotten to the part where Neo decides to take the red pill when the front door opens. Brooklyn walks in and Jess jumps up off the sofa after pausing the movie, startling Gouda, who lets out a sharp bark.

A myriad of emotions roll over Jess's face in quick succession; surprise, anger, hope, love, apprehension. He crosses the living room to where she stands. "What are you doing here?"

"We need to talk."

Gouda paces, sensing the tension in the air, and I stand. "Come on, Gouda, we'll go for a walk." I'm shocked when she trots over and retrieves her leash from a spot by the door and brings it over to drop at my feet. I squat down and chuckle, giving her a scratch behind the ear. "Good girl."

Brooklyn's head snaps in my direction, and her brow furrows, her eyes narrowing. She examines me with something like suspicion before blinking and returning her attention to Jess when he moves his face in front of hers. "No, we don't. I said everything I need to say, Brooklyn."

"Please, Jess. I just want to talk. You wouldn't even answer my texts."

He heaves a sigh and as I slip my shoes on to take Gouda on said walk so I won't be in the way, they're halfway down the hallway toward his room.

Thirty minutes later, Gouda is practically dragging me back to the house and I don't have my phone anyway, so I have nothing to do. Reluctantly, I step back into the house, hoping I don't hear screaming when I open the door.

Oh, I hear screaming all right, but not the kind from fighting. I hear the kind that comes from fucking. Paired with the shrieking, above even the loud music playing—probably in an attempt to drown out said shrieking—the headboard of Jess's bed bangs against the wall.

"I guess they made up," I mutter down at Gouda, who must be used to these types of sound. All it reminds me is that it's been longer than I'd like since I've gotten laid and need blooms low in my abdomen.

The sounds stop and I flinch, recognizing I've been glued to my spot. I walk over to the kitchen and fill up the kettle and set it on the stove and crank the temperature to high, needing something—anything—to occupy myself. Spotting my purse on the opposite counter, I snatch out my earbuds and plug them into my ears, pretending to be listening to anything except what I was so blatantly eavesdropping on.

Does Jess still make that face when he comes? Does his head fall back and his eyes look like they nearly roll back in his head? Does he still pull that crooked grin? Does he look at Brooklyn with that same look on his face when she sucks him off? All those years ago, even a hundred feet away, I could see it plain as day. I've got eagle eyes, my father always said.

And now, that face is all I can imagine, even as I press my thighs together as I stand at the stove.

CHAPTER FIVE

JESS

I pull Brooklyn into my arms and she rolls to face me with a smile on her face. "Better?"

Although nothing is resolved, we talked, and she's agreed not to move. Brooklyn spoke with the CEO and they've agreed to let her telecommute as long as she still does travel blogs as usual.

Somewhere deep down, I know this is probably the beginning of the end for us, because if she doesn't want the same things I do, what are we even doing? But fuck, I love her. So, for now, I push that inevitable end date out a little further, fully aware it makes me a cowardly chicken shit. But if I can choose to feel pain now or later, give me later all day long.

I look down at her and give her a soft smile and drop a kiss on her forehead. "Yeah."

She presses a kiss to my chest and rises from the bed, beginning to pull on her clothes. "Good."

When she puts on her shoes, I frown in disappointment. "You're not staying?"

She sits back down on the edge of the bed and continues to

adjust the slip-on shoe, making sure the back is pulled up over her heel. "Well, since I told them I would telecommute, I have to go to Asheville to get all of my credentials and stuff. They want me there tomorrow afternoon. But I'll be back next weekend."

"So you can't stay tonight? It's only a four-hour drive."

"I have to pack and call Allison. She's gonna shit a brick when she finds out I'm leaving."

"You can still stay tonight. Leave early in the morning. We just made up, babe."

She rolls her eyes. "And there will be a lot more making up next weekend." She piles her hair on top of her head and secures it with a hair tie. "What do you know about Ophelia?"

Tugging on my boxer briefs, I frown and scratch my chin. "What do you mean?"

"What do you know about her? Her background?"

I blow out a breath. "She told me today that she has nine brothers and sisters. She grew up super religious and sheltered, and when she decided to leave for college, her family disowned her. She didn't even kiss a guy till she was twenty. She's never seen *The Matrix* and doesn't understand a lot of pop culture and stuff since she grew up without TV or internet or even any books besides the Bible until college. Why?"

She shakes her head, her brows drawn down in contemplation. "There's still something really familiar about her. I can't put my finger on it. It's bugging me. I'm sure it's nothing. So she's really never seen *The Matrix*?"

"Nope. We were watching it when you showed up." A tea kettle whistles from the kitchen. "Guess she's back from walking Gouda."

Brooklyn winces. "Oh, God. You think she heard us? I would imagine she's pretty vanilla."

I shrug. "She said she's not a virgin, and she reads a lot of smut, so I'd say she's not gonna have a fainting spell."

"How do you know she's not a virgin?"

"Because she's thirty. And because she told me. I was trying to get to know her. You've seen how she dresses; I was just curious. And when she said she hadn't kissed a guy till she was twenty and how sheltered she was, I didn't ask, but she could see the question on my face. I didn't ask it, but she volunteered the information."

"Does she have a boyfriend?"

I shake my head. "No. She's pretty shy, I think. Says she has a hard time relating to people with the way she grew up. People look at her like she's weird and they ask her a lot of insensitive questions. She didn't say that last part, but that's the picture she painted."

"Well, maybe we can find her someone. She's pretty cute. You know, if a little frumpy."

"I said something about getting Josie to help her pick out some new clothes. I asked her if she liked the way she looked and she said she'd never really tried another look and that jeans and tee shirts were about as risqué as she got. You know, since she had to be super covered up growing up so men wouldn't be tempted to sin or something."

Brooklyn's jaw clenches and she shakes her head, disgusted. "Such patriarchal bullshit. I swear, purity culture causes so much trauma for girls. They're expected to remain completely innocent and pure and are told sex is this dirty, awful, sinful thing. At least, right up until the moment some man who's been told his wife will obey his every sexual whim slips a ring on her finger. And then, she's expected to completely forget that sex is dirty and be some kind of sexpot; like flipping a switch. It's a total mind fuck."

I nod. "Yeah, she said she could only unpack one religious

trauma at a time and sex was more important to her than unlearning extreme modesty."

She laughs. "Can't argue with that."

"Right?"

After I redress, we make our way out to the living room. Ophelia is on the couch with her earbuds in and is reading on her Kindle, cup of tea in hand. Gouda's head is in her lap, but when she sees us, the dog perks up, causing Ophelia to also look our direction.

She doesn't have any trouble meeting our eyes or look uncomfortable or give any indication she heard Brooklyn and me. Her eyes fall to Brooklyn's and my joined hands and she smiles. Standing, she says, "I'll let y'all have the living room to watch TV. I can read in my room."

Brooklyn chuckles. "You don't have to go anywhere; I'm not staying. I have to get ready to go on a work trip. Plus, you have to finish *The Matrix*. It's Jess's favorite," she says, giving my hand a squeeze. She gives me a kiss and sighs. "I'll see you next week, okay?"

Although disappointment flares in my chest, I give her a smile and one last kiss before she walks out the door. I walk over to the kitchen and drink a glass of water and look out the window toward the back yard.

"For a guy who just got laid, you don't look to happy about it."

I choke on my water and sputter liquid down my chin. When I turn, Ophelia is laughing, her hip propped against the counter. I mop my hand down my face, heat creeping into my cheeks. "Sorry you heard all that."

She waves away my apology and rolls her eyes. "Oh, please. I grew up on a farm and I'm the oldest of ten. Even if I were a virgin, I still would be immune to *that* sound." Her expression neutralizes. "But y'all made up, I assume?"

I nod. "It would seem so."

"That's not a very enthusiastic answer."

I shrug, not wanting to get into it. "We still have a lot to work out."

Ophelia nods and gestures to the TV. "Do you feel up to finishing the movie, or would you rather be alone? Or, I can go to my room if you'd prefer to watch something by yourself."

"I'm good. I'm not gonna bail on you. I mean, I know I did bail on you when Brooklyn got here, but I'm okay. And if you're already watching something, I wouldn't take the TV away or anything."

"It's your house; your TV. You'd be within your rights."

"You pay rent, so you have rights, too. I'm not an asshole. I have a TV in my room if there was something I was dying to see and you were using this one. Please don't feel like you can't take up space here, Ophelia. Really, if you're living here, this is your home, too. You're welcome to the TV and Netflix and Hulu and any other streaming services that are on there."

She nods slowly, considering, and I can't help but ask, "Aside from your family, were your cousin and her boyfriend the only people you've lived with?"

"Yeah. My apartment before this was a studio and when I lived with my cousin, we split everything three ways. And if you want to split the cost on those services, I'm happy to pay for that. Just let me know."

I shake my head. "That's not why I asked. I already factor that stuff into my budget. And whether or not you were here, those are things I would have, so I'm not gonna expect you to shell out for it. Now, if we decided together to get another streaming service, that would be one thing, but this is stuff I've had for years."

"Okay."

"Can I ask why you moved back here after college? Why didn't you stay in North Carolina?"

A look I'm not sure how to read flits through her gaze, but it's gone so quickly, I have no clue what the emotion is. She swallows and shrugs. "It just didn't work out. And I think part of me always hoped I'd reconcile with my family at some point. Hard to do from there."

"I'm sure. Have you had any luck with that?"

"No. The one time I went to the house, they wouldn't even open the door. And that was five years ago, so I'm not up to trying again just yet."

"Sounds to me like you did try. If they don't want to have you in their lives, that's their loss."

She sighs. "That's what I tell myself."

Over the next few weeks, Brooklyn is true to her word and I end up getting to see her every weekend. It's more time, it seems, than we've spent together in years. And although I offer to stay at her place so we can have more privacy and not subject Ophelia to the sounds of us making love, she insists we stay at my house. And honestly, my bed is more comfortable than hers, so I really can't complain.

Today, we have the house to ourselves while Josie insisted on dragging Ophelia shopping once she found out she might be open to a new look. Sitting curled up on the sofa, it's nice to have time to simply talk. "Maybe since Ophelia is gonna have a better look, she'll finally find a date. Has she been out at all since she moved in?" Brooklyn asks as we eat lunch.

I shake my head. "No. From what I gather, she's a home-body. I made her a list of all the best movies and she's slowly been working her way through them. She just finished watching all the *Police Academy* movies and *Ghostbusters*."

"You're kidding. She hadn't even seen *Ghostbusters*?"

"No. But she loved it. She texts me and we talk about them while I'm on my first break."

"So, it's working out with her being here?"

"Definitely. Don't tell Josie, but she might even be a better roommate than her. She doesn't leave her girly stuff sprinkled all around the sink and she cleans her hair out of the drain after she showers. She doesn't paste it to the wall like some people I know," I say and give her an accusatory side-long glance.

Brooklyn laughs. "Wow. Sounds like you love living with her."

"I do. She's started cooking and man, she's got this great recipe for chili. I have no clue what all she puts in it, but it's the best I've ever had. And she made some homemade apple butter that was good enough to eat straight out of the jar. I think I've gained ten pounds since she moved in."

"Well, I'm glad it's working out."

"You know, you could always move in with us. You and Ophelia get along and you're here every weekend, anyway."

She gives me a forced-patient smile. "We've talked about this, Jess. I'm not there yet. I still like having my own place."

"Then why don't we ever stay there? I've offered every weekend. And yet, you never want to be there."

"Your place is bigger. It's closer to the interstate. There's a bar right around the corner."

I huff a laugh. "Sounds like great arguments in favor of you moving in."

"Jess, stop," she demands, annoyed. "I'm not moving in here. Drop it."

"Brooklyn, this is—." The front door opens and I clamp my mouth shut since I refuse to argue in front of guests or Ophelia.

When she enters, Josie has a huge grin on her face and Ophelia is laughing about something as she trails behind her, arms loaded down with shopping bags.

She's still dressed in the same jeans and tee shirt she was wearing before she left, but her hair is a lot shorter. Brooklyn and I both gape at Ophelia, our fight forgotten. Brooklyn jumps to her feet. "Oh, my God, Ophelia. Your hair, it looks amazing."

Josie nods enthusiastically. "Right? Doesn't she look awesome? It's just a color rinse, but it's like it pulled out some honey tones she had in there."

Brooklyn fingers Ophelia's now shoulder-length locks and elbows me. I don't even remember standing. "Jess, don't be rude. Tell Ophelia how great she looks."

I blink, coming out of whatever stupor I've been in as I look at Ophelia. The shorter hair makes her look more confident somehow and her smile seems even more radiant than normal. "Oh. Yeah. It looks great. I bet it feels lighter, huh?"

Ophelia laughs. "No joke. Alright, y'all, I've gotta put these bags down. My arms are about to fall off. Josie, thank you so much for today. I never knew shopping was actually supposed to be fun."

Josie grins. "Well, duh. Anytime spent with me is fun. Just don't forget about next weekend."

"What's next weekend?" I ask as Ophelia walks into her room.

Josie's smile turns wicked. "It's when Ophelia goes on the prowl. She's going out with Hensley and me."

My eyes go wide. "No. You cannot subject her to Hensley. That is a terrible idea."

"Why, because she might actually get laid?"

Brooklyn's expression brightens. "Ooh, can I come? We can make it a full-blown ladies' night."

Josie smiles. "Perfect." Turning to me, she pats me on the shoulder. "Looks like you're on your own next weekend."

THE CONFESSIONS OF IVY SINN
EPISODE 77: THE NEIGHBOR

Last night, I heard my neighbors fucking. And voyeur that I am, I couldn't help but stop and listen. It reminded me that it's been so, so long since the last time someone touched me. Since I had a good, hard fuck. Since someone pulled my hair or made me call out their name. And God, I miss it.

Listening to the animalistic sounds coming from next door was enough that for the next few hours, I was so turned on, it was all I could do to wait until I was able to touch myself.

And again, it made me think of you. Whoever you are. As long as I've done this, I've never really had a clear image of who you are. I often wonder what you imagine me to look like. And honestly, I'll never tell. I'd hate to ruin what you picture when you hear my voice.

But tonight, as I touch myself and you listen, I imagine you are my neighbor. I imagine it's us next door and you're making me produce those sounds. It's us making the headboard slam against the wall with such force it rattles the photos on the other side of the wall.

And I have to tell you, just thinking about that has my pussy dripping and I'm already sliding my hand between my thighs. Will you touch yourself, too? Will you imagine it's us in that bed? Fuck, my panties are soaked and I'm just barely getting started.

Take off your underwear and touch yourself for me. Are you dripping for me yet? Did you moan when you dragged your hands over that spot that lights you up? Oh, God, I'm so close already.

Usually, I pull out my vibrator, but tonight, I think I only want to use my hand and imagine it's your hand. I just need that connection. Fuck, my clit is sensitive.

If you fucked me with your hand, would you bring it to my lips and make me taste myself? Would watching me lick off my sweetness make you need to taste me yourself? Oh, God, it's sweet. And Jesus, thinking about your face buried in my cunt has me wanting to come so badly. Oh, fuck, I need your fingers, too.

But you know me, I'm a greedy girl. Would you give me another finger and another until you were stretching me so good I screamed? Fuck, it's so good.

I need more. Please, I promise to be a good girl. Will you fill me up? Take away this ache from needing someone to touch me? Will you make me scream?

Oh, God. Please. I'm so close. Come with me, baby, please. I love it when we come together. I need to hear you. Fuck. Oh shit, I'm coming. Please come for me. Now. Fuck.

Thank you for hearing my confession.

CHAPTER SIX

JESS

As is my custom on Saturday mornings, I sit down to pay my bills at the computer and check my emails. This morning, though, I'm multitasking and talking to my mother while I peck at my laptop keyboard.

"Yeah, Mom, the house is fine."

"And things are still working out with the new roommate?"

I roll my eyes. "Yes, it's great."

"And Brooklyn really doesn't care that you have a woman living with you?"

"No, Mom. Josie lived with me for two years. Brooklyn isn't a jealous person and she and Ophelia get along great. And actually, they're all going out tonight." I'm not thrilled it's with Hensley since she's such a partier and is liable to ditch the other women to go home with someone and leave them stranded. Don't get me wrong, Hens is one of my best friends, but she's self-destructive and seems content to take others down with her.

"I just don't understand your generation. You'll live with

one woman, carry on with another for years without a commitment and think nothing's wrong with that picture."

"Mom, we've talked about this. There's nothing wrong with having a roommate. And Ophelia is great. Maybe if you ever came to this side of town, you could see how well everyone gets along."

My mother says something, but I'm distracted by the sight of Ophelia coming into the kitchen, earbuds lodged into her ears, mouthing the words to some song. She jogs almost daily, but this is the first time I've been home to see her leave since she and Josie went on that shopping trip last week. And I nearly choke on my coffee when I take in what she's wearing. I'm honestly not sure what shocks me more, the fact that she's wearing shorts and a tank top, the fact that she's pouring a cup of coffee, or the fact that she has a tattoo on her right shoulder blade.

I've not heard a word my mother says, but I interrupt her. "Mom, I'll talk to you later. Love you." I disconnect the call and drop my phone on the table and stare at Ophelia, physically unable to take my eyes off of her.

This cannot be the same girl who first moved in a month ago in shapeless slacks and wearing a brooch and had hair down to her ass who was afraid to even cook something in this very house. And now she's drinking coffee? What the hell?

She obviously catches me looking at her and gives me a puzzled expression. "What's with your face?"

"You have a tattoo."

She snorts a laugh. "Yeah. I got it in college."

"Can I see it?"

Ophelia nods and walks toward the table and I stand. "Honestly, I thought you'd be more stunned because I'm wearing shorts. Or that I'm drinking coffee."

"Yes, well, those facts do intrigue me, but I can't believe you have a tattoo."

"Stick around, pal. I'm full of all sorts of surprises," she says with a playful smile. Along with the inches of hair and hemline she's apparently shed, so too has she shed the quiet, standoffish woman she was when I first met her. She turns to let me see her inked skin and I can only make out about half of it.

"What is it?"

"What, you can't see it? You might have to pull my tank top to the side to see all of it."

I stick my index finger under the fabric of her tank top and sports bra and drag it in toward her spine. With my touch, goosebumps pop on Ophelia's skin, but I'm struck more by her tattoo. It's a bird cage with the door open, a single bird flying free. The thought of her finally breaking free of her upbringing makes me smile. "This is great," I remark, letting go of her shirt.

"Thanks. Do you have any tattoos?"

"Yeah."

She turns to face me. "Really?"

"Yeah." I pull my left arm out of my tee shirt and show her the tattoo that spans from my sternum across my left peck and up to the front of my shoulder.

She examines it and then frowns. "What is it? I mean, I know it's some sort of chemical compound from what I remember in my college chemistry class."

I smile. "It's an oxytocin molecule. Oxytocin is the love hormone." I slip my arm back into my shirt.

"Is it some sort of message to say that love is only a chemical response? You don't really believe in love?"

I shake my head. "No, the exact opposite, actually. Love is a chemical response, but I think it's also a lot more complex than that. You also have to choose it. You can love someone and them still not be the right person. Someone can love you and you not be their right person. And as much as hormones play a part in attraction and physical reaction to another person, you still have to choose that other person every day; put them first. And they have to choose you, too." I sigh with the last sentence because right now, I'm feeling like I'm choosing Brooklyn, but she's not really choosing me.

Ophelia nods thoughtfully. "Do you think they could bottle that hormone?"

"They do. They give the synthetic version to people in labor to make things progress. It's also the hormone the body naturally releases when someone nurses to help them bond with their baby. It's also released during sex; so some people have a hard time telling the difference between love and simply chemistry. It's a very complicated hormone."

"I'll take your word for it." She says, stepping toward the sink and filings up her water bottle.

"What, you've never been in love?"

She shakes her head. "No. Can't say that I have. Not sure I'd even know what it looked like."

"Really? Not even with your boyfriends from college or after?"

"No." She looks away for a beat, as if thinking, and her eyes come back to mine. "Most of those were more physical relationships than anything. The way I see it, unless you know yourself, how can you expect someone else to know you? And if they don't know you, how can they truly love you? I've spent the last ten years getting to know myself. Maybe someday, someone else will know me, too. And maybe then, I'll finally see what all that oxytocin business is about."

"That's pretty profound and self-aware." She smiles and starts toward the door and I call after her. She pivots with her hand still on the knob. "A word of advice about tonight?" She shrugs. "Don't let Hensley talk you into continuing to drink.

She's a lot of fun, but she forgets sometimes that not everyone likes to get blackout drunk every Saturday night and wake up with a different person every morning. I love her to death, but she thinks everyone has a hollow leg."

"Got it. You're working today, right?"

"Yeah, getting ready to leave in about a half-hour. If y'all get in any trouble, holler at me."

"Will do. Have a good day."

Because I'm running on about four hours of sleep from working last night and picking up half a shift today, I'm dead on my feet by eleven PM. I'm trying to wait up for Brooklyn and Ophelia to see if they had a good night and maybe finally get some actual quality time with Brooklyn. I know if I lie down, I'll pass out, so the sofa it is.

For the past week, she was on a camping trip as part of an assignment and there was no cell service. And since she got in last night, I was getting ready to leave for work. I'm honestly surprised she didn't just stay at her place. Especially since she had some errands to run on that side of town this morning. So I also didn't see her before I left for work today or before the girls all went out and I miss her.

I must doze off, because some time later, the front door crashes open and I'm instantly on alert and up on my feet. Brooklyn and Ophelia both stumble in hanging off of one another and they're both drunk and laughing hysterically.

Rubbing the sleep from my eyes, I shut the door they left open and evaluate them both. Brooklyn is dressed in her normal club wear of faux-leather pants and an off-the-shoulder tee shirt, combat boots, and her hair in wild curls. That, I expect. What I don't expect is what Ophelia has on as they shuffle toward the kitchen, completely ignoring me.

She wears a tight black dress cut right below her ass that is so low in the back you can see the dimples on either side of the small of her back. Sparkly, silver, strappy stilettos complete the look and she has on a ton of makeup, her hair in tight curls and braided back on one side. She doesn't even look like herself and I'm not sure what to think. When she turns, finally noticing me, I catch a glimpse of a deep v-neck and a whole lot of cleavage. Good God, how did she keep from flashing everyone all night?

"Jess, hey," Ophelia slurs with a big grin and tries to walk toward me, but her heels must be too high and her steps falter, and I rush forward to catch her.

Supporting her around the waist and grabbing her forearm to keep her upright, I shake my head. "I guess I should just be glad you're a happy drunk and not an angry one."

"Happy and hor—. Hey, is that a *Ghostbuster's* shirt? I've seen that movie."

I could nearly catch a buzz from her breath and start guiding her toward her room. Seeing that Brooklyn's fallen into one of the chairs around the kitchen table and laid her head on her folded arms, I know I can leave her for a moment. "Come on, Birdie, let's get you to bed."

"Okay," she says dreamily. "I drank a lot."

I snort a laugh. "I know. Did you leave any tequila for the rest of us?"

"Probably not. I really like tequila. I forgot how good it is. I think I should have tequila all the time."

"I think I like you just fine sober."

"Everyone liked me okay drunk, too."

I open her bedroom door and guide her over to the bed. "Well, the right people will like you exactly how you are, no booze needed."

"Okay." She falls onto the bed and rolls onto her side, her dress hiking up to clear past her ass, revealing a black lace thong. I quickly avert my eyes and proceed to take off her shoes before pulling the covers up around her.

I stalk back to the kitchen, where Brooklyn is up on her feet at the kitchen sink, drinking straight from the tap, sans glass. I chuckle. "Classy, babe."

"No dishes to wash," she quips as she shuts off the water and mops her hand down her chin.

I step forward and take her face in my hands and examine her appearance. "You doing okay there, babe? You seem a little better off than Boozy McGhee in there."

She smiles, but her eyes are glassy and her breath smells strongly of cinnamon and I know she's been hitting the Fireball tonight. And from experience, I know in about an hour, she's gonna be puking. Great.

"You should have seen her, Jess. She was so much fun."

"Who, Ophelia?"

She nods sleepily. "All these guys wanted to buy her drinks and dance with her and she got asked her number so many times, I thought we were gonna have to form a line."

"Well, maybe she'll find a nice guy out of the horde. Did y'all eat any supper, or were you all just mainlining alcohol all night? You need some carbs? Want me to make you a grilled cheese?"As if my words have triggered her gag reflex, Brooklyn shoves me out of the way and heaves over the side of the sink. Sighing, I hold her hair back until she's finished and grab her a paper towel and a glass of water. "You good?"

She nods and when she stands upright, while still looking a little green around the gills, her eyes look more clear. "Yeah. Take me to bed? I've got an early morning tomorrow."

"For what?"

"I have to start my next assignment. I have a flight in the morning."

She begins to step past me and I get in her way. "What do you mean, you have a flight? You aren't scheduled to leave until Monday. The weekends are supposed to be mine, Brooklyn."

Brooklyn rolls her eyes. "What's a few hours, Jess.?"

"A few hours? It's a whole day. Plus today. We've not spent any time together this weekend and you were out of cell range for a whole week. We've not had an actual fucking conversation in over a week."

She heaves an exasperated groan. "Because all you want to talk about is the same old shit."

"The *same old shit?*" I ask, the words stinging. "What 'same old shit' would that be? Our future?"

She drops her head to my chest. "I can't do this right now. I'm drunk. I don't want to fight. Please? Can we just go to bed?"

Letting my forehead fall to the top of her head, I let out a soft, resigned sigh, feeling the minute hand tick closer to our end date. "Alright." Leading her to my room, I turn down the bed and she shimmies out of her pants, only for them to get hung up on her boots. Accepting defeat, she simply lies down on the bed.

Stepping around to her side of the bed, I sit and pull her feet up into my lap and untie her boot laces and work them off her feet before dropping them on the floor. I drag her pants down the remainder of the way and discard them on top of her boots.

Scooping her up and depositing her farther up the bed, I pull the covers down and tuck them up around her. I strip down to my underwear and crawl into bed beside her and shut off the lamp. When I lie down, Brooklyn rolls toward me and buries her face in my neck, kissing her way down toward my chest. She snakes her hand down my stomach and into my boxer briefs and I snatch her hand away. Not that I don't want to make love to her, but I'm hurt and angry and she's drunk and none of that makes for a good combination.

"Come on, baby. Let me make you feel good." She pulls her hand from mine and resumes sliding her fingers down, giving my cock a rough stroke. And despite my feelings, my body betrays me and hums to life. "See," she says, a smile in her voice. "You know you want it."

"Brooklyn, no. You're drunk. We had a fight."

Kissing her way down my chest and stomach, she whispers against my skin. "So let me make it up to you. I'm not *that* drunk. Please?" When she gives the head of dick a squeeze, I can't bite back a groan. And at this moment, it'd just be easier to give in and pretend we'll be fine, even if I know we won't. Our problems will still be here and she'll still not want to marry me or move in with me or have babies with me.

And yet, I don't stop her when she tugs down the front of my boxer briefs and slides her lips over my cock. Where it would normally feel like ecstasy, tonight, it only feels like some sort of consolation prize. Thankfully, half-drunk as she is, Brooklyn doesn't notice how detached I am from this moment. And although it only takes me a few minutes to get off, it feels hollow and nothing like all the other times she's given me head. Because now I feel nothing.

Approximately two minutes later, Brooklyn is snoring on the other side of the bed and I lie awake for a lot longer than I should. And try as I might, I can't keep the tears from rolling down my face knowing I can't keep doing this. I'd never want to keep her from her dreams, but what about mine? If we stay on our current path, I'll still be here waiting patiently five or ten years from now. Simply because Brooklyn has said what she wants.

I'm still awake when her alarm goes off. I feign sleep and

pretend to barely stir when she gives me a goodbye kiss and I mutter something incoherent when she says she'll call me later.

CHAPTER SEVEN

OPHELIA

After the worst hangover of my life, I'm nursing a cup of coffee —I have to say, Jess's coffee is really smooth and almost drinkable, even black—and skipping my run. I have blisters from the high, high heels I wore to the club and my boobs are irritated from the tape I had to use to keep my dress from landing me an indecent exposure charge.

Feeling marginally better after a shower, my head is still pounding. Curled up on the sofa with no TV on, I've almost nodded off again when heavy footsteps sound from the hallway. Jess doesn't say anything and he's dressed in gym clothes and sneakers as he walks toward the coffee maker.

Surprised to see coffee already made, he looks around and I lift my mug in salute when his eyes meet mine. He jerks his chin up in acknowledgement and pours himself a cup of coffee before coming to sit on the opposite end of the couch. He wordlessly sips his coffee and seems sad.

"You okay?"

He shrugs. "Undecided."

"Brooklyn still in bed? She didn't drink nearly as much as me, so I'm shocked she'd still be sleeping it off."

He doesn't look at me and shakes his head. "She left. She had a flight to catch."

"Oh, right. I think she mentioned that last night at the club. Something about heading to Napa, maybe."

He huffs a disappointed laugh. "Well, glad to know she told someone."

My brows rise in surprise. "You didn't know she was going?"

"Not until y'all got home last night. And we got basically no time this weekend and with her assignment last week, we didn't talk because there was no service."

"I'm sorry. I'm sure it's hard with her being gone so much. Y'all seemed to be doing better."

He takes a long sip of his coffee. "Not really."

"Oh. Well, that sucks. She's great. And you're great. And y'all seem great together."

He blinks and I'm shocked to see he's near tears. "Yeah, she is great. She's amazing and fun and beautiful and I love her. But..."

When he trails off and shakes his head, I find myself wanting to comfort him, but have no clue how. I try to think about anything I can do to brighten his day, but not much comes to mind. So I toss out the only idea that formulates. "You're off today, right?"

He turns his head, giving me his full attention. "Yeah. Why?"

"Because you don't need to sit in this house and dwell on everything going on. It won't you do any good. You and Brooklyn will talk and hopefully work everything out again, but you're only gonna feel worse if stay inside. Come on a drive with me."

"Where?"

"Does it matter? Anywhere would be better than this."

Jess considers. "I guess. Okay. Let me brush my teeth."

"So you were gonna go to the gym with yuck mouth? Gross."

He scoffs. "You're one to talk. You came in smelling like you'd let Jose Cuervo have his way with you six ways to Sunday."

I snort a laugh. "You're probably not far off. I don't remember much past the first few shots. I'm a lightweight."

Twenty minutes later, after I drag on a pair of jeans and a tank top, sandals, and a ball cap with my ponytail threaded through the back, I back out of the driveway, Jess in my passenger seat.

"So, where are you taking me?"

"What, you don't like surprises?" I ask, trying to keep my tone light. He's still in a foul mood and I'm determined that by the end of the day, he will smile at least once.

He props his elbow on the door and rests the side of his head on it, looking out the windshield. "Not really."

"Well, too bad because it's a surprise."

"Alright." His tone sounds resigned and again, because I'm terrible at comforting people, I don't have words to give him in this moment. We're both quiet for a long beat and his head eventually lolls in my direction and he sits up straighter. "Can I ask you something?"

"Sure."

"Did you have fun last night?"

I smile. "Yeah, it was fine. Why?"

"You didn't look like yourself, so I didn't know if you were comfortable."

Unsure of his meaning, I press for clarification. "What do you mean?"

"Well, I've never even seen you drink before and you stumble in the house three sheets to the wind and were passed out before you even landed on your bed. You had on a shit-ton of makeup, which I've also never seen you wear. And you can't tell me your feet aren't killing you today. Those were, what, five-inch heels?"

I shrug and grip the steering wheel, unsure how to feel about his assessment of me. "So, I looked bad? Is that what you're saying? Because I'll have you know, I got lots of attention and my phone hasn't stopped buzzing from texts."

He frowns. "No, looked beautiful. That's not what I meant. And just because you got attention, doesn't mean it's necessarily good attention."

Feeling somehow both bolstered and annoyed by his comment, I glance at him, trying not to read too much into his words. "Okay, well, there's a lot to unpack with what you just said. And honestly, I'm not sure if I should be insulted or flattered. On one hand, you said I was beautiful, so thanks. On the other hand, it sounds like you think because of the way I looked, you assume any guys I met last night will think I'm easy or a slut or any of those other words men like to label women to make them feel smaller or bad about themselves."

He blinks rapidly and scoffs. "That wasn't what I was implying, but if you go out with these guys, they're gonna expect the girl you were last night, not who you are normally."

"Wow. Okay. So now I'm catfishing, is that what you're telling me?"

He's obviously flustered and sputters. "N-no. That's not what I'm saying." He pinches the bridge of his nose. "Can you pull over? I can't have this conversation while you're driving. The way you're gripping the steering wheel, I'm afraid you're gonna veer into oncoming traffic simply to make a point."

Thoroughly pissed off, I clench my jaw and turn on my

blinker to pull into a shopping center. I slam the car into park and turn toward him, arms folded. "Okay, so if you weren't saying that men are gonna think I'm slutty because I wore a short dress and high heels and had on makeup, what were you saying, Jess?"

He takes a deep breath and seems to attempt to collect his thoughts for a beat before looking me in the eye. "I only asked you if you were comfortable last night. And that was the only concern I had. You were the one who said extreme modesty was your default. I know I nudged you to maybe branch out, but there's nothing wrong with the way you look. Even exactly how you are now. You have really nice hair and good skin and the right guy won't need you to look a certain way to give you attention. Not to mention, you're obviously intelligent and resourceful and a lot of fun to hang out with."

Still miffed, if a bit less venomous, I raise a brow. "Jess, you talk to me like you think I'm this innocent little virgin whose virtue needs to be protected. I'm not. Trust me. I'm fully aware what men who asked for my number last night were looking for. How do you know I'm not looking for the same thing?

"Just because you haven't seen me bring anyone home doesn't mean it's out of the realm of possibility for me. All it means is, I haven't found anyone I like well enough that I could see bringing them home. You work at night. For all you know, I'm hooking up with four different guys a week at their place. And for your information, I was very comfortable with the exception of the giant blister I now have on my pinky toe. Maybe your 'nudge' did exactly what you wanted it to. It helped me build my confidence and bring me out of my shell. I think having friends can do that, too, though.

"Don't assume because I grew up the way I did and was late to the party that I don't know my way around. I am not naïve and haven't been in a long, long time. I'm also not your sister, so I don't need you to pretend to be my big brother. I'm a grown woman and don't need you to hold my hand."

He nods slowly, letting my words sink in. "You're right. I'm sorry. And it's none of my business what you do with your private life. But I'm your friend and I don't want to see you get taken advantage of. And I'm also in a really shitty mood today. It's no excuse, but I'm letting my mood turn me into this negative person and you don't deserve my attitude. I know you're just trying to cheer me up and I appreciate it. I'm sorry I'm ruining it."

"Thank you for your apology. And you are forgiven. Now, can I take you to your surprise?"

He gives me a small smile. "Sure."

Twenty minutes later, I pull in at the animal shelter and Jess's brows draw down in confusion. "So, your solution to my sour mood is to bring me to a place with lots of homeless animals?"

I roll my eyes. "Just trust the process, okay?"

We climb from the car and I push him toward the door. When we get inside, we're greeted by Camille, one of the regular staff members. Her eyes light up when she sees me and a huge grin crosses her face. "Ophelia! Hey. So good to see you."

"You, too." I gesture toward Jess. "My friend here is in dire need of some vitamin P. Got any to spare?"

Camille nods. "Of course. If y'all want to get signed in, you can go on back. You remember the way?"

I huff a laugh. "It's only been a couple of weeks. I couldn't forget if I tried."

"Alright."

Although confused, Jess signs the sheet and doesn't question what vitamin P is or ask where we're going as I lead him down a hall toward a block of large walk-in kennels. I look from cage to cage, my heart sinking when I see that Garth is still in residence. I let out a sad sigh and open the kennel. Jess puts his hand on my arm, stopping me. "Are we allowed to open that?"

I nod and give him a reassuring smile. "Yeah. Come on."

He still looks hesitant and his eyes dart to the giant mass in the corner of the kennel. "Is it aggressive?"

"No. He's sweet."

As I open the cage, Jess asks, "You know this dog?"

"Yeah," I reply, sad. "This is Garth."

Entering the kennel, I cross to where Garth is lying on his elevated bed, head resting on his massive paws.

"You don't sound happy to see him."

"I'm not. For me to see him means he's still here."

I drop to sit, legs folded, in front of the dog. Garth's sad amber eyes lift to mine, but he makes no move to rouse, even as I get closer so his nearly deaf ears can pick up the sound of my voice. "Hey, buddy. You remember me?" The dog simply lets out a huff, making his considerable jowls flap.

"What's wrong with him?"

"Nothing. He's just old." When I reach my hand within range of his nose, he perks up considerably, his large tail beginning to thump. "There he is," I say with a smile. When Garth realizes it's me, he whines and hauls himself to his feet and bumps my outstretched hand with his muzzle. He steps off his bed and walks over to me, his whole body wagging with happiness. I can't help but laugh at how excited he is.

I glance up at Jess, who's still standing near the entrance. "Come say hello." He seems to snap out of whatever trance he's in and steps closer, dropping to sit next to me. "He's almost completely deaf," I explain. "So you have to be really close to his ears and speak loudly if you want him to hear you."

He extends his hand toward Garth and lets him sniff his

fingers. The dog considers the offering and gives Jess's hand a lick. "You're in," I tell him.

He chuckles. "Well, alright. So, if nothing is wrong with him, why is he here?"

"His owner passed away a couple of years ago and didn't have any family or friends to take him. He's thirteen, so no one wants a dog who will kick the bucket at any moment. I've been coming here since I moved back to Knoxville and I've hated seeing him every single week since he was brought in. I kept hoping someone would take him and he'd get to spend his last days knowing love."

"You come here every week? I didn't know that."

I shrug. "It started as just something to do to get out of my apartment. I've always loved dogs, but couldn't have one at the apartment, so I'd spend my free time coming to give the misfits and rejects attention. Everyone wants puppies and the friendly dogs. Senior dogs and ones who need a little more time to warm up to folks or need specific living arrangements are harder to place."

"What breed is he? Some sort of mastiff?"

I nod. "Yeah." I pick up a nearby weathered tennis ball and let Garth sniff it before tossing to the opposite corner. As usual, it takes him a bit to see and sniff it out, but momentarily, he obediently retrieves it and drops it in front of me.

"What's vitamin P?"

I give Jess my attention as I continue to toss the ball for Garth to fetch. "What?"

"You told the woman up front I needed vitamin P. What's that?"

I smile. "'P' as in, perspective. The first time I came here was right after I'd gone back to the farm to see my family. In spite of the way I was raised and stuff, they're still my family and I missed them. But when they wouldn't even answer the door, I was sadder than I can ever remember being in my whole life. I was driving down this road and happened to see some volunteers out in the outdoor space exercising some of the dogs. There was nothing I wanted more in that moment than to play with some puppies and forget about all the shit with my family.

"I was still crying when I walked in and asked if they needed any volunteers to play with the puppies. Camille looked at me and said, 'No, but it sure looks like you could use some vitamin P.'

"She brought me back to this area and said if I wanted to volunteer, they were always needing helpers on 'Misfit Island' as she called it. That maybe if I spent some time with the seniors and those with less than stellar pasts, I might gain some perspective into my own life. That no matter how bad it got, my life would still always be better than a reject dog's."

Jess scoffs. "Well. That's a pretty shitty way to look at it."

I nod. "Yeah, and sometimes, people do have worse lives. And really, I didn't fully grasp her meaning until I moved into your house. I haven't had anyone since I left North Carolina. For five years, I was pretty much an island unto myself. And I know a lot of that is my own fault, but until then, I felt like Garth here. There's nothing wrong with me, but no one really wanted me." I sigh. "Well, almost no one. And those that did, didn't want friendship or even a relationship, so I really did start to feel like a reject.

"But given a good friend and a place to thrive, you gain perspective. So, even though things with Brooklyn are messy right now, hopefully you'll work it out. And even if you don't, that doesn't mean you have to go to Misfit Island because you have friends. Good friends who will be there for you."

I clear my throat and peer down at Garth, who's grown tired and has laid down on the floor and rested his head in my lap. I rub his ear and he sighs contentedly. "Sorry. It's probably a stupid analogy. I'm no good at pep talks."

Jess reaches over to run a hand down the dog's back. "No, that was really good, actually." After a beat, he asks, "How come you haven't come to adopt him since you moved in?"

I blink at him, confused by his question. "I guess it never occurred to me that it was an option."

"And what if it were? Would you?"

"I didn't bring you here to guilt trip you into adopting a dog, Jess. That wasn't the purpose of this visit."

"I know. I wouldn't think you'd do something like that. But you like him; he obviously likes you. I'm sure once he got to know me, I'd definitely be his favorite, but you know, baby steps," he says with a grin and nudges my elbow with his.

CHAPTER EIGHT

JESS

Ophelia continues to consider my suggestion to adopt Garth, but still looks to be hesitant. "What's causing you to doubt adopting him? Trust me, I wouldn't have asked if I didn't think there was a good possibility of this dog going home with us."

"I promise I didn't bring you here to give you some sob story in the hopes that would be the case."

I roll my eyes. "I know that. You already said that. I love dogs. I got used to having Gouda around when Josie lived with me and honestly, I've been missing someone to clean up after in the yard," I say with a wink. "But for real, no one should be alone in their last days, not even big, dopey dogs who will probably drool all over my sofa and pee on my rugs."

Ophelia smiles. "He's housebroken."

"Well, that settles it. He's coming home with us. Go start the paperwork. We'll have to go home and get my car since yours is a sardine can on wheels and there's no way he'll fit in there."

She huffs a laugh. "Do not mock the tiny car. You should see the gas mileage that thing gets. I can go over a week on one tank of gas and I look cute in it." Her expression grows serious. "Are you sure, Jess?"

I nod, because I am. If for no other reason than to never see that look of despair on her face when she saw Garth was still here. That look was not one I ever want to see again. And Garth is pretty cool and maybe Ophelia and I can give him some great last days.

Her face morphs into a mask of pure glee. "Oh, my God. Thank you."

"Anytime, Birdie."

She blinks. "What?"

I huff a laugh. "What, you never had a nickname before?" After thinking for a beat, she shakes her head. "Well, now you have. So, go do the paperwork and we'll stop by the pet store and get all the things on the way back to get him."

Two hours later, we're settling in at home with Garth and he's currently sniffing every inch of the living room after already christening the backyard. Satisfied he's smelled every smell possible, he lumbers over to the sofa and climbs up, planting himself on the cushion between us. He has his head laid in Ophelia's lap and she peers down at him with such affection, I know bringing him home was the right call.

"Thank you for today," I say a moment later.

Ophelia shakes her head. "I should be thanking you. I can't believe Garth finally got to find a home."

"Still, I appreciate you trying to cheer me up."

"Anytime." Struck by a thought, she asks, "Do you have any family?" I nod. "Do you speak to them?"

"Yeah. I was talking to my mother when you walked into the kitchen yesterday. My dad passed while I was in college. I also have a brother and we talk, but since he lives out of the country, I really only get to see him at holidays. He's also pretty tech-adverse, so he doesn't do much social media. We talk about once a month, but don't have much in common."

"Where does he live?"

"France."

Her eyes go wide. "France? Wow. Have you ever been to visit him?"

I shake my head. "No. Other than the vacations we went on as a family, I haven't really been anywhere. I'm not like Brooklyn or Flynn—that's my brother. I don't need to go anywhere to feel like I'm somewhere. I don't have insatiable wanderlust. I enjoy being home. I'm a bit of a workaholic, but that's only because I want to get my house paid off so that when I get married or have kids, I don't have a mountain of debt hanging over my head."

"What will you do if your wife doesn't want to live here? I mean, don't get me wrong, it's a great house, but she might want something different."

I shrug. "If this house is paid off and Br—." I clamp my mouth shut because I was about to say Brooklyn's name as if she'll be the one helping me decide where we should live, but I already know it won't be her. I sigh and drag my hand down my face and start again. "If this house is paid off and whoever I marry doesn't want to live here, I can always rent it out and make passive income. There's really no downside to having it paid off."

Ophelia nods slowly and says quietly, "It still might be Brooklyn, you know."

My chest growing tight with emotion, I shake my head. "No, it probably won't." I drop my head to the back of the couch and a few seconds later, feel the weight of a very large, warm mass settle into my lap and I grunt when he steps on my legs.

She laughs, and the sound makes me smile, despite how shitty I feel. "Looks like he's trying to be there for you."

"He's there, alright," I say with a pained breath as Garth leans his entire body against my torso, all nearly two-hundred pounds of him. After a long moment of Ophelia downright cackling at my discomfort, she guides him off of me and I finally take a full breath. "Jesus, he really makes you feel the love, huh?"

"I'll say."

I laugh and hop up off the couch and head toward the kitchen, planning on starting supper. "You have plans tonight?"

She follows me into the room and washes her hands after filling Garth's water bowl. "No. Why?"

I shrug. "I didn't know with all those guys you gave your number to last night. I thought maybe you'd already set something up with someone. I was gonna fix supper, but wanted to check with you before I did. I can make plenty and we both have some for our lunches tomorrow."

She gives me a warm smile. "Oh. I still don't have plans."

"Alright. Well, in that case, you get to help."

She snaps my arm with the towel she's been using to dry her hands. "You're acting like I don't already help if we eat together."

"Ouch. Damn, you aim is lethal with that thing," I say and rub the spot, already forming a welt.

She winces and grabs my arm, examining the damage. "I'm so sorry. I was actually aiming for your shoulder. I've got some salve I can put on it."

I'm about to protest, but she's already jogging around the corner to her room and is back before I even have a chance to notice she's gone. She steps forward and screws the top off a small jar and sets it on the counter before digging out a pea-sized amount and lifting my arm again, massaging the ointment into the skin. Her thumb makes small, gentle circles around the inflamed area and I have to swallow, because after a moment, I don't feel the sting, I only feel her hands on my skin and it begins to feel a bit too intimate for my liking.

She must come to the same realization as me at nearly the same time because she drops my arm and clears her throat, focusing her attention on recapping the jar. "It's coconut oil, beeswax, honey, and lavender, so it's good for your skin."

"Thanks. Feels better already."

Ophelia nods, not making eye contact, and heads back to her room.

The following week, I'm about to walk out the door for work when my phone vibrates with a text. I pull it out and examine the screen as I continue to walk toward the garage and my car.

> Brooklyn: Won't make it to town this weekend. There's a party at HQ I'm expected to attend.

I sigh and hang my head. After our fight last weekend, things have been a bit chilly between Brooklyn and me. I don't want to argue, but how long has she known about this party? Since she didn't tell me about interviewing for the job, what else doesn't she tell me anymore? I hate that my ability to not question everything has been compromised by her omission of truth.

As I slide behind the wheel of my car and my phone connects to the bluetooth, I call Brooklyn. When she answers, I try to keep my tone light. "So, what's the deal with this party?"

"Oh, you know. Billionaire flexing his muscles. And now I somehow have to track down a cocktail dress to wear, even though the venue is casual. They're doing it at that brewery that makes your favorite beer.

"Highland Brewing?"

"That's the one. Are you on your way to work?"

"Yeah. Did you just find out about the party? A couple days seems like short notice."

Brooklyn sighs. "No, I've known about it for a couple of weeks, but I thought I'd be able to get out of it. And I'm sure, if Hanson wasn't coming, I could."

"Who's Hanson?"

"The CEO. I'm sure I've mentioned him before. He's the tech-guru genius. But he's putting in an appearance, so I have to, too."

Disappointment floods me that there's no way I'm gonna get to see her this week. "Well, it sucks I'm not gonna see you, but I get it. What's your assignment for next week? It gonna put you anywhere you might be able to sneak home for a day?"

"Nope, can't say that it will."

"Alright. Well, I'll talk to you later. I'm getting ready to pull in at the hospital."

"Okay. Have a good shift."

As we say our goodbyes and I get parked, I'm surprised to see Ophelia standing beside her car door. And she's not alone. She's talking with a man and they're laughing. A sense of unease fills me because I know the guy she's talking to; a surgeon by the name of Drake Samson. He's a player and has made the rounds of the entire surgical floor.

Ophelia sees me as I'm almost past them and waves. "Hey, Jess."

I stop and give her a tight smile. "Ophelia." I give Samson a quick jerk of my head. "Dr. Samson."

"Good to see you, Jess."

I focus my attention back on Ophelia. "I took Garth out right before I left and fed him, so he should be good for a while."

"Okay. Thanks."

I check my phone and know I can't stand around. "See you at home."

"Alright. Have a good night at work."

And if my ears aren't deceiving me, as I walk away, I hear Samson asking for Ophelia's number and if she has plans for the weekend. My stomach clenches and I can't stop from rolling my fingers into a fist.

None of your business, Jess.

The next morning as I'm coming in from work, Ophelia is filling her travel mug with coffee. I'd gone back and forth all night about whether or not I should give her a heads up about Samson, and as her friend and roommate, I decided I should tell her.

"Hey," she says with a smile. "How was work?"

I drop my lunch box on the counter. "Fine. Do you have a second?"

She screws the lid on her travel mug and I notice her nails are painted. *That's new.* "Sure. What's up?" She tucks her hair behind her ear and I also see she has on earrings. *And makeup?* I examine her more fully and see that while her clothes would still be considered business casual, they're more form fitting and the blouse she wears has a v-neck that showcases a bit of cleavage and the pencil skirt she wears has a long slit up the back that showcases a lot of thigh when she walks across the kitchen to grab her purse. In high heels? *I guess she's ditched the flats.*

"Jess? You were saying?"

I shake away the thoughts about how Ophelia shouldn't be going to work looking like this. Not that there's anything wrong with the way she looks; not in the least. But it's verging on "sexy" territory and I'm not sure what to think. "Oh. Right. Sorry, I'm tired. I wanted to talk to you about Dr. Samson."

"What about him?" she asks and takes a sip of her coffee.

"I heard him ask for your number and if you had plans."

"Yeah? So?"

"You don't need to go out with him."

Her eyes narrow. "And why's that?"

"Because he's not a good guy. And just because he's a prestigious surgeon does't mean you shouldn't look at the bigger picture."

"You're acting like the big brother again, Jess. I'm a big girl."

I sigh. "I'm not trying to act like your brother. I'm trying to be your friend, Ophelia. I work with the guy. He's worked his way through every nurse on the surgery floor and probably more, for all I know. I just don't want to see you get hurt."

"Jess, I haven't even gone on a date with the guy and I'm not going to."

Relief floods me. "You're not?"

She shakes her head. "No. I know about his reputation. Just because I don't have any friends at the hospital doesn't mean I don't hear a lot. For years, I was practically invisible, and you'd be amazed at what people will say when they think no one is around." She takes a step closer to me. "And the fact that he's a womanizer doesn't bother me. It's the fact he cheats on his wife to do it."

I blink, my brain glitching with shock. "He's married?"

She nods. "Yeah. I was never gonna go out with him. He

saw me walking to my car and probably thought I was new or something. He walked out with me and he's charming and funny, but I don't do cheating. And besides, I already have a date this weekend."

"Oh, okay. Well, good for you. I guess Garth and I will just have to have a guys' weekend."

She frowns. "Brooklyn's not coming in?"

I sigh. "No, she has to go to this work cocktail event thing."

"Since when?"

"Yesterday."

"She didn't invite you to go with her?"

I shrug. "She probably thinks I wouldn't go anyway and it would lead to an argument. I've not been the most accommodating lately," I admit.

"Okay, so go anyway. Rent a hotel room, surprise her. Show up looking entirely dashing and show her you're still willing to put in the effort. Do you know where the event's being held?"

"Yeah. I do, actually."

"Alright, so what do you have to lose? I know you don't like to travel, but it's Asheville, not L.A. You've already got the time off, so do the grand gesture thing and sweep her off her feet."

I consider. "Not bad. I'll have to think about it. So, date, huh?"

"Yeah." After a beat, she amends her statement. "Well, really, it's just drinks at 35 North."

"Cool place. Josie and I used to go there all the time. Right down the road, too."

"Thus the appeal." She taps her phone screen. "Shit, I have to go. See you later."

CHAPTER NINE

JESS

Following Ophelia's advice, I've stepped entirely out of my comfort zone and rented a hotel room in Asheville and have the one good suit I own in a garment bag hanging in the back seat. And nervous as I am as I made this drive, I hope if Brooklyn can see I'm still willing to put forth some effort, we'll be able to start making our way back to where we were.

Freshening up at the hotel and getting dressed, I decide, last minute, to forgo the tie so as not to appear too stuffy. Satisfied I'm presentable in my navy suit and light pink button-down, I blow out a breath and head out the door to the venue.

Pulling up at Highland Brewing Company at little after nine PM, I'm struck by how large the building is. I've been drinking many of the beers Highland produces for several years, but have yet to make a trip over to see the brewery itself. It's a beautiful industrial building with a large wooden deck out front stung with Edison lights.

More than a bit nervous as I walk toward the entrance to their dedicated events space, I try to take some calming breaths and hope there's not some check-in process. I smooth my hair and tug on my cuffs as I enter the building and take in the large space, again strung with Edison lights that cast a warm glow around the room. Several standing banners advertise the travel website and Brooklyn's photo is on several of them, showcasing many of her adventures.

"Excuse me." I turn to see a man in a suit in his early twenties and offer him a smile. "Can I help you? Are you on the list?"

I shake my head. "Probably not. My girlfriend, Brooklyn Hill, is supposed to be here. I came in to surprise her."

His face lights up. "Oh, you're Brookie's man." He gives me an appreciative scan. "Very nice." Extending his hand, he continues, "I'm Zane, Brooklyn's newest very best friend. And you must be Jess. I've heard so much about you."

Not wanting to tell him Brooklyn hasn't ever mentioned him, I shake his hand and smile. "Hopefully good things."

He arches one sculpted brow. "Oh, trust me. Very good things. She should be around her somewhere." Gesturing toward the bar, he leans a bit closer. "Why don't you go get a beer. It's open bar—thank you, Hanson—and I'll see if I can track her down."

I nod. "Sounds good." I make my way over to the large bar and order my standard—the Oatmeal Porter—and survey the crowd. It's an eclectic bunch. Some people are the high-fashion, stereotypical corporate types. Some are more nerdy-techie. Some are just average joes. But none of them look as good to me in this moment as the woman walking toward me dressed in a dark red, strapless cocktail dress. Her hair is styled in a knot of some kind and she's toned down her makeup. In truth, her whole look seems to be toned down and more mainstream than I've ever seen.

She closes the distance between us and I notice she even has on high heels and her hair isn't navy anymore, it's a dark brown. I'm unsure how to even comprehend her transformation because she doesn't look like herself. First Ophelia and now Brooklyn? Is there something in the water? Her smile is warm, but something in her eyes doesn't give me the warm and fuzzies or the impression that she's happy to see me. Another puzzle to figure out, I guess.

"Jess, oh my God. What are you doing here?"

I pull her in for a hug and give her a kiss on the cheek and her posture is stiff for a brief moment until she returns my embrace. "What, a guy can't, out of the blue decide, to do something completely out of character and show up unannounced to surprise his girlfriend?"

She chuckles, but it sounds forced. I pull back and take her face in my hands. "What's wrong? Did I break some big rule by showing up? Will this cause problems for you?"

"No. You're fine. I just wish I'd known you were coming. I'm gonna have to schmooze all night; so I won't be very good company, that's all."

I shrug. "I'm fine." I lift my glass with a smile. "Couldn't be better, actually." I lean in and brush a kiss under her ear. "I also got a room, so as long as you can tell me we can go back there and I take this dress off you after this thing, I will be a very happy camper."

She huffs a laugh. "Sounds perfect. Okay." She lifts a brow. "And actually, if you wanted to go ahead and go and wait for me, that's fine. If you're here, I might feel incentivized to stay, but if you're waiting for me in a room with a bed in the same city as me, I will bust my ass to get out of here a lot sooner."

Smiling, I lift her hand to my lips and kiss her palm. "I'm gonna finish my drink, but sure, I can do that."

After a quick kiss, she scurries off to continue doing whatever it is her job demands of her at this thing. Finishing my first beer, I go ahead and order one more, knowing I won't stay past that. I'm lifting my glass to my lips as a guy in his early forties in a suit that possibly costs more than my car walks by but stops short when he sees me. I'm not sure what to make of his reaction, especially as he comes closer, blatantly sizing me up.

I pull myself to my full height and set my glass down. "I don't know you," the man says.

Caught off guard by his words, I can only shake my head and answer honestly. "No, I don't believe you do."

He comes closer and continues to examine me. Seeing my confusion, he smiles. "That only means you don't work for me. I have all the faces and names of my employees committed to memory. So that either means you're with someone who works for me or you gatecrashed."

I huff a laugh. "Or, both," I admit and extend my hand to the man I now realize must be Brooklyn's boss. "Jess Tate. Brooklyn Hill is my girlfriend. I drove in for the weekend to surprise her."

He nods, a wide grin on his face. "Well, Jess, it's great to meet you. Hanson Culpepper. Brooklyn has become a great asset to Culpepper Media. We appreciate you letting us steal her away from Knoxville."

Not like I had a choice in the matter.

I keep my smile in place and nod. "Well, I sure miss her, but she seems to be enjoying it here."

"I sure hope so. Can't have my Vice President of Online Presence for our travel division being unhappy."

I frown. "I'm sorry, what title did you say?" He repeats himself and I think I'm surely misunderstanding him. "Are you sure we're talking about the same Brooklyn Hill? She's a travel blogger."

"Not anymore. Well, she still travels plenty, but it's mainly to interview the talent she's bringing onboard. That was the title we agreed to when she came to work here. Didn't she tell you? It's a huge leap in her career path. Now, she's the one making the decisions about where our bloggers go. You should be proud of her. Also, have you seen her new place? I'm so glad she took my advice about the tree in the front yard. Cutting it down is gonna add so much to the value of the property in the way of curb appeal."

"I'm sorry, her *place?*"

He nods, clearly confused by my incomprehension. He continues nodding slowly. "Yeah, her new house. She'd been waffling about cutting down the oak tree."

Something hot and feeling a lot like rage settles into my chest. I try to breathe but I'm not sure I remember how. Hanson must see something on my face that says he's fucked up because he gives me an apologetic smile before looking across the room. "I'm so sorry, I see someone I need to speak with."

I don't respond and simply nod. I'm not sure I can form words in this moment. And it's not until Brooklyn enters my line of sight that I actually move at all. I guzzle the remainder of my beer and angrier and more hurt than I've ever felt before, walk over to her. The fact she's laughing with someone while she's been lying to me for months makes bile rise in my throat.

Unable to wait for a break in the conversation or even apologize for interrupting, I step next to her. "We need to talk. Now."

Her head snaps in my direction and she searches my face. After a moment's hesitation, she nods and excuses herself from the crowd of people she'd been entertaining. And no matter how much I'm hurting in this moment, I'm still not about to embarrass her and have this fight publicly.

I pivot and walk outside, not even glancing behind me to see if she's following. The click of the heels I've never seen her wear tells me she is. Once we're both outside and the door shuts, I wheel on her. "Vice President of Online Presence? You bought a fucking house? Were you even gonna tell me?" Her mouth falls open in shock that I know and I realize she wasn't. Especially when she makes no move to explain. I press forward. "Makes sense why we couldn't stay at your apartment on the weekends. You let it go, didn't you?"

"Jess, I can explain."

I fold my arms. "Okay, go ahead."

"When I interviewed, it was for a travel blogger job. But during my second interview, Hanson offered me the VP job. It was twice as much money as the blogger position. How was I gonna turn it down?"

"You didn't even fucking tell me. You didn't tell me anything. Made me look like a real tool in front of your boss. He must assume I either don't pay attention or don't give a shit because I knew fuck all about your job or your house."

I drag my hands through my hair and swallow against the tightness in my chest and throat. "You bought a damn house, Brooklyn? You put down fucking roots? What happened to needing to travel and not settle down? Guess for the right amount of money, you will though, right? For almost two months, you've been coming to my house on the weekends while you fucking live here. *Live* here.

"What was your plan, just continue to visit me and lie about going on assignment? You sit behind a desk in a corner office and change your hair and your clothes and your entire philosophy of life for money? You'd lie to me for fucking money? I would have moved with you. You know that."

She nods, her eyes welling with tears. "Yeah, you would have. And then you would assume because I'd settled down that I wanted to get married and pop out those babies you're so desperate for." She takes a step closer and grips my face. "I love you. I didn't want things to change between us but also didn't want us to keep fighting."

Tears burn my own eyes and I pull her hands from my face. "I'm not fighting you anymore, Brooklyn. And things changed between us the minute you decided to start lying. You don't want to get married or have babies? Fine. I could've probably accepted that. But I can't accept the fact that you've willfully been deceiving me for fucking months. You don't do that to someone you love."

I don't wipe the wetness from my cheeks or try to disguise the hurt in my voice. "I hope it was all worth it. I'm sure your new house is perfect. I hope it's big enough to house all your success and ambition because God knows you're probably not ever gonna let anyone else in there." Realizing I'm still grasping her hands in mine, I drop them and turn and begin walking down the stairs.

"Jess, wait. Please," Brooklyn calls after me. "We can talk about this."

I stop and turn so abruptly, she nearly runs into me. "The fucking time to talk was when you decided you wanted roots but didn't want them to include me. You wanted to keep me interested so you'd have some weekend fun and good dick but not have me interfere with any of your plans. I have nothing else to say to you, Brooklyn. Go back to your party. We're done."

"Jess, I'm sorry. Please. We can fix this."

I huff a disgusted laugh. "You're not fucking sorry. You're sorry you got caught. Like I said, we're done."

This time, when I turn to leave, she doesn't follow and I waste no time sliding behind the wheel of my car, driving back to the hotel to collect my things and heading straight home.

Although I'd started crying when I was with Brooklyn, no additional tears come. In fact, all I feel is numb. And even though I knew it would probably end sooner or later, I didn't expect it to be like this.

It's nearly three AM by the time I pull into the garage at home. I drop my bag in the laundry room before opening the door that leads into the kitchen. As I enter the room, I stop in my tracks when I see an unfamiliar man standing at my kitchen sink dressed only in a pair of jeans.

The guy, a tall blonde in his late twenties or early thirties, chokes on the water he's drinking and the color drains from his face. "Fuck, I didn't know she had a boyfriend. I swear."

I shake my head, annoyed I have to talk to anyone when all I want to do is fall into bed. "I'm not her boyfriend. I'm her roommate."

Relief floods his features and he resumes drinking his water. "Cool." He grabs a shirt I hadn't noticed from the counter and tugs it on. Pulling out his phone, he checks the screen. "Gotta go. Uber's here. Tell Olivia that Nash said bye?"

I blink at the name he used. For all I know, that's the name Ophelia gave him. I shrug. "Whatever."

CHAPTER TEN

OPHELIA

After a less than satisfying night of sleep following an even less satisfying sexual encounter—dear God, I wish they would make knowing the location of the clitoris required to pass high school science—I rise and dress to go for a run. I start a pot of coffee and take Garth out into the backyard to allow him a few minutes to anoint the roses. Ensuring he's happily occupied with his chew toy, I dig around in my purse, attempting to locate my earbuds before remembering I left them in my car.

Heading out through the laundry room, I stop short when I see Jess's car in the garage. Why is he back? When did he get back? Knowing it will bug the hell out of me during my run, I head back into the house and through the kitchen and down the hall. When I get to his room, I notice his door is wide open and he's face down on his bed.

I take in the scene and know immediately the trip to Asheville must've not worked out. His shoes are still on but his shirt isn't. He has his arm wrapped around an empty jar and his pants are halfway down his legs. But the thing that catches my eye the most is that his boxer briefs are pulled down just enough that his whole ass is out for all the world to see. And yeah, it's a nice ass. One of those asses I'd want to take a bite out of. But I can't do that. Because he's not single.

And even if he were, it would be awkward because we live together; even if almost all of the people I imagine listening to my confessions as of late have been Jess. Ever since that day I popped him with the towel and rubbed the salve on his arm and I heard his breathing change, I've been ultra aware of him. It was as if that moment affected him as much as it did me. I realized in that moment I'd never touched him before and I liked it way more than I had any right to. I tried to tell myself it was only because it had been so long since I'd touched anyone, but I know that's not all it is.

But I'm not a cheater. I don't even look at attached men. And thankfully, with Jess's work schedule and mine, that hasn't been an issue.

I also assumed that if I went on a date and finally got laid, I'd be able to stop thinking about Jess. But all that did was make me think of him while I was having sex with Nash.

And now, Jess is half naked and I can't take my eyes off of him. But immediately, guilt slams into me because he's unconscious, and I grab a blanket from the shelf in his open closet and drape it over him before backing out of the room and shutting the door. I head back toward the living room and give Garth a scratch behind the ear. "Keep an eye on him, boy."

When I return from my jog, Jess still hasn't made an appearance. I take a quick shower and after getting dressed, proceed to make pancakes. I'm not sure if he'll feel like eating, but I figure having some carbs to help soak up whatever booze is left in his system can't hurt, right?

And as if summoned by the flapjacks themselves, he wanders into the kitchen just as I'm pulling the last one out of the skillet. "Well, how about that? He does live."

Jess winces and squints at me. "Birdie, I'm gonna need you about five thousand decibels lower."

"Feeling that good, huh? What did you drink?"

He drops into one of the chairs at the kitchen table and puts his head in his hands. "I drank all my beer and found a jar of moonshine Josie left when she moved out."

I set a plate with some pancakes and sausage links down in front of him, along with a bottle of syrup and cup of coffee and ruffle his hair. "Well, the pancakes will help. Eat up, buttercup."

I retrieve my plate and join him at the table and he side-eyes me. "Why are you in such a good mood? Because you got laid? By the way, some guy named Nash said to tell *Olivia* goodbye. Did you give him a fake name?"

I snort a laugh. "No. He's a dumbass. He was already not getting added to the roster due to his lack of game, but he couldn't even remember my name? Even more reason."

"Lack of game? That sucks."

It could also be that I was thinking of you.

"Yeah. He was a good kisser. The skills did not carry over." I drizzle some syrup on my pancakes and ask, "Do you want to talk about what happened? Or do you want to never talk about what happened?"

Jess shrugs and takes a bite of his pancakes. "Not talking about it won't change what happened, so sure. I broke up with Brooklyn last night. For good."

I have a bite of food halfway to my mouth and freeze. "What happened? Was she mad you showed up or something? Did y'all get in a fight?"

He takes a long drink of coffee and rubs his eyes. "She's

been lying to me for weeks. When she took that job in Asheville, it wasn't a travel blogger position. It was some VP of online presence or some shit. It's an in-office position. She's been working out of the Asheville office this whole time. She bought a fucking house."

My mouth falls open in shock. "But I thought she was so adamant about traveling and not settling down? What changed?"

He gives me a sad smile, his eyes full of pain and heartache. My chest grows tight with the expression I see on his face. "Money. The VP position paid twice as much as the blogger position, which already paid three times what she was making at her old job." He blinks and drags his thumbs along his lash line as his eyes well with tears. "And the kicker is, she wasn't even the one who told me. Her boss assumed I knew and asked how I liked Brooklyn's new place."

"What did Brooklyn say?"

He looks down at his plate, but I know he's not seeing anything. "She said she knew if she told me she'd settled down and bought a house, I would think she'd eventually want to get married or have kids and we'd fight. She said she loved me and didn't want things to change between us."

"Oh, Jess. I'm so sorry. Truly. I never would've suggested you go if I had known how badly it was gonna turn out."

He shakes his head. "It's not your fault. I was on borrowed time with her anyway. I just can't help but wonder how long she would've kept up the ruse. She lied to me for weeks, months even. She had no problem looking me in the eye and never mentioning anything. Who can do that? Lie to the person they supposedly love?"

"Still, I'm so sorry you had to find out that way. That's really shitty."

"Yeah. It is." He heaves a sigh and takes another bite of his pancakes. After he swallows, he looks over at me. "These might be the best pancakes I've ever had."

I huff a laugh. "I think you might still be a little drunk."

He shrugs. "They're still good. Thank you for cooking."

"Anytime."

"So was that guy really terrible?"

I nod. "Yeah. You ever ask someone to scratch your back and they almost get the right spot and then veer completely away from where you're directing them?" He lifts a brow and I nod. "That was my night."

Jess laughs and I nudge him with my knee. "It's not funny. First time I get laid in two years and he was probably the worst I've ever had. And that includes my first time. At least that guy knew what he was doing. Sweet Jesus. How can a guy be thirty and not know what to do? I mean, really. It's not that difficult."

He laughs harder. "Damn. That's like watching a house burn down and the fire department coming to spray water on the one next door."

"That's exactly what it's like. Ugh. I hate dating. Especially if *those* are the pickings."

"I guess you have to kiss a lot of frogs and all that."

I level him with a gaze. "Frogs I can deal with. I'm not even getting frogs, though. These are more like nematodes or some lesser life form. All guys either only want to hook up or want someone to mother them."

"We're not all like that. I don't need a mother and I don't just hook up. Well, not since high school."

Nope. Jess definitely isn't a nematode. He's also not a frog. Jess is the kind of guy you want to think about growing old with. Or, at the very least, someone you picture spending lots and lots of time in bed with.

I nod. "I know. I wasn't referring to you. You are one of the good ones. I'm sorry about how things worked out with Brooklyn."

He blows out a breath, his smile falling. "Me, too."

When we're almost done eating, Garth trots over and lays his head in Jess's lap. He absentminded reaches down to rub the dog's soft, floppy ears. I can't help but ask, "Do we need to go get you some more vitamin P?"

Jess snorts a laugh. "No. I'm sure we'd come home with four more Garths and he already eats us out of house and home." He gives me another one of his sad smiles. "I'll be okay. I think I'd already started grieving after that last big fight we had. I knew it was probably only a matter of time. And although I hate that she lied, I can't fault her for doing what she thinks she needs to do. I just wish I didn't feel like she would have continued to string me along simply so she'd get all the physical benefits of a relationship without having to invest anything emotionally. I feel like, if she truly cared, she would've cut me loose. Or, at the very least, been honest and let me decide for myself."

I nod. "So, what kind of day do you need it to be? Is it a leave all the lights off and listen to the score from *Schindler's List* and drink until we run out of booze kind of day? Is it an eat our feelings kind of day? Or is it laugh until you cry until you laugh kind of day?"

Jess considers. "Can it be all three?"

"Absolutely. Do we need to invite Josie over to make it a real party?"

He shakes his head. "She's on the road with Ford."

"What kind of work does he do? And does she always go with him on business trips?"

He chuckles. "He's a coach for a minor league hockey team. Until last year, he was in the NHL."

My eyes go wide in shock. "So, he's, like, famous?"

He nods. "He's got a lot more anonymity here, but yeah. Josie said when they went to San Jose a couple months ago to visit a friend who's also a player, they were swarmed at the game."

"Did she know that when she met him?"

He snorts. "No. For months, she had no clue who he was. She didn't want a relationship, so she was content not knowing anything about him. But, as things usually go, she caught feelings, and after a lot of drama, they seem to be really happy."

"Wow. I can't imagine being with someone famous."

Jess shrugs. "Ford's actually pretty normal. He's not a big fan of the celebrity that came with his status. I think he likes Knoxville so much because he can walk around without most people knowing who he is."

I stand to take our plates to the sink and he smiles up at me. "Thank you for breakfast and for also not mentioning that you saw me both cheeks out this morning. Definitely not my finest moment."

My face flames and I huff an uncomfortable laugh that he knows. "No problem. I'm sure you would've done the same for me."

"I would. But for real, thank you for being my friend."

"Anytime, Jess. Thank you for not making fun of me for all the things I don't know about pop culture."

He shakes his head as I step into the kitchen. "Never. In fact, what's the next movie on your list? I'm sensing a marathon. I'm sure, the drunker we get, the funnier the movies will be."

I drop the dishes into the dishwasher and pull out my phone, sorting through the list he sent me. "Um, the next movie is *The Mummy*."

His eyes light up. "Yes. Oh, my God, yes. I'm so glad I get to see you experience that classic for the first time."

I can't help but laugh at his enthusiasm. I also know he's probably trying to project that's he's okay. Most likely, he's heartbroken and pushing it down. "Well, I know it's bound to be good if you've seen it who knows how many times and still react that way."

He nods and begins to run some dishwater for the skillets and mixing bowl and utensils I'd used to cook. "It's so good. Ninety percent of the actors in that movie are hot and Brenden Fraser is always gonna be the GOAT."

I blink. "The what? The *goat*? As in livestock?"

He snorts a laugh. "No. The greatest of all time. The G-O-A-T. He's awesome and talented and if I were into guys, he'd totally be a smash."

"A what?" I sigh. "God, I feel stupid when you talk sometimes."

"Sorry. A smash is someone you find attractive. Someone you'd smash sexy bits with."

Oh, so you. Got it.

"Gotcha. I swear, every time I think I've got all the slang down, I'm reminded I *so* don't."

"Do you have any kind of social media? Instagram, TikTok, Twitter?" I shake my head. "Well, that's your next assignment. Get some socials. I guess, if you wanted, you could do Facebook, too, but it's mostly for groups and businesses anymore. I can't believe you didn't get into anything in college."

I shrug. "I didn't have a phone then. I had to use the campus library computers to research and write all my papers and Rosalind's apartment still had a landline."

Jess's expression morphs into one of amazement. "You must've really wanted your education. That takes dedication to be willing to be at the mercy of the school library."

"I did," I admit. "It's a shame I'm not using my degree, but I'd never regret having it."

"Definitely not. You should be proud of yourself and what you've accomplished."

"My parents would say that pride in one's own accomplishments is a sin."

He lifts a brow as we finish washing up the dishes. "I'm sure your parents would say a lot of the things you do now are a sin, right? What's one more?"

I nod, laughing. "Too true. Lord help if they ever knew I was living with a man. My mother would surely die of shame." As we sit on the couch to watch the movie after taking Garth out for a potty break, I turn my body toward him on the sofa with my leg pulled up under me. "Do you want to hear something stupid?"

Jess grins. "I'm sure if you're gonna say it, it's entirely not stupid because you're not stupid, but sure."

"Do you ever imagine yourself doing something, like what you'd do if you only had the nerve?"

"I mean, sure. Doesn't everyone? Why?"

"I think sometimes about what I would have said to my parents if they had opened the door that day I went back to the farm after college. I wonder if I would've begged for their forgiveness and returned to that way of life. Or, if I would've finally told them exactly what I thought about the way they raised me and my siblings."

"Do you ever think about still going?"

I think for a minute. "I think if I went and saw my brothers and sisters still there, still living that way, it would break my heart. My parents weren't really cruel. They were just backward and wrong in their way of thinking. I worry if any of my siblings are still there and if any of them are gay, what kind of shame are they living with because they think something is wrong with them. That God must've made a mistake when they were made because the way they are is sinful. Even more so than just lust, which is painted as the worst of all the sins. But to be told the way you love is an abomination? I can't imagine what that would do to their self-worth or mental health.

"And it might be sexist, but I never worried about my brothers as much as my sisters. In purity culture, boys are treated so much differently. The sin is placed on women. If a man sins sexually, it's because a woman tempted him. She showed too much of her body or wore makeup or something equally preposterous. They're not really taught to take accountability for their own actions."

He's quiet for a moment, absorbing my words. "You seem to have escaped mostly unscathed."

I huff a laugh. "This is ten years out. It's taken me a lot of self-examination and reflection to unlearn all of that toxic behavior." After a beat, I add, "And lots and lots of smut."

He chuckles. "Nice.

CHAPTER ELEVEN

JESS

The following weekend, following a shitty week at work as I tried to work through my thoughts about everything with Brooklyn, I realize on my first break that I've forgotten my lunch. Knowing I can take a couple minutes off my lunch to make up the time, I drive the ten minutes home to get it.

I don't bother pulling into the garage, since I'll be in and out, and slip in the front door. I stride across to the counter where my lunch box sits and just as my hand touches the handle, the bathroom door opens and Ophelia comes out in only a towel and I freeze.

Understandably startled, she screams and brandishes an empty wine bottle like a sword in one swift move, holding it by the neck of the bottle, blunt end pointed at me. In her haste to wield her weapon of choice, the towel wrapped around her comes loose and drops to the floor.

As if in slow motion—at least that's the way it feels in my mind—the terrycloth flutters to the ground, revealing every bit of Ophelia's fucking gorgeous body and my mouth falls open. I am completely enthralled at the sight of her full, round breasts with taut, dusky nipples. Her trim waist flaring to wide hips and down to a tuft of manicured dark hair. I take in the scenery until a split second later, when common sense kicks in and I immediately spin around. "Oh, God. Sorry. I forgot my lunch. I didn't mean to scare you."

She laughs nervously and clears her throat. "My fault. I shouldn't be listening to my music so loud in the tub I can't hear the front door open. I'm decent now."

Sure my face is about fourteen shades of red, I turn and make sure to keep my eyes only on her face. "I'm gonna go. Sorry again."

She shrugs. "It's fine. Nothing you probably haven't seen before."

I nod. "Right. Well, I'll see you tomorrow."

"Sure. Have a good night at work."

I grab my lunch and practically sprint out of the house. My whole shift, as I prep surgical kits, the only thought running through my mind is, *Ophelia looks like* that?

Granted, Ophelia is a beautiful woman. I thought she was cute when she first showed up at my house, but over the last several weeks, she's really blossomed in her personality and confidence and it's been wonderful to see. She's a lot of fun and I enjoy spending time with her.

I knew from the way she's been dressing in recent weeks and from the night she went out with the girls that she's got a great body. But this was something completely different. This wasn't a flash of cleavage or a butt cheek and a thong. This was her whole-ass naked body. Her whole-ass gorgeous naked body.

I'd be lying if I said I didn't spend my entire shift trying to avoid a hard on from picturing Ophelia naked. I really shouldn't be doing that. There are so many reasons me thinking about Ophelia naked is disastrous. I really, *really* shouldn't be doing that. She's my roommate. She's my friend. She's not someone I could fuck and it have no consequences. I also just got out of a long-term relationship.

Plus, who's to even say she would even like me like that? For all I know, her type is the kind of guy she brought home the previous weekend; blonde and skinny without chest hair and doesn't want a commitment. None of those things are me. I'm definitely not skinny or without chest hair. I definitely pursue women with a future in mind. Not that I'm pursuing women right now. Not yet. Probably not for a while.

But there's no harm in fantasizing, right? Even if—especially if—I never act on it? Right. There's no harm in imagining what it might be like to squeeze those luscious tits in my hands. To imagine what she tastes like. To imagine the sounds she makes when she comes. To imagine sliding my cock into that sweet—.

Stop it, Jess.

But alas, my dick doesn't get the memo and is instantly harder than I can recall in possibly years. I try to think of gnarly surgeries and pus and broken bones to stop thinking about Ophelia naked. By my last break, I'm almost in pain from the ache that's settled into my balls. My body screams for release and, unable to not do something about this issue, I slip into one of the bathrooms and lock myself behind the door of one of the stalls and lean my forearm on the wall as I practically rip the drawstring loose on my scrub pants and pull out my cock.

For someone who prides himself on his stamina, it's embarrassingly quick how fast I come. And try as I might, I can't get the image of Ophelia out of my head during the ten quick strokes I give myself before I'm spilling into my palm with a quiet gasp, my heart racing.

Thankfully, Ophelia has already left for work when I get home, and neither of us is forced to have an awkward conversation about what happened. Before heading to bed, I take Garth out and spend a few minutes letting him track down his ball.

My phone vibrates in my pocket and I pull it out and my eyes go wide when I see the picture Josie just sent me. I immediately call her instead of texting, and she answers on the second ring. "I didn't know if you'd still be up."

"What the hell is that giant thing on your finger? Holy shit."

She laughs down the line. "Ford did good, right? I was so shocked."

"What happened?"

"Well, you know we went up to the cabin with Ada and Silas, right?"

"Yeah."

"So, we were lying in bed Saturday night and I was in my feelings because Silas told me Ada's pregnant."

"Oh. Wow. Yeah, I know that was probably hard for you."

She sighs. "It was, and it wasn't that I was upset, not really. I told Ford it was just hard. Also, you can't tell anyone. I'm not sure when they're going to announce the pregnancy, so keep your trap shut."

I roll my eyes. "Will do. Okay, so then what happened?"

"He asked me if it would cheer me up if he asked me to marry him. I laughed and said, 'sure', because it's been this whole thing between us lately and he got really serious and asked. Like, *asked* asked. I nearly choked when he pulled out the ring."

"Well, your weekend definitely trumps mine. Actually, my last two weekends. We haven't talked in forever."

"I know. I'm sorry. This coach's girlfriend thing is a lot

more involved than I thought it would be. I feel like a team mom. What's going on with you?"

I give her the rundown of my breakup with Brooklyn and it's getting easier to talk about, so that's good, right? "Also, I saw Ophelia naked last night. Total fluke, but now I'm afraid things are gonna be weird."

"Oh. Well, that is some excitement. She's hot, right? I swear, she has come out of her shell so much since she first moved in with you. She's all confident and stuff now. She's got a great sense of her own personal style and seriously, that honey-colored hair *and* it's natural? Damn. People pay good money for that shade. And those big blue eyes? I'm telling you, if I was into girls, she could totally get it."

"Josie," I groan. "Focus."

"Right. Sorry. It's not that big a deal. You're both adults. It happens. It probably won't happen again. I mean, unless you want it to happen again. Do you want it to happen again?"

"Considering I just broke up with Brooklyn five minutes ago, no."

"But if that wasn't something you needed to think about, do you think you'd like her?"

"I do like her. As a friend. She's great. She's funny; she's easy to talk to. I enjoy spending time with her and yeah, she's hot."

"Do you only think she's hot because you've now seen the goods?"

"No," I admit. "I thought she was beautiful before that."

"Okay, so what's the worst that happens if y'all hookup?"

"Besides the fact that we live together and I just got out of a serious relationship and I don't *just* hookup anymore. I mean, what if she doesn't like me like that? What if I'm not her type? She hooked up with this guy last weekend who was this super skinny, blonde guy who probably waxes his chest. You could see his fucking ribs."

"Okay, for starters, you are every girl's type. You are strong and smart and have great hair. Chest hair is sexy and so are you. You are a phenomenal cook, you have a stable job, you own your own home. You are the total package, my friend. Do you think you're having this crisis of confidence because of what happened with Brooklyn? Are you maybe feeling a little inadequate?"

"Probably."

"At least you're self-aware. For the record, you are not inadequate. You just weren't the right person for Brooklyn. And you've known this breakup was coming for months. Hell, you already broke up with her once. You'd already be over her if she hadn't come over that next day and waved her vagina in your face.

"I know you're upset about Brooklyn, but she was never gonna be the right woman for you. And it's okay if you find someone else sooner than you think is acceptable or whatever. Look at Silas and Ada. They were engaged a year after Cole died. A lot of people thought they were callous and uncaring or that it was disrespectful to Cole's memory, but the people who matter will never fault you for being happy. Not if you truly are.

"Who knows, maybe your brain and your dick were shocked into some kind of state since it's the first naked woman besides Brooklyn you've seen in real life in over three years. Maybe you're just confused. Maybe you don't actually like her like that. Maybe don't think too hard about all of it until you give yourself adequate time to fully grasp how you feel about your relationship with Brooklyn ending. Maybe go to a strip club and see if you have the same reaction."

I let Josie's words sink in. "You're a wise woman, Josephine Campbell."

"I'm glad to hear you admit it. Don't do anything hasty, but also don't hold yourself back from potential happiness, okay? It does no one any good. Look at all the shit I put myself through trying to keep Ford at arm's length. I swear, if he hadn't persevered, I'd still be miserable.

"You're the only one who knows your heart, Jess. You're the only one who can know how you truly feel. Give it some time. And go get some sleep."

"Okay, Mom."

Josie laughs. "You know I don't have a mommy kink, but I will be happy to tell you when you're being dumbass. Right now is not one of those times. I'll talk to you later, okay?"

"Alright. Congrats, Jos. I'm so happy for you."

"Thanks, Jess."

And I am happy for Josie. After everything she's been through, she deserves a break. If you had told me she'd be getting married before me, though, I would've laughed in your face.

I sigh and after getting Garth's attention, we go inside. I ensure he's got food and water and give him a scratch behind the ear before heading to bed.

THE CONFESSIONS OF IVY SINN
EPISODE 80: THE NEIGHBOR, PART 2

I had a dream that I was locked out of my apartment. I'd gone to get the paper—although, does anyone actually still read the paper—and had just gotten out of the shower. I was wrapped only in a towel and when I stepped out into the hall, you were there.

I was so startled because you're usually at work that time of day and I'm always alone on our floor. But when you scared me, I accidentally let my door close and it locked, and then, I accidentally dropped my towel.

You saw me in all my glory and as long as I've known you, you'd never looked at me the way you did this day. Your eyes dragged down my body and my skin prickled with the way your gaze lingered on my breasts before dropping to my pussy. And, God, I was so turned on in that moment, I would've dropped to my knees to suck that beautiful cock of yours.

Gentleman that you are, you apologized and turned away to give me privacy to wrap myself up again. And because you're such a helpful neighbor, you had the spare key to my apartment. Although I invited you in, you couldn't stay.

When I woke up, I was so wet, I was dripping. I had no choice but to think about the way you looked at me in the dream. I had no choice except to drag my fingers through my folds and up to my clit to try to ease this ache. It's so bad anymore. I think about you more than I should.

Do you think about me, too? What it might be like if we finally gave into temptation? Oh, God. That's good. I pretend my hands are your hands. God, I wish they were.

I think about what it would be like to feel you on top of me; inside of me. The way it would feel to have you pound into me. Fuck, I'm so close. I want you to take out your cock and stroke it. Think about my lips closing around it. I would take you so deep. I'd want you to fuck my mouth; make me feel it and let me know I'm yours.

Would you come down my throat or would you want to see your cum leaking out of my pussy once you'd fucked me so well I couldn't move? Oh, shit. Fuck, baby. Can you get there with me? Just thinking about feeling your cum drip down my thighs for hours is so hot. I'm close.

Or, are you a dirty boy? Would you lick my cunt after you dirty it up? Would you taste us mixed together and kiss me so I could taste it, too? Fuck. Fuck. Yes. Oh, fuck.

Thank you for listening to my confession.

CHAPTER TWELVE

OPHELIA

For two weeks after "the incident", all I can think about is the way Jess looked at me. I repeatedly tell myself that it was simple shock because I was naked and not that he could possibly find me desirable. Besides the fact that he just got out of a long relationship, I'm probably not his type.

Brooklyn was edgy and worldly and a lot of fun and, judging by the sounds they both made during sex, good in bed. And despite my extracurricular activities, I'm not exactly a sex kitten. *Confessions* has, more than anything, helped me heal from the trauma of purity culture more than actually giving me any real bedroom skills. I know what I like and have read enough smut to make me feel as though I know my way around a penis, but in truth, I'm not *that* experienced. I have a hell of an imagination, but that only gets you so far.

In reality, I've only had one actual relationship, which only lasted a few months, and it was the first guy I ever slept with. He was sweet and gentle and talked me through a lot of things and helped me get to know my body and walked me through my first orgasm. And had he not graduated and moved across the country, we might still be together for all I know. Every sexual encounter since has been to primarily scratch an itch.

Well, that's not entirely true that I've only had one relationship, but I refuse to count *him* after the hell that came from that. Especially after everything he cost me.

But knowing what I do about Jess, that's not something I could do with him because I actually like him. I'm not sure if that translates to having feelings for him, but he's a great guy and a good friend. And if I slept with him and it got weird, I wouldn't only mess up my relationship with him and it possibly result in me being homeless, it would also jeopardize all the other new relationships I have in my life. I definitely don't want to lose out on my friendships with Josie and Hensley, as surface-level as those still are.

Maybe the next thing I should do is find some more friends. Friends who don't have anything to do with Jess. That way, if somehow, anything happens between Jess and me, I'm not left without some sort of support system. I refuse to be that lonely again. But that's a task for another day.

Today, I'm thankful things aren't currently weird between Jess and me. We haven't talked about "the incident", but it's also not tense or anything at home, leading me to believe even more that seeing me naked had no effect on him.

And maybe I should be thankful for that, because it's actually the first day we've both been home together since it happened and we have errands to run. "So, I'm thinking groceries, feed store, and back home. I'm also thinking that because we'll be too exhausted to cook after the hell that is grocery shopping and obtaining a hundred pounds of dog food, we DoorDash supper. Thoughts?" Jess asks as we drive the two miles to our regular grocery store.

"Fine with me. Can we also tick off another movie, or do you have plans?"

"No plans. A movie sounds perfect. What's next on your list?"

I pull my phone from my back pocket and open up my notes app, where I've put the substantial list of movies, books, and music he thinks I should experience to make me a well-rounded member of current society. "Looks like *Tremors*. What's that one about?"

He grins. "It's a campy horror movie. Used to terrify me as a kid. It's great."

I lift a skeptical brow. "I don't know about horror. I really didn't like *Saw*. Pretty sure I didn't sleep for a week after you made me watch that one."

"I promise, this one's not like that. It won't mess with your head like *Saw* did."

"I'll take your word for it. But if I can't sleep, you will pay."

"Aww, don't worry. If you have trouble sleeping, I can always sing you a little lullaby."

I huff a laugh, even though the idea of him being anywhere near me when I'm trying to go to sleep makes my skin prickle. "I'll hold you to that."

An hour later, we've piled our groceries into the back of Jess's car and after weaving through congested midday traffic, make it to the farm feed store.

It only took us having Garth for a couple of weeks to see that buying his food on our weekly grocery runs was gonna get real expensive real fast. Knowing the feed store was where we always got our food for our farm animals growing up—even the domesticated ones—I knew it was a lot cheaper.

As usual, I get caught up looking at the collars and leashes and toys and he rolls his eyes. "I'll go get his food. Why don't you finally get him that braided collar you've been eyeing for weeks? Make him look all pretty," he says with a grin before heading a couple of aisles over to get a bag of food.

I smile and pull down the collar he's mentioned, along with a matching leash. I'm reaching for a squeaky toy on the opposite shelf when I stop, my hand in midair. A voice from the next aisle over has me frozen. But in the next breath, I'm walking toward the end of my aisle and peeking around the end cap, already knowing who I'll see.

My father hasn't changed at all, it would seem, in the years since I last saw him. His hair is still buzzed and even from where I stand twenty feet away, I can see he's still using that same safety razor he has my whole life, if the razor burn on his jaw is any indication. He wears the same type of tan work shirt and patched jeans he's always worn, along with those same scuffed boots.

He's also not alone, and my chest tightens. Although he's older, I'd recognize Ajax anywhere since I practically raised him for the first five years of his life. Not to mention that distinctive café au lait birthmark on the side of his neck that always looks like a splash of coffee that's spilled onto a piece of paper. For fifteen, he's tall and rangy, probably working the farm the same way my other brothers did.

And I never imagined it would hurt so much to see someone I loved nearly as much as a mother could love any child. I spent so many nights rocking him to sleep and ensuring he was clean and happy, and when I left, I had to lock away the thoughts of worrying about who was taking care of him in my absence. It didn't stop the ache, but it assuaged the guilt a bit.

My father looks at something in my direction and our eyes meet and my breath catches. There's no question of whether he recognizes me, and I instantly want to shrink under his gaze. Knowing I'm wearing cutoff shorts and a tank top and my hair is almost too short to pull into a ponytail and I'm wearing makeup, I'm not shocked to see the disgust in his eyes. I'm also not shocked to feel the sting of it.

For a long moment, he just drags his eyes up and down my body, still with that same look of disdain, and I stand there and let him. Ajax seems not to notice this silent stand off and I'm thankful.

"You ready to go home, Birdie?" Jess's cheerful words cut through my trance and I blink and turn my face toward him, even though I'm not sure I can move my body. He must see something in my expression, because he drops the dog food without another word and steps closer and puts his hand on my shoulder. "What's wrong?"

I shake my head, trying to blink back the sudden tears I feel burning my eyes. "Ophelia, what is it?" The worry in his own gaze makes something twist in my chest and I'm about to tell him I'm okay, when I see movement out of the corner of my eye and turn to look over at my father and brother again.

Ajax is looking at me, probably triggered by Jess's use of my name. His eyes go wide and he smiles and attempts to step toward me, but my father stops him just as he passes him. My brother looks at my father, confused. "But, Dad, it's Ophelia. She's here."

Jess's grip tightens on my shoulder and it feels like his hand is the only thing tethering me to this existence. Especially as Ajax's next words leave his mouth.

"Can I go say hi? Please?"

"No. We should go."

My throat goes tight and I hang my head, knowing my father is still exactly the same as he was nine years ago. He's never going to see me as a person. He's only ever going to see me as a sinner; a disobedient daughter who doesn't deserve to have any contact with my family because I've gone against his wishes for my life. I take a deep breath and look back up at Ajax. "Hey, Jax. I miss you." My voice is shaky and I wish it wasn't so my father wouldn't know how much this moment is killing me.

Again, my brother tries to step forward and my father grabs his arm. "I said no, son. Don't make me tell you again."

Before I can blink, Jess drops his hand from my shoulder and steps forward, extending his hand toward my father. "You must be Ophelia's father. It's nice to finally meet you."

He says it like he was always gonna meet my parents at some point and I'm not sure whether to laugh or cry at this moment. My father seems equally perplexed, but his upbringing won't let him snub a handshake and he takes Jess's hand in his for a brief shake. "And you are?"

I step forward, jolted from my trance by Jess's small act of kindness on my behalf. "This is Jess, my roommate."

And although I knew when I said the words what kind of reaction my father would have to hearing them, the reality is still painful. Especially when he curls up his lip in a sneer. He's about to say something, but Ajax pipes up. "But it's a sin to live with someone of the opposite sex if you're not married or related to them."

And were it anyone but Ajax, I might educate him on how *sinful* I truly am, but hearing him parrot words my parents have said my entire life only makes me see how sad my life was. It makes me see even more that the only things I knew were the things *they* told me. It only makes me pity Ajax and any of my other siblings still in that toxic environment.

My father's sneer turns into a smug smirk. "That's right, Ajax; it is. So, as you can see, it would seem your sister has fallen even farther than we feared. We'll continue to pray for her. Let's go."

He turns and I take another step forward. "Still just as self-righteous as ever, I see, Dad. Tell me, does knowing you disowned your own daughter for simply disagreeing with you make you feel superior? Last I checked, the Bible was pretty clear about how fathers are supposed to treat their children."

He narrows his eyes as he turns to face me once again. "You want to get into a debate with me about the Bible, little girl? I think we both know who'd win that one."

I lift a brow, angry bitterness settling in and fueling my ability to speak. "Careful, Dad, someone might think you're being prideful. Then what would that do for your witness? Hard to point out the speck in someone else's eye when you have a plank in your own, isn't that right?"

"I see we're still picking and choosing which verses we want to embody, Ophelia."

"Pot meet kettle. You're one to talk. The one verse I think you've always been quick to toss out is the one in Colossians about children obeying their parents. You always forget to read that next verse along with it; the one that says fathers shouldn't provoke their children, lest they become discouraged. It would seem to me that our sins cancel each other out."

My father's jaw clenches. "I'm so glad your mother is no longer here to see what a mouthy, disrespectful whore you've become."

Jess steps forward and his hand rolls into a fist, but I grab his arm, my mind still trained on what my father just said. "What do you mean, Mom's no longer here?" He eyes Jess with disdain and keeps his mouth shut. I raise my voice. "What do you mean, Mom is no longer here?"

Ajax, seeing my father is not going to explain, opens his mouth. "Momma died. Four years ago."

My inhale of breath is sharp and my stomach drops and I bring my eyes back to my father. "Mom died? And you didn't tell me?"

"I don't have to tell you anything anymore, Ophelia. It was a family matter. You are no longer family. You made that choice. These are the consequences." He looks at Ajax, his expression neutral. "Let's go, son. We've got chores."

I don't even realize I'm trembling until Jess puts his arm around my shoulder. "You're shaking. Let's go home. Garth has enough food for another day or two."

Unable to even respond, I let him lead me out to the car. I have no memory of the drive home or even walking into the house. I don't register him guiding me to my room and helping me into bed after pulling off my shoes. I am completely numb as I try to process that my mother is gone.

It's not until Jess returns to my room, presumably after putting away the groceries, and crawls into bed next to me, do I register anything at all. He doesn't pull me into his arms or hold me or anything, he simply lies facing me and tucks a stray hair behind my ear. "I'm really sorry you had to find about your mom that way."

As if a switch has been flipped, I burst into tears. He does put his arm around me then and pulls me into his chest. I wrap my fingers into the front of his shirt and sob. For long moments, I'm unable to stop and he rubs my back and runs his fingers through my hair and lets me get it all out.

CHAPTER THIRTEEN

JESS

In this moment, as Ophelia cries in my arms, it's all I can do not to find out where her father lives and track him down and beat the living shit out of him. It's not the fact that he looked at her like she was worse than a piece of chewed-up gum stuck to the bottom of his shoe. It's not the fact that he wouldn't even let her brother talk to her—and God, seeing the hurt in her eyes nearly killed me. It's not the fact he called her a whore, which, had Ophelia not held me back, I would've gone to jail. It's the fact her mother has been dead for four years and she never knew.

I suspected just from the things she's said about her upbringing that it was bad, but having seen her father with my own eyes and the disdain he has for his own daughter; it's even worse than I could've imagined. It makes me marvel even more at how Ophelia has turned out as well-adjusted as she is.

After a while, her sobs subside, but she doesn't pull away and I'm not about to let her go if she still needs to be held, so I make no move to release her. Her breathing begins to level out, and I realize she's fallen asleep. Her hand is still gripping my shirt and her face is wet from her tears, tracks of mascara running down her cheeks. And even red-faced and puffy, she's beautiful.

Ever since that night her towel dropped, I've had such a difficult time keeping my eyes off her when we're in the same room. And although I feel like everything is the same, everything is somehow different. I'm more aware of the way she moves and eats and cooks and jogs. Oh, sweet Jesus, the jogging.

And I thought it was simply a physical attraction. But when I saw her face at the feed store as she turned her anguished expression in my direction, something twisted painfully in my chest and I only wanted to make it better for her.

Some could argue that my need to comfort her in this moment is something any good friend or roommate would do and they wouldn't be wrong; I've done it for Josie. But despite our shared history, I don't have more than platonic feelings for Josie anymore. She's one of my best friends and I love her, but I don't see myself *with* her. I'm probably so fucked, because I can see myself *with* Ophelia.

And the feelings I had while Ophelia was arguing with her father were not platonic feelings. They were you're-hurting-someone-I-care-about-and-you-must-pay feelings. They were feelings I recognize from when Brooklyn would tell me about some asshole she met on one of her trips and I went into angry boyfriend mode.

As I stare down at her while she sleeps, the feelings are still there. I don't know what to do about them or if I even can do anything about them. She seems so unaffected by my seeing her naked, it's as if she doesn't care. And hell, maybe she doesn't. Maybe she doesn't watch me the same way I do her.

But for now, I'll simply lie here since she has a death grip on my shirt. I'm not complaining and I'm thankful I took Garth out before I came back in here so I wouldn't have to risk leaving her. For now, I'll just pull her closer and listen to her leveled breathing and hope I can sort out my feelings about her soon.

Ophelia stirs next to me and I jerk awake. I definitely hadn't meant to fall asleep, but when she pulls back and looks up at me, her eyes still puffy from where she's cried, her lips are only a few inches from mine and I have to make myself not look at them.

"Sorry about that," she says, her voice quiet.

I frown in confusion and brush a stray hair out of her eyes. "What do you have to be sorry about?"

"I didn't mean to hold you hostage. I was still holding onto your shirt when I woke up. I didn't mean to fall asleep or keep you with me."

I shake my head and give her a gentle smile. "I was more than happy to be your hostage. Best nap I've had in years, actually."

She huffs a laugh and sniffles. "I didn't mean to fall apart on you."

I blink, confused and more than a bit taken aback. Does she think she's supposed to be some sort of robot? "Birdie, you found out your mom died and that she's been dead for years and you had no clue. How do you think you're supposed to react to that news? Your reaction was entirely appropriate."

She looks down, her eyes welling with tears again. "I don't know. I thought I'd processed everything with my family essentially exiling me. But seeing my dad and Ajax and finding out about my mom, it was a lot."

I swipe away her tear with the knuckle of my index finger.

"I'm sure. I gotta say, though, I was proud of you for the way you stood up to your dad. I'm sure that was hard, too."

She nods. "It was. But hearing Ajax spew the same kind of garbage I did at his age made me angry. So fucking angry. I wanted to grab Jax and shake him and tell him the world isn't just what they say it is. But he'll probably turn out to be exactly like my father. And who knows about my other brothers and sisters? Are they married and believing the same bullshit we had shoved down our throats growing up? Are they raising their own kids that way?"

I sigh. "You can't make people take the red pill."

"They haven't even been given the option of a red or blue pill. They're stuck. And at what point, given the choice, would it not matter? At what point in their lives, if they continue the way we were raised, will they simply stop questioning things? If they ever did in the first place."

"You're not responsible for their actions. You can only do what you feel is best for you. And as much as I'm sure it hurts to see people be ignorant, it's obvious your brother knows no different. He might never know any different. Even if you presented him with a different viewpoint, he may never be open-minded enough to hear what you say. Especially if your dad is as toxic as he appears."

"He is. God, it's a wonder I made it out."

"I'm glad you did."

"Me, too. Can you imagine all the great orgasms I would've missed out on?" she asks with a laugh.

Even as the thought of what she looks like or sounds like or feels like when she comes makes need settle into my groin, I laugh. "I'm glad you can still see the glass as half-full."

Her expression sobers. "My mom is gone, Jess."

"I know, Birdie."

"I never got to say goodbye." She lets out a shuddery breath and her eyes well with tears again. "Did she think I never thought about her? Did she think I stopped loving her because I left?"

"There's no way. I think moms have to know, right? Some kind of biological tether that transcends time and distance. And I'm sure you were on her mind when she went. Wishing she would've been able to see you one last time. And you don't know, maybe she even asked for you and your father refused her. That's on him."

She begins to cry again and buries her face in my chest and again, I hold her, even as my own throat grows tight and I'm forced to swallow the lump that's formed seeing how much pain she's in. "I'm so sorry, Ophelia." I don't have words for her. I don't have anything but my presence to offer her at this moment. And I can only hope it's enough.

Sometime later, after we've both fallen asleep again, Garth lets out a low, rough bark from the living room, waking me. Ophelia is still asleep, and I carefully extricate my shirt from her iron grip and drop a kiss onto the top of her head as I climb from the bed.

I run my fingers through my hair and rub my eyes with the heel of my hand as I walk into the living room. Garth drops off the couch and trots over and I give him a scratch behind the ear. "Come on; let's go out." I motion for him, since I know he can't hear well, and he follows me to the back door. I let him outside and knowing it's not hot enough outside to be detrimental to his health if he's left out there for more than a few minutes, I open the fridge, trying to determine what to make for supper.

"I thought we were just gonna DoorDash?"

I look over my shoulder and Ophelia is just coming into the kitchen, her arms folded across her chest. "I can cook."

She sighs. "Would you care if we stick with our original plan? Maybe it'll help me feel normal again."

"You're not supposed to feel normal; your mom died."

She nods, her expression turning stony. "Yeah, she did. But I'll never find out how or be able to see her grave or do anything at all to get closure, so it doesn't matter."

"Why would you say that?"

"Because, if I know my father, he buried her on the back side of the farm where all the dead babies are buried and there's possibly not even a record of her death."

My mouth falls open. "I'm sorry, did you say *dead babies*? Want to back that train the fuck up?"

"None of us were born in hospitals. My father or my aunt delivered all of us kids. There are no records of any of our births. My mom suffered several stillbirths and there are no records of those, either. They buried the babies on the farm in the family cemetery. I don't even have a birth certificate."

"How is that possible?"

"If you're not born in a hospital and your mother receives no prenatal care and your birth is attended by only a family member and you never go to doctors or public schools, why would you ever need one?"

"Still, that's wild."

"Tell me about it. Getting my GED and applying to college were both a bitch. I didn't even have a social security number until I was twenty."

"Okay, I just have to ask. Did your parents grow up the way they raised you?"

She shakes her head. "Mom grew up in a 'normal' family, as far as I know. I know she had a sister, but I never met her or my mom's parents. I know now it's because they probably spoke against the way my father was; the life he wanted us to lead. My dad grew up baptist, but from what my cousin Rosalind said, she overheard her mom—my dad's sister—say, he felt like the church had gotten too soft. So they formed their own branch of things. My dad, his sister, and her husband began a home church.

"My dad and his family are from Wilmington and when things first started, as far as I know, they weren't so stringent. I can remember us having a phone in the house and even a TV when I was really little, maybe around three. But then, it was gone and things got more serious.

"I think it even caused tension between my dad and aunt and uncle. They felt he was too harsh; too fervent in his practice. And that's when we moved here. But we'd still make a trip to Wilmington once a year, just because my dad still communicated with his parents and wanted to see them. Rosalind's parents had a TV in their house, but when we were there, it was unplugged and covered with a sheet."

I shake my head. "And here I thought my family was out there because my grandfather was a priest who fell in love with a nun and they ran away together."

Ophelia's mouth falls open. "You're kidding."

"Nope. Totally true."

"Well, what a pair we make, huh?"

I nod. "Yep." After a beat, I ask, "You sure you wouldn't rather me cook?"

"Yeah. Pizza? And alcohol. So much alcohol."

"Well, pizza we can do, but we're out of booze unless you've got a bottle of wine stashed somewhere. I was planning on picking some up on my way in to work tomorrow because I didn't figure you'd want to drink since it's a work night."

Ophelia shakes her head. "Nope. No work for me tomorrow. I haven't called in once in five years. I'm thinking I'd much

rather get really drunk and forget about this day." Her eyes
light up as if she's had a big idea. "How about, instead of Door-
Dash, you take me to the bar and get me drunk?"

A mourning, drunk Ophelia sounds like a recipe for disas-
ter. "I don't know, Birdie. I do have to work tomorrow."

"Yeah, but not until six. That's all day to recover from your
hangover. Please? I want to not feel this right now. And the
alternative is, I take myself to the bar and someone else buys me
a drink and I end up having, at best, mediocre sex with a guy
whose name I can't remember. And I really don't want to do
that."

I want her to do that about as much as I want someone
sticking bamboo shoots under my nails. But who am I to tell her
how to grieve, right? If this is what she needs, I can give her
this. "Are you sure?"

"Yes. The best revenge I can get on my shitty father is to
have a good time in memory of my mother. To live since she
can't anymore."

"Okay. Bar it is."

CHAPTER FOURTEEN

JESS

An hour later and Ophelia and I are pulling up at the nightclub closest to the house. Now, am I a nightclub guy? Not at all. But Ophelia feels the need to let loose, and the least I can do is keep an eye on her drink. I can also try my best to not think about what she might look like dancing with other men. Although, I'm sensing that mental battle will be a futile one.

After parking and paying the cover charge, we immediately head for the bar. For a Sunday night, it's pretty busy, but early enough that there are still a few pairs of stools left. We take our seats and I order a beer while Ophelia opts for a double shot of tequila. Thankfully, we stopped and got burgers on the way over, so I'm not worried about any booze she drinks hitting an empty stomach.

"When you were in college, did you go out like this a lot?" I ask. "Or since you moved back to town?"

Ophelia downs her shot and sucks her lime and shakes her head. "Never."

"Not even on dates?"

"No. I dated one guy in college for a few months and then

he graduated and moved across the country, so we broke up. I went to a few parties, and that's how I met other guys. And I've only gone on a few dates since I moved back to Knoxville; usually some guy I met at the store or something. You know, until I went out that night with the girls. But I think I've learned my lesson," she says, eyes wide in an expression that can only be described as slightly horrified.

"And what lesson would that be?" I ask, amused by the look on her face.

She signals to the bartender and orders a margarita with extra salt and pushes her shot glass across the bar. "Don't let beer goggles make your dating decisions for you." She gives an exaggerated shudder and I laugh. "That guy a few weeks ago?" I nod and she continues. "Too skinny. Way too skinny. I didn't remember him being that skinny at the club that night. And he was all right that night we first met, so you know, benefit of the doubt and all that, but I'm pretty sure I got bruises from how sharp his hipbones were. Never again."

On one hand, the fact she thought he was too skinny makes me feel better about my chances that she might be okay with my build. On the other hand, although I already know she slept with that guy, I really don't want to think about her knowing how his hipbones feel.

"What about you?" she inquires, taking a sip of her drink.

"What about me what?"

"Dating. Before Brooklyn. Did you go out clubbing a lot?"

"No. I was a little wild in high school after Josie and I broke up, but I calmed down after college. I worked all the time and really didn't go on many dates at all. I'd actually met Brooklyn in college. She was taking some photography classes to go along with her degree in journalism and I was taking an entry-level photography class for an art elective.

"We did several projects together, but she had a boyfriend

at the time, so I didn't even think about making any moves. Not my style, you know?" When she nods, I take a pull of my beer and continue the story. "I dated a couple of women when I started at the hospital, but after beginning to make the rounds a bit, I decided I didn't much want to shit where I ate, so I stopped. I was leaving the hospital one day and Brooklyn and I ran into each other. She was in the ER for a concussion from zip lining or something. I was single, she was single, and the rest is history."

"Gotcha. Have you heard from her?"

I shake my head. "No."

"Does that bother you?"

I give her question serious consideration and I'm surprised to see it doesn't bother me nearly as much as I assumed it would have. "It sucks that she hasn't reached out, simply because if she cared, she would. But it's not as upsetting as I thought it would be."

"And how do you feel about it not upsetting you?"

I shrug. "It probably means I knew it was coming and had already started distancing myself from her and processing the breakup before it even happened. Could be worse, right?

"Right." She drains the rest of her margarita and spins on her stool. "I'm going to line dance. Wanna come?"

I shake my head. "I'm still way too sober. I'll watch and join you in a bit."

She shrugs. "Suit yourself."

Hopping off the stool, she joins the lineup of dancers filling the floor. She watches and slowly begins picking up the steps and thankfully, no one decides she needs "help" and I don't feel the need to jump up and enter the fray. Caught up as I am, I don't see a tall, blonde figure step up and take Ophelia's vacated stool. Not until said blonde nudges me in the ribs to get my attention and I reluctantly pull my eyes from the dance floor.

I'm instantly annoyed until I see who it is that's prodded me. "Hensley. Should've known you'd be out tonight."

She lifts one shoulder in a half-shrug and gives me a small smile. "One of the perks of being able to call all your time your own, I guess. What are you doing out? I mean, other than eye-fucking Ophelia."

I choke on my beer and she laughs. "It's okay. I won't tell Brooklyn." She looks out to the dance floor. "She's hot. Who could blame you?"

Mopping my hand down my chin, I clear my throat. "Brooklyn and I broke up."

Her eyes go wide and her mouth falls open. "Shut up. Well, well. So, are you planning on doing more than just using your eyes on our new girl?" I blow out a breath and turn my attention to the dance floor and can't keep the smile off my face as Ophelia laughs with a tiny, elderly woman when they both flub the dance steps.

"Oh, shit. You really like her." I level Hensley with a gaze and she lifts a brow. "What, are you saying you don't like her? Because from where I sit, you can practically see the cartoon hearts circling your head." I don't say anything and simply drink the rest of my beer and order another. "So, what are you gonna do?"

"I don't know," I admit.

"Well, there are worse things than falling for your room-mate. I mean, look at Silas and Ada. Just saying, if we're talking about cringe factor, this doesn't even rate."

I give her my full attention and lift a brow. "Is that jealousy I detect in your voice, Hens? And who are you jealous of, Ada or Silas?" Her cheeks turn bright pink and she blinks and clamps her mouth shut. I sigh. "Hens, when are you finally gonna—"

"Hensley. Hey," Ophelia interrupts and if I'm not mistaken, I see Hensley visibly relax since I wasn't able to finish my question. I give Ophelia my attention and offer her a wide grin. Her fair skin has a pleasant flush and a slight sheen of perspiration. She grabs my arm. "Mind if I steal Jess away? He owes me a dance."

Hensley shakes her head. "Have at it. I'll watch your drinks. Well, unless some hot thing comes to sweep me away."

I reluctantly let Ophelia drag me out to the floor. "You realize I can't dance, right?"

"You can't be any worse than me."

"Yeah, I think you're underestimating exactly how left both my feet are."

She laughs, pulling me along. "I don't care. This dance requires a partner. They said they'd call out the steps."

"It's your toes, Birdie." And yet, I let her line us up in the quickly forming circle of couples. Following the command of the instructor, Ophelia faces me and places her right hand in my left and her left hand on my shoulder. I slide my hand around her waist and settle my right hand under her left shoulder blade.

I keep my eyes on her face and she's grinning wildly. Upon further instructions announced from a speaker, I take two quick steps forward, leading with my left foot to guide her back, followed in quick succession by two slower steps. I breathe a sigh of relief when I don't step on her toes.

She lets out a surprised laugh as we continue the steps. "Oh, God, you really are a bad dancer, aren't you? You looked like you just defused a bomb."

"Not far off," I admit.

"Do you hate it? We can go sit down and I can wait for the line dances to start again."

"Nah, this is fine." I step forward with my right foot and it lands squarely on top of her left one and I wince. "Sorry."

She grunts but shakes her head. "It's okay. You'll get it." She gives my hand a squeeze. "You just need to relax." She runs the hand she has planted on the outside of my shoulder to over my trapezius muscle and squeezes there, too. "You're really tense."

I try to breathe but the task has been made all the more difficult because she's squeezing parts of me and I like it too much to actually focus on the task at hand. But somehow, after a few more times around the circle, we've got the steps. The instructor commands a new step in the dance itself and I shake my head. "No way. I just barely got these."

Ophelia laughs. "Fine, we can stay just like this. What are they gonna do, kick us off the floor?"

"Good point."

After a few more minutes, they add some music into the mix and it's loud and her lips move and I know she's saying something, but I can't make it out. I tug her a bit closer and lower my mouth to her ear. "What did you say?"

I bend so she can repeat herself and her breath is warm on my skin and smells of lime and tequila and I suddenly don't ever want to smell anything else ever again. "I asked why you shook my father's hand."

Nodding, I rest my cheek on the side of her head as I speak. "Even though I knew he was probably an asshole, just based on what you'd told me before, I wanted him to know I'm not. Had I known it was gonna go downhill the way it did, I might've saved the handshake and just punched his lights out."

She pulls back and gives me a small smile. "Thank you for

wanting to stand up for me. But thank you for letting me stand up for myself. I needed that."

I nod. "I know."

CHAPTER FIFTEEN

OPHELIA

After we finish dancing, we make our way back to the bar and order fresh drinks, as our old ones are nowhere in sight. I'm nearly out of breath and Jess is sweating profusely. As the evening has progressed, the club has filled up more and the temperature has risen considerably. But I'd be lying if I said I wasn't having a great time. In spite of how shitty this day is, Jess dancing with me—regardless how terribly—was the best part of today.

He sips his water and I take a long gulp of my margarita. "Thank you for dancing."

"Anytime." He leans in so he won't have to scream. "You're a really good dancer."

"And you're terrible," I say with a laugh.

He grins. "I tried to warn you."

Halfway through my margarita, physical and emotional exhaustion hits me with the force of a Mack truck and I touch Jess's arm. "After I finish my drink, would you care if we call it a night? I think I've had enough fun."

Examining my face, he nods. "You've got it." I pull out my

wallet and Jess waves it away. "I already gave them my card. You can buy next time we go out."

"Are you sure? I think I have some cash."

"Yes. Now finish your drink. If you're good, I'll still let you see *Tremors* tonight."

"Why, so I can have nightmares?"

He laughs. "Don't worry, I'll protect you, Birdie."

Even though I laugh along with him, I like the thought of Jess protecting me—being there for me—more than I'd like to admit.

When we get home, we spend a few minutes outside with Garth and I can't stop yawning. Jess lifts a brow. "I don't think you're gonna make it through a movie. Why don't you go on to bed? I'll keep an eye on our boy." I'm about to protest when a huge yawn escapes again. "See? Told you. Go to bed. Did you already call out for tomorrow?"

I nod. "Yeah. Okay. I'm gonna grab a shower and turn in." After a long shower that seems to only zap even more of my energy, I drag on my pajamas and after drying my hair, head to bed. I wave to Jess as I walk down the hall and he turns down the TV a bit as I step into my room.

As I lie in bed, the day replays on a loop in my mind and all I can see is Ajax telling me our mother died. In spite of her making no effort in the time before she passed to reach out to me, I'm still struck with such an overwhelming sense of loss, a choked sob wells up in my chest.

I think about the first memory I have that includes my mother. I was four and she was making chicken pot pie. She was heavily pregnant with—it had to be Angelo—and she was rolling out pie crust on the kitchen counter. She let me sit on the counter next to the dough and she was singing some old classic country song. Maybe Tanya Tucker. She had such a sweet, pure voice.

As she put the crust into the pie plate, she tapped the end of my nose with her index finger as she finished the last line of the chorus of "Two Sparrows in a Hurricane", a gentle smile on her face. And God, I never realized how much I look like my mother until I think about her on that day.

I also remember something else. How, when the garage door opened, her entire demeanor changed, and she helped me down from the counter. "Be sweet, Ophelia. Let's be really good for Daddy, okay? Can you go check on Juliet for me? You're such a good big sister."

Where only a moment before, her face was relaxed and she was happy—seemingly genuinely happy—it all changed the moment she knew he was home. Did she feel trapped by her life? Did she have ambitions and dreams that were discarded because of marriage and children? The thought makes me weep even harder and try as I might to stay quiet, Jess must be able to hear my sobs from the living room because a moment later, he's in my room and crawling into bed with me once again.

It should seem strange, him being in my bed, but in this moment, it's only comforting and I welcome the feel of his arms around me. He pulls me into his chest and I cry even harder and can't bring myself to care. He rubs my back and presses a kiss to the top of my head and I should probably examine that, but I can't.

He doesn't say anything or even do more than simply lie with me, lending me the comfort of his presence. And in this moment, it's more than I could ever ask for.

When I wake, it's morning and even with how tired and puffy my eyes are, I can clearly make out the dust motes that dance in the stream of bright sunlight coming in through the crack in the curtains, letting me know it's later than I normally sleep.

An arm is draped around my waist and a large hand I know must belong to Jess is under my tank top, splayed over my stomach. Sometime in the night, I rolled away from him and he spooned up against me. Puffs of warm air brush down the side of my neck and his nose is buried in my hair.

I try not to let it register how wonderful it feels to sleep curled up with someone, and specifically Jess. I don't give myself permission to enjoy the rather large bulge pressed into my ass. I don't think for a long, long moment about staying exactly where I am for the rest of all time.

Closing my eyes, attempting to nod back off and stay in this bubble, I've nearly succeeded when Garth barks and scratches at my bedroom door. The hand on my stomach flinches, and I don't move.

A couple of minutes later, the dog barks more insistently and Jess stirs. It's probably a cop out to pretend to be asleep, but I'm just too comfortable. He slides his hand off my skin and I hear him let out a soft sigh just before I feel his lips gently graze the skin under my ear. I make myself not react to the kiss, even though my mind and heart races with what it might mean.

For all I know, it was simply a supportive, friendly kiss. But it felt way more intimate than that. Paired with the fact that he didn't exactly snatch his hand away from my body when he realized he was touching me, it didn't feel like he was too alarmed about the situation. Am I reading too much into everything, or can all this mean anything?

After feigning sleep for a few more moments, I reluctantly rise and stretch and make my bed, wondering for a moment if the side Jess slept on smells like him. *Guess I'll find out when I go to bed tonight.*

I hurriedly change clothes before stepping across the hall to brush my teeth and work my hair into some low pigtails. When I make it to the kitchen, I see a full pot of coffee and glance out the back door to see Jess outside with Garth. After pouring myself a mug, I join them outside.

Jess is on the phone and when I take a seat next to him on the stairs, he jerks his chin up in acknowledgment of my presence. He nods and grins in agreement at whatever he hears on the other end of the phone line and sips his coffee. "Sounds good. Thanks for letting me know and I'll see you tomorrow." Seconds later, he disconnects the call and turns to me. "So, I have news."

"Oh?"

"Yeah. A few months ago, I'd applied for this position at the outpatient surgery center next to the hospital. Salary is pretty equal to what I'm making now, but I'll be permanently on days, Monday through Friday."

My eyebrows rise in surprise. "That's great. And how do you feel about it?"

"Awesome. I can always pick up extra shifts at the hospital if I want, but a steady Monday to Friday has always been the goal. And days is a dream."

"Well, good for you. When do you start; tomorrow?"

"Yeah. And my hours are gonna be great, too. Seven to three, so I'll be able to have supper finished most days when you get home."

Touched by his thoughtfulness, I smile. "You don't have to cook all the time. I mean, not unless you want to. You are really good at it, but we could take turns or cook together, too."

He nods, considering. "True."

"Is it going to be weird for you to be on a set schedule like this?"

"Nah, I've been hoping I got this new position for a while, so I'm excited." Garth walks over and lays his head in Jess's lap. He grins down at him and scratches his ears.

"He loves you."

"Eh, he just knows who gives him the best treats." After a beat, he changes the subject. "Sorry I fell asleep in your bed."

I feign ignorance. "Oh, did you?"

He nods. "Yeah. I was just gonna stay until you fell asleep and I guess I did, too."

"No problem." *So, probably definitely only a friendly kiss. Good to know.* "I didn't mean to fall apart again."

He stops petting Garth and turns his face toward me. "Don't ever apologize for the way you feel. Your feelings are valid, Ophelia; especially in a situation like this. I can't imagine what yesterday was like for you."

I shrug and draw my knees up and rest my chin on them. "I just got to thinking about the first memory I have that includes my mother. She was pregnant with the oldest of my brothers. She seemed happy. She was singing and cooking and then the garage door opened and it was like a flip switched because my father was home."

He nods. "You don't think their marriage was happy?"

"Looking back, I think he kept her pregnant for most of it. My mother would've never spoken against my father and the older I got, I rarely heard her speak at all. It was like her personality completely vanished." I blow out a breath. "And I can't help but wonder if I had stayed in that life, would I have become her?"

"No telling. But something tells me no, since you actually got out. You are strong, Birdie. Stronger than you even know, I'm sure."

"Well, thank you for being there for me last night. It meant a lot."

"Anytime. What are you feeling like for breakfast? Pancakes, French toast, eggs benedict?"

I huff a laugh. "You can make eggs benedict?"

"Of course, can't you?"

"No. No, I cannot. I'm not that good a cook."

"So, is that what you want?"

I shrug. "Why don't you surprise me?"

"Can do."

An hour later, he's setting a plate down in front of me. "This is crepes."

He laughs. "Well, you did say to surprise you, right?"

"Absolutely. I love crepes." I cut into them and my eyes go wide. "Are these stuffed crepes?"

"Yeah," he says with a wide grin as he takes his own seat. "My take on strawberry cheesecake crepes."

I take a bite and he watches for my reaction and I nearly moan as I chew. "Holy shit," I remark around a mouthful of food. "This is amazing. Tell me why you're not a chef instead of a surgical tech?"

"Because food is a passion, not a career for me. I think if I had to do it for work, it would lose all its appeal. Instead, I will wield my culinary skills like a secret weapon."

I chuckle. "Well, your secret is safe with me."

After a relaxed rest of the day spent simply watching movies and later, a supper of grilled chicken and roasted veggies, I'm curled up on the sofa while Jess does who knows what in his room. And even though I know he's probably not doing anything scandalous, it's hard to keep my mind on my e-reader and not on his closed door.

It's not until he comes out with his arms loaded down with laundry that I finally feel like I can breathe again. I drag my focus back to my book and reread the same paragraph for the fifth time, this time actually comprehending what I've read. What is wrong with me? I'm antsy and I'm unsure why.

Jess falls onto the sofa and once again, I lose my train of thought about this book. "What are you reading these days?" he asks after I lay the reader on the end table with a sigh.

"It's a romance, of course. A 'why choose' about this girl who is a vet and these three billionaire friends bring their pets to her and convince her to come be their personal vet at their big compound."

"A 'why choose'? What's that?"

I give him a wicked grin. "Where she's with all of them."

His eyes go wide. "Like *with* all of them? So, she's just out here getting her back blown out by three different guys? At the same time?"

I nod. "Sometimes. She has a full-blown relationship with all of them. Each guy usually brings their own component to the relationship."

He blinks. "What about jealousy? What about logistics?"

I snort a laugh. "You are thinking way too hard about this. It's fun. Don't overanalyze it."

He shrugs, still contemplating. "I'm genuinely interested. Are the guys also *together*? Or, are they just with the woman?"

I nod. "Yeah, sometimes it's actually polyamorous, where everybody's in love with everybody. Sometimes, it's just the heroes sharing the same heroine. And usually, there is one hero who is the definite alpha and there's a lot of jealousy on his part until he works through it. There's usually a really broody one and a nurturing one. And most times, one of them is artistic; either an artist or musician. A lot of them are usually darker in nature, but I actually read one recently that was a rom-com. It was great."

He frowns and shakes his head. "I can't see something like that ever working."

I laugh. "It's called fiction for a reason. Just because you read about something doesn't mean you actually want it to be your reality. I find the idea of having one partner to be pretty daunting, let alone multiple. If you think about it too much, it becomes less fun. I don't. I will be content to disassociate and imagine what it might be like to have three partners entirely devoted to my every need. In reality, that would drive me up a wall."

Jess nods, considering. "Okay. I guess. It's still weird. What else to do you read?"

"Lots of things. Monsters, aliens, fairies. Some taboo stuff, like priests falling in love with their parishioners," I say, wiggling my eyebrows.

He shakes his head. "Nope, couldn't do that. I'd be forced to think about my grandparents. Pass."

"What do you normally read? Or do you read? I don't think I've ever seen you."

"Some. Mostly audiobooks. Mostly historical—biographies and stuff. I read the Ron Chernow book that *Hamilton* was based on. It was really good."

"I see. So you're, like, a *smart* reader."

He laughs. "You say 'smart', but it sounded like you were saying 'pretentious'. We don't yuck other people's yum, Birdie."

I shake my head. "I wasn't. It just appears we have two different goals when we read. You read for enrichment, and I read for entertainment."

He lifts a brow. "It can be both, you know. Have you ever read any non-fiction?"

"Not outside of the context of school," I admit.

"Okay, so don't knock it until you try it. How about you recommend one of your whacked-out smutty books and I'll recommend something non-fiction to you and we'll see how we do?"

I consider. "Okay. Deal."

CHAPTER SIXTEEN

JESS

I don't know what I expected when Ophelia and I agreed to send each other book recommendations. I know I certainly didn't expect I'd get horny reading her smutty stuff. I certainly didn't think I'd be taking mental notes about some of the things I read.

And while the book she sent me reads like porn a lot of the time, it also has a distinctive love story element and I enjoy it more than I'd like to admit; especially the dirty talk. I really like the dirty talk.

Of course, then my mind wanders to that place where I think about what Ophelia might like. Does she enjoy dirty talk and having someone take charge in bed like the women in the books she reads? Or, is it like she said and simply because she reads it in books doesn't mean she'd like it in real life? Fuck if I don't want to find out.

And reading these filthy books, paired with how much more skimpy Ophelia's clothes seem to be getting as the weather warms, I can't stop watching her. Most of the time, it makes me feel like some sort of creep. Like I'm this pervy peeping Tom in my own house.

Not that I act on my increasingly indecent thoughts where she's concerned. I make sure to keep my distance so I don't accidentally get close enough to smell her shampoo; the smell of which is permanently embedded into my brain from the night I slept in her bed with my nose buried in her hair. I also keep my distance so I don't kiss her again. Regardless of the fact the kiss I gave her was only under her ear, I enjoyed it way too much. And I probably shouldn't have done it, but that spot was just too inviting to resist. Oh, God, now I really do sound like a creepy perv.

Get it together Jess. She's your roommate, not someone you should be considering sleeping with.

The thing is, though, I don't only think about having sex with her. I think about what she looks like when she wakes up in the morning, one arm tucked under her head. I think about the way she looked when Garth nearly tackled her that day we went to the shelter and she laughed. I think about holding her as she coped with the death of her mother. I think about how I hate to dance, but I'm happy to dance with her. I think about how she becomes fully enthralled in a new movie and how, at this point, I can tell thirty minutes in if it's one she's enjoying.

I also think about her lying in bed, just down the hall and how I'm lying wide awake because I've not had a decent night of sleep since the night I fell asleep with her. And hard as I try, I'm only able to toss and turn and try to find a comfortable position, even an hour after I wished Ophelia good night.

After another five minutes of staring into the dark debating the merits of continuing to lie here and be miserable or getting up and going to have a bit of something to drink in the hopes it makes me drowsy, I sigh and roll out of bed and tug on my pajama pants. Not wanting to wake Ophelia, I quietly open my bedroom door and tiptoe down the hall, freezing when I hear what sounds like hushed voices coming from her room.

At first, I assume she's talking to someone, even though I have no clue who it would be. But then, I hear a moan and my heart stops. I take a step closer to her door, wondering briefly if she's fallen and gotten hurt, but then I hear the moan again and my mouth falls open in surprise. Is Ophelia watching porn?

Adding additional points to the creepy perv category, I can't stop myself from moving closer to her door; until my ear is only inches from the wood. I hear it again and I realize it's *her*. Ophelia is making those sounds. I'm not sure how I know it's her, but I do. And unless she snuck someone in—the idea of which I find utterly improbable because she's a grown woman and doesn't need to sneak around—she's by herself.

The thought of her being in her room, alone, making those sounds, makes my breaths come more quickly. The thought of what she might be doing and, more importantly, how, is enough to make my dick stand at attention. "Oh, fuck," I hear from behind her door, followed by another moan, and my cock jerks in response.

I can't stop from reaching down to grip my dick through the outside of my pants, my eyes falling closed. Hard as I am and as much as I continue to want her, I know it would only take minutes for me to get off. And with the addition of her increasingly more audible sound effects, probably even less.

Feeling like I can pretend she's thinking about me or wants me to hear her—even though I'm sure it's absurd—I imagine we can get off together like this. And as dangerous as it is, I slip my fingers into the front of my pajama pants and take myself fully in hand.

Not that I know what she sounds like when she comes, of course, but judging by how much higher pitched her moans are becoming and the sheer number of expletives spewing from her mouth, she can't be too far from the edge.

I fist my cock, wanting more than anything to share this moment with her, even if I'm the only one who ever knows. Even if I never get to hear those sounds for real. Even if this is all I get from her, I want it.

I'm right on the edge, sweat popping on my brow and my breath coming in quiet sighs, but I refuse to finish before she does. Whether from simple pride or the knowledge that if I were *with* her, I'd never allow myself to get off before her, I can't say. But when I hear a final, choked cry fall from her room, along with some last muffled words, I know she's come and I give myself permission to let go, the image of Ophelia's face in my mind as I spill into my fist.

Suddenly wiped out, I head back to my room and clean up using a towel I pull from my hamper. I fall into bed and I'm out as soon as my head hits the pillow.

During lunch the following day, I receive a text from Ophelia and I can't help but feel bummed as I read it.

> Ophelia: I have plans tonight. Wanted to let you know so you don't hold supper for me. Sorry for the last minute heads up. See you later.

And bummed as I am, I don't have any right to feel that way. She's not mine any more than Josie was mine when she was my roommate. Granted, I didn't want Josie when we lived together. I very much want Ophelia. But I also don't want to fuck up what we have. So, in spite of the possible knowledge that Ophelia could be on a date and the way they makes me feel, I try to be a good friend to her.

> Jess: Sure. No problem. If you need me, call me.

She only sends me a thumbs-up emoji and all that does is make me feel even more that she probably only sees me as a roommate and friend. The thought of sitting home, stewing in those thoughts, is utterly depressing.

Knowing Josie is on a road trip with Ford for a couple more days, I call one of the only people I know who doesn't have a life. Well, not one they can't do whatever they want with. Hensley answers on the third ring.

"What do you want, loser?"

"Nice, Hens. You're such a sweetheart."

She huffs a laugh. "What, you never call unless you don't have anyone else, so spill."

"Are you doing anything tonight?"

She's quiet for a minute. "Jess, you know I think you're hot, but I'm not gonna date you. We both know you're not my type."

I snort a laugh. "It's not a date, Hensley. Jesus. I need someone to talk to and Josie's firmly lodged up Ford's ass—not that I'm not happy for her."

"How could we not be happy for her, did you see that massive rock? Shit."

"Right?"

"And what about that roomie of yours, you can't talk to her?"

"No," I answer immediately.

Even through the phone, I can hear the smile in her voice. "Oh, I see. Because it's about that roomie of yours."

"Yes," I admit.

"Alright. Sure. I assume you're at work?"

"Well, yeah. Some of us do have day jobs. We can't all be people of leisure like yourself."

She huffs a laugh. "Yes, but were I not a woman of leisure, who would you get to listen to your tales of woe?"

I sigh. "It would seem my options are limited."

"I'll choose to take that as a compliment. I'll choose to believe you're seeking my immense wisdom."

"Sure, Hens."

"Just come over after you get off work. I'll have the chef make extra if you're gonna stay for dinner. You like sushi?"

"Okay. Yeah, sushi's fine. I'll be off at three."

"Sounds good."

CHAPTER SEVENTEEN

JESS

I don't bother changing out of my scrubs before heading to Hensley's house, or rather, Hensley's parents' house. A house that is more estate than simple home. There is a full-time staff and stables and a Hensley has an entire wing of her own.

And in spite of her family's immense wealth, Hensley has mostly stayed grounded. Well, except for the not working and the massive parties she regularly throws and the cars, clothes, and trips. But in reality, I've long suspected a lot of her bravado is simply a façade to try to hide her loneliness. She's an only child whose parents have never been around for her.

The housekeeper, Mrs. Hicks, greets me with a warm smile. "Well, Jess Tate, long time no see."

"Yes, ma'am. How are you these days, Mrs. Hicks?"

The woman, who is perpetually in her fifties and hasn't aged in the twenty-five years I've known Hensley, shrugs. "Oh, you know me, still kicking. I suppose you're here to visit with Miss Hensley?"

"Yes, ma'am. Would you happen to know where she is?"

"Out by the pool, I think." She gestures toward the back of the house.

"Thanks, I know the way."

"I'm sure. Holler if you need something."

"Will do."

I make the trek through the expansive home with its marble floors and ornate, hand-carved wooden trim and large, formal oil paintings of a much younger Hensley and her parents. Huge chandeliers light the opulent space and while it's beautiful, it also feels cold and sad.

By the time I make it through the kitchen and out onto the back patio, I feel as though I've walked a mile. Hensley is swimming laps and has loud music blaring from a bluetooth speaker on a small table. I take a seat on the end of one lounger and turn the volume down while I wait for my host to finish her swim.

Ten minutes later, Hensley climbs out of the pool dressed in a bikini that looks more like pieces of floss connecting minuscule patches of fabric. It leaves nearly nothing to the imagination and while Hensley is gorgeous, I feel nothing even remotely resembling attraction for her. Yep, it's only Ophelia.

Hensley retrieves a robe from a nearby chair and wraps herself in it before taking a seat on the lounger next to me. She lifts a wooden box from under her seat and opens it, the distinctive smell of marijuana wafting from the direction of her lap.

I don't remark as she rolls a joint and lights it, but when she extends it my direction, I shake my head. "Suit yourself," she says on an exhale, blowing smoke away from me. "So, what's up?"

"I think I like Ophelia."

She rolls her eyes. "I thought we already established that. You mean you still haven't made any moves on her since that night at the club? She was primed for the picking. Y'all looked great together while you were dancing."

I nod and Hensley reaches down into a cooler between our chairs and pulls out a bottle of my favorite beer and hands it over and I give her a smile. "Thanks."

She takes another deep inhale from her joint and holds it in for a long beat before blowing the smoke away again. "So, what's the problem?" she asks, picking a stray fleck of pot from her tongue.

"I don't know if I want her because she's awesome and beautiful and kind and sweet or if I'm only confusing attraction for actual feelings." I relay the story of how I saw Ophelia naked and how, although I thought she was beautiful before that, I'm not sure if I had feelings before that.

She considers as she finishes her joint and drops the tiniest sliver of a roach into an ashtray. "Okay, my first question is, how hot is she? I mean, I know I've seen her in club wear, but seriously, how stacked are we talking?" I level her with a gaze and her eyes go wide. "That good, huh? Nice. So, what's the worst-case scenario here? If you hook up with her and it's terrible?"

I sigh and drag my hand down my face. "Well, for starters, I don't know if she even likes me as more than a friend and roommate. Secondly, I don't want to fuck stuff up between us. I enjoy being her friend and I love living with her. She's fun and easy to live with."

"I think she likes you."

"Based on what?" I question.

Hensley pulls out a beer for herself and sips it. "Based on my gut. It's never steered me wrong. I knew when I hooked up with Silas back in high school that he was into Ada. Of course, my ego didn't much care for him calling her name during sex, but whatever. Truth be told, I was thinking of her a lot of the time, too, so I can't be all that pissed."

"Your gut is hardly a reliable scientific measurement."

"Attraction isn't all that scientific either, Jess. So, the worst that happens is that you lose your roommate. You and Josie hooked up and it ended and y'all are still friends."

"I don't just hook up anymore. That's not what I want. I want a future with someone. If I just look at Ophelia as a hookup, then I would've been better off staying with Brooklyn."

"Then I think you have your answer. You can go all in hoping it works out, but you know nothing is a sure thing." She looks out toward the pool. "Look at me. I thought for sure I would've found someone to spend my life with by now. And yet, all I have are parties and nights out." After a beat, she says, her voice quiet, "My parents are demanding I get married."

I snap my head in her direction. "What?"

"They said they're tired of me wasting what good child-bearing years I have left."

I snort a laugh. "What is this, the eighteenth-century? Do they have a dowry for you and everything?"

She shrugs, one brow ticking up as if to say, *pretty much.* "They already have a suitable gentleman picked out and everything."

My eyes go wide. "You're joking."

She gives a resigned shake of her head. "No."

"And what if you don't want to marry him?"

"I'm not sure it matters what I want at this point."

"And what if you wanted the opposite of a gentleman?"

She scoffs. "Yeah, I'm not sure that would fly. Dabbling is one thing. Parading a full-blown relationship with someone who they don't approve of is totally different. They couldn't care less who I fuck, and honestly, they're probably hoping I'm able to 'fuck away the gay'. I figure they think if I get enough now, I won't want it later."

"Please tell me you're joking, Hens. They do know that's not how it works, right?"

She drains her beer and pulls out another. "Like I said, it doesn't matter. I either do it, or they'll disown me."

"So start planning your escape. Yeah, you'd have to get a job and stuff, but you'd be fine."

"With what skills would I be *fine*, Jess? I've never worked a job a day in my life. I've never done anything of note. All anyone sees when they look at me is a pretty face with nothing going on in my head except what my next party theme will be."

"And whose fault is that, Hensley? You let people think that. Just like you let them think you're straight all these years. You're the only one who can change what people think about you."

"It's easy for you. You've got a great mom and brother who only want what's best for you. You've never had an issue standing up for yourself or going after what you want. Well, apparently, until now. If you want Ophelia, go after her."

"Any chance you're gonna take your own advice, Hens? Because it would be one thing if you actually liked the guy your parents are trying to set you up with, but you and I both know you stopped liking dick about the same time you and Silas broke up."

"It's not that I don't like dick, I just like pussy the same amount. Okay, sometimes more. I'm selective about my dick. It has to have more than just skill. It also has to be attached to a guy with an exceptional personality. Unfortunately, all the dick I've encountered in recent years are duds."

"But why do you keep up the ruse that you only like guys when we're out? Do you honestly think any of our friends would give a shit?"

"What else am I supposed to do? Sometimes, I wish you'd never found out and I could still pretend."

"Trust me, it's not like I wanted to walk in on you and Paige that night. I mean, don't get me wrong, I'm glad you got your sexuality confirmed, but I would've preferred if it hadn't been with my prom date."

She shrugs, a nonchalant smile on her face. "Sorry. She was really hot, though."

I laugh. "Yeah, she was."

Her smile falters. "She got married last year."

I nod. "I saw that on social media, I think."

She blows out a breath. "She came to see me before the wedding."

My eyes go wide. "She did?"

Hensley nods, her eyes welling with tears. "She asked me to give her a reason not to go through with it."

"Hensley, God. I had no idea. What did you do?"

"All I could think was that after everything I put her through, she still wanted me? I think that might have been the lowest moment of my life. I didn't even have the balls to let her love me when she was offering to throw away a wonderful life with someone else. I was a coward."

"So change. Stop being a coward and stand up to your parents. What good is this grand life of yours if you're essentially a prisoner? You're gonna marry some guy you'll probably be able to tolerate—at best—and pop out a couple kids just because you're worried about having to actually work for what you want? Please tell me you're not that shallow?"

She gives me a sad smile and a small shrug. "I don't know how to do anything else, Jess. I'm scared."

"So learn, Hens." I watch as she pulls her knees up and rests her chin on them. "Am I still the only one who knows? I mean, besides your parents?" She nods. "Not even Josie?"

"No."

"Why not?"

"The only reason you and my parents know is because you've seen me with women. If you'd never seen, I probably wouldn't have told you. They keep hoping it's a phase. I thought if I came out to them, it would make a difference, but it didn't."

"Well, all I know is, you're thirty-five and you're still in the closet. You go out and pretend to be straight and only ever leave with men. One of your best friends doesn't even know you're bi. You're obviously gonna have to come to terms with it yourself before you can ever hope other people accept it. And there are worse things than being disowned by your family. Ask Ophelia about that."

She frowns. "What do you mean?"

"She was disowned from her family because she chose to go to college. She hasn't seen any of her siblings or her parents in nine years. Well, until the other day when we were at the feed store and ran into her father and youngest brother. Her father called her a whore because she lives with a man she's not married to. She found out her mother died four years ago, and they didn't even tell her."

Hensley's eyes go wide. "Jesus. Is she okay?"

I shrug. "She cried, and I tried to be there for her, but I think it's still a lot."

"You really care about her, don't you?"

I nod. "I do. I just don't want to fuck this up. She's not someone I could sleep with and there'd be no consequences. And I honestly don't think I could only do it once and get her out of my system. Especially after last night."

She lifts one brow. "Oh? What happened last night?" Blowing out a breath, I recount the events of my midnight eavesdropping masturbation session and her mouth falls open. "Holy shit. That's hot. I bet she sounded sexy, didn't she?"

I nod. "Better than I would've imagined."

"Sounds to me like you know what you want, friend."

"And what about you? What do you want?"

She looks out toward the pool. "To be able to be honest with my parents and not have them look at me like there's something wrong with me or I'm defective in some way."

"You know you're not, right? You know you're perfect exactly the way you are?"

"Most of the time."

"Well, most of the time, I think you're pretty great. I think you drink too much and smoke too much pot. I think the only reason you do it is to try to numb the pain you feel from the shame and self-loathing you have from not being your most authentic self."

"Ouch. I could've done without the truth bomb, Jess. Fuck. And besides, it's easy for you. You are a beautiful, straight, white man. You're never gonna have to worry about being ostracized for who you love. You're never gonna have to face public ridicule."

I shake my head. "No. I'm not. I have no clue what it's like to have to walk in your shoes. But I know the people who care about you won't give a shit who you choose to spend your life with. The people who deserve to be in you life will love you. Full stop. No 'in spite of' or 'regardless'. They will simply love and support you."

I rise from my lounger and step over hers to straddle it and face her. I take her face in my hands and look into her eyes. "And if you need family at the end of the day, I will be your family, Hens."

Tears well in her eyes. "Why can't I just love you? You're so great, Jess." I press a kiss to her forehead and pull her in for a hug. She returns my embrace. "And if Ophelia doesn't see how great you are, that's on her."

"Thanks, Hens." My phone vibrates in my pocket, and I

pull it out to look out at it. I frown when I see I have three missed calls from Ophelia.

"What's wrong?"

I shrug and shake my head, already returning her call. "Not sure."

"Jess?"

"Everything okay, Birdie?" I glance at Hensley, who mouths *Birdie* with a raised brow.

"I'm at the hospital."

My stomach drops and I jump to my feet. "Which one? I'm coming. What happened?"

"I'm okay. I just need a ride. I was in a car accident."

My heart seems to stop and try as I might, I can't keep the worry out of my voice. "I'm coming. Which hospital?"

"Tennova."

"Closest to home?" I confirm.

"Yeah."

"Okay. I'm coming."

"I'm okay, Jess. I promise."

She disconnects the call, and I try to breathe. "What happened?" Hensley asks, concerned.

"Ophelia was in a wreck."

"Oh, God. Is she okay?"

I pat my pockets to make sure I have everything. "She said she was. She drives one of those tiny car things that looks like a clown car, so it's probably a wonder she's in one piece."

"Do you need me to drive you? You don't look great." I pat my pockets again and Hensley grabs my wrists to get my attention. "Do you need me to drive you?"

"No."

"Are you sure? I know you're worried, but chances are if she called you herself, she really is okay."

I know she's right, but I still can't help but worry. "I know."

I blow out a breath. "I'm okay. I can drive. She's close to home already, so I just need to swing by and pick her up."

"Be careful. Call me if you need anything. I don't mind coming and give sponge baths," she calls toward my back with a chuckle.

"Bye, Hens."

CHAPTER EIGHTEEN

OPHELIA

I debated even calling Jess, but honestly, he was the only person I wanted to see when they gave me the all clear. I guess I could've called an Uber, but I hate to admit that I've never used one of those ride share apps and it sort of freaks me out. And when Jess returned my call, I was struck with such relief that it made me forget how sore I'm gonna be tomorrow.

And now, as I sit in the waiting room of the emergency room, I roll my neck and shoulders. Turning my head from side to side, I catch a glimpse of a familiar face and feel my eyes go wide with how fast Jess is running. Part of me is flattered he'd run so quickly to get to me, but another part of me feels guilty for the worry I see etched into his face, even from fifty feet away.

He's forced to slow considerably when the automatic doors don't open as quickly as he probably wishes they would. As he makes it into the ER, he stops for a second, his breathing labored, to brace his hands on his knees to catch his breath. He begins to stand and walk over to the reception desk and I call his name.

His head snaps my direction and he jogs over to me, dropping to his knees in front of me. He looks as though he's afraid to touch me and his eyes examine my face and every part of my body he can easily see. Blatant relief flooding his features, he takes my hands in his. "God, you scared me to death."

The concern in his tone makes warmth fill my chest and my eyes unexpectedly fill with tears and I blink them back furiously. "I told you I was fine."

"I know, but still, your car is a sardine can on wheels. What happened?"

"A big SUV ran a stop sign and I didn't get stopped in time."

He releases my hands and runs his own up my arms, seemingly wanting to reassure himself I'm in one piece. "But you're okay? You're sure?"

I nod. "Just sore. I wasn't going that fast. I don't even have any whiplash."

He lets out a ragged breath and grips my face. "I was terrified, you know that?"

His words and the way he's touching me seem like more than friendly concern but I try not to read anything into it. Jess is a caring guy. I'm sure he'd react the same way if it were Josie or Hensley or any of his other friends. "I'm sorry I scared you."

"Can you walk? Are you ready to go home?"

I nod and rise from my chair, already feeling stiff. Jess hurriedly stands and takes my lunch box and purse, even as I protest. "I can carry that stuff."

"You can also let me carry them." He offers me his arm for support and although I shouldn't, I take it.

We're quiet as we walk out to the parking lot and I lean closer to him and whisper, "Why do you smell like pot?"

He huffs a laugh. "I was at Hensley's."

I nod, unsure how to feel about that fact. I don't want to

feel jealous, but that's my first reaction. And really, who could blame Jess if he's hanging out with or hooking up with Hensley? She's stunning and a lot of fun. They'd make a beautiful couple. I realize Jess is still speaking and I focus my attention back on his words.

"I'm surprised you even know what pot smells like."

"And I'm surprised I keep having to tell you I'm not as naive as you think I am. I went through a pothead phase in college."

A bark of laughter falls from his mouth. "Oh, really? Well, color me shocked."

I shrug. "I mean, it was only for about a week, but yeah."

He laughs even harder as we get to his car. He opens the passenger door for me and helps me slide inside. I try not to wince with the pain, but the soreness is quickly descending and I'm so glad they've written me out of work for tomorrow.

"So, what do you want to do for supper? I was supposed to eat at Hensley's, but I ran out when you called."

"If you want to go back over after you run me home, that's fine. I'm okay, Jess. I don't want to wreck your plans."

"They weren't really plans to begin with. I called her after you said you had plans and she asked if I was gonna stay for dinner. Speaking of which, I'm guessing your plans got ruined?"

I nod, but stop when it hurts. "Yeah, I was supposed to meet someone for drinks, but obviously that didn't work out."

"Oh? Was it a date?" His tone is neutral when he asks the question and is just one more reminder that he only views me as a friend. It's doesn't seem to bother him that I might have a date. I hate the way it twists my guts to think he wouldn't be jealous.

And yet, I answer honestly. "No. One of the girls from over in billing. She complimented me on my shoes, I complimented her on her purse. I guess that makes us best friends? We were supposed to have drinks before she met her husband for dinner."

His only reaction is a swallow before he nods. "Well, I'm sorry you had to bail. Hopefully, you can reschedule. So, I'm thinking something simple for supper. Maybe some spaghetti or homemade pizza? We've got that Italian sausage that needs to be cooked."

We've got Italian sausage. Somehow we are a *we* but we're also not. I don't know if it's that the pain I'm in is making me more aware of the things he says or his body language, but I'm confused. I don't want to read too much into things. I don't want to assume and end up making things awkward at home.

Home. That's another one of those words that makes me think *things.* Because, in truth, Jess's house is the first place that actually feels like home in more years than I care to admit. Before this, I would have said Rosalind's, but that was ruined by everything that happened right before I graduated college. So, yeah, Jess's is home and if I throw myself at him or give any indication that I'm interested when clearly all he wants is a friend, I may lose that home.

Jess's hand on my arm brings me out of my thoughts. "I'm sorry, what?"

He gives me a small smile. "I asked if you had a preference for supper? Although, I'm sure you're pretty out of it, huh?"

I nod. "Yeah. Sorry. You said spaghetti?"

"I can do that. Or something else if you're not up for that."

"Jess, I'm fine. I'm sore and I'm sure I'll feel worse tomorrow, but I'm okay."

"I'm guessing they didn't give you anything for the pain, did they?"

I shake my head. "No. They said I could take some Advil or Tylenol, but that's about it."

"Well, there's some epsom salt, so you could take a long soak and it should help loosen everything up."

"Not a bad idea." I sigh, struck by a thought. "Shit."

"What?"

"I have to get a car. Mine's totaled."

"Okay, we'll figure it out. You don't have to do it today."

"I'm only getting tomorrow off, along with the weekend to recover, so it's sort of a pressing issue."

He chuckles. "Like I said, we'll figure it out. You have insurance, right?"

I nod. "Yeah, full coverage."

"Okay, then tomorrow, we'll call the insurance company and they can get you a rental to use until they send an adjuster to check the damage and cut you a check. Then, we can go find you a new car. Preferably one that doesn't look like a clown car."

"Hey, I thought we agreed you wouldn't bash on my car."

"No, you said that. I never said that. Besides, Garth can't even fit in your car. And not that I care to drive anytime we all go somewhere, but don't you want something the dog can ride in? He likes adventures, too."

"Fine," I say, knowing I'm not winning this argument because, in all honesty, he makes some good points.

A moment later, he's pulling into the garage at home and I'm trying not to grunt with how much pain I'm in. Jess levels me with a gaze as I walk into the house. "You don't have to be stoic, Birdie. I'm sure you're in so much pain it's not even funny."

"I'll be fine."

He sets my stuff down on the counter and hustles to let Garth out in the yard so he can do his business. "Come on, I'll run you a bath and start supper. You'll feel better once you have a good soak and get some food in your belly."

I move gingerly toward the bathroom and he jogs ahead of me to start the bath. I try not to think about him being so nurturing and kind to me. Granted, Jess is kind and I keep reminding myself he'd do this for anyone, not just me. That he's only being a good friend.

Attempting to bend to take off my shoes, I inhale sharply as pain radiates through my torso from where the seatbelt restrained me. Jess turns, having just finished dumping some bath salts into the water. "Here, I can get it." He drops to his knees and gently unbuckles the ankle straps on my high heels and slips them off, one by one, offering me his hand for balance when I lift my foot from the shoe.

Again, I remind myself that this is just who Jess is. He's kind, he's genuine, he's a good friend. Even as he looks up at me from his knees with a smile and I think about other reasons he could be on his knees. Apparently, even being in massive amounts of pain doesn't stop me from wanting him. "Thanks," I say, trying to keep my voice even.

He stands. "Sure. You think you can get in by yourself?"

I huff a laugh. "What, you didn't get enough of an eyeful last time?"

He blinks in surprise, his cheeks going pink. "I was just—I mean, I know you're in a lot of pain and—."

I cut him off with a laugh, even though it hurts. "I'm joking. I know. Knowing you, you'd probably offer to keep your eyes closed to protect what think is left of my virtue." I lower my voice. "Spoiler alert: I have none."

He chuckles, the blush still coloring his cheeks. "I would, you know. It would be difficult, but I'd do my best. Besides, I've got a pretty good memory," he says with a grin.

It's my turn to blush, but thankfully, he doesn't see it as he bends to shut off the water. When he looks at me again, his face is free of playfulness and any kind of humor. "Seriously, do you want help? I can keep my hands to myself. I'm a medical professional, you know."

"I think I'm alright. Thanks, though."

He nods, his expression still neutral. "Okay. Well, I'll leave you to it. For real, though, if you need help, yell. I don't want you getting hurt worse by trying to be brave."

"I will," I confirm.

Jess examines my face one last time before stepping out. I take a moment to unbutton my blouse, trying to breathe through the pain of moving my arms. I let it fall from my arms and attempt to reach behind me to undo my bra and let out an involuntary whimper and I can't do it. Reaching up to push the straps off my shoulders in preparation of just sliding the clasp around to the front is even too much, and tears of pain and frustration spring to my eyes.

Jess's voice comes through the other side of the door a second later. "Ophelia, let me help you. Please? I promise not to look."

Yeah, I'm pretty sure I wouldn't mind, buddy.

I'm also pretty sure he doesn't want to look, and that's okay. He's just trying to be a good friend. I grab my towel off the hook and cover my front. "Okay," I say with a resigned sigh and turn away from the door.

He opens it and steps inside and out of the corner of my eye in the mirror, I see him approach. He takes a deep breath, as if steeling himself to touch me and it's in that moment, in spite of what he said about his memory or the way he looked at me when he came to the hospital, I realize he truly doesn't want me. He can't. Not if he has to prepare himself before putting his hands on me and the expression on his face is that of pinched concentration. He makes quick work of the clasp and drops his hands just as fast and knowing I can't make him want me or look at me as more than simply a friend and roommate, I give him a tight smile over my shoulder. "Thanks."

He returns my smile. "Anytime. Are you good? Or do you need help getting in?"

I shake my head. "I'm fine."

"Alright. Well, holler if you need help."

I wait until he retreats again before gritting my teeth and as fast as I possibly can, shove my skirt and panties down my hips and to the floor. Breathing through the pain, I climb over the edge of the tub and lower myself into the warm water and close my eyes as I lean back.

As I soak, I contemplate how my life might be if all Jess is to me is a friend. He's a great friend, so I could do a lot worse. And it would hurt like a bitch to watch him start dating again after he gets over Brooklyn but I could still be his friend.

I just have to lock it away and remind myself he's not mine and never will be. Even as tears threaten, I remind myself that I will be fine. And when my lease is up, I can move. I can find a new place that doesn't feel like home, but also doesn't remind me of Jess.

Good lord, I'm acting like—well, I'm acting like I love him. That's not possible, right? I mean, is it possible to love someone you're not in a relationship with? And besides, would I even know what it looks like to love someone?

I let my mind wander to what I was taught love was. Obedience, meekness, long-suffering, selflessness; just to name a few qualities. No one ever told me about this ache. They didn't tell me I wouldn't just think about his body pressed against mine. They didn't tell me about the completeness I'd feel when I'm with him. They didn't tell me how safe I'd feel or how much more *me* I would feel because of him. They didn't tell me how I'd picture what it might be like to watch his hair turn gray or his steps slow as he ages. No one told me I'd think about what a child with his green eyes and my blonde hair would look like.

I was taught to be a good woman, you needed to defer to a man. That desire is a sin until you say some vows. But how can the way I feel about Jess be wrong? Despite knowing he doesn't think of me that way, he's still treated me better in the few months I've been here than anyone else in my life.

Some might say I've not been around the block enough to recognize a good man from a bad one. And to that, I say, I grew up with a father who isn't half the man Jess is, so I recognize plenty. But despite being able to see how wonderful he is and know he'd be a good partner, none of that matters since he doesn't see me the same way.

I allow myself to wallow for the time it takes the water to drain once it's gone cold. And then, I rise with great effort and difficulty and wrap myself in a towel and head toward my room. After slipping into a pair of leggings and an oversized tee shirt with the neck cut out that hangs off one shoulder, I shuffle out to the kitchen, where Jess is putting the finishing touches on the spaghetti. The scents of Italian sausage, garlic, basil and tomatoes fill my nose and I smile. "Smells great."

He gives me a big grin. "Thanks. Go ahead and sit. I'll bring the plates over. I went ahead and poured a glass of wine for you so it could breathe."

I take my seat and sip my wine. Were the circumstances different, I could convince myself this is a romantic dinner. Alas, it is not. It is merely two roommates enjoying a delicious— and platonic—supper. Jess sets my plate down in front of me and takes his own seat and looks at me, his expression turning concerned. "What?" I ask, confused by the look on his face.

He reaches over and brushes his fingertip across my collarbone and my breath catches, goosebumps scattering down my arms. "You've got a burn from the seatbelt. You should put some of that salve on it."

I can only nod and take another sip of my wine.

Only friends. Only friends. Only friends.

"Does it hurt?"

I shrug. "Not bad."

"Do you think the bath helped?"

"Yeah, I'm sure."

He gives me a quick smile and reaches into his pocket, pulling out his phone as he takes a bite of spaghetti. He chews and taps on the screen before setting it facedown on the table. "Hensley was asking how you were."

Probably wanting to ensure there's no funny business between us.

"Tell her I said thanks for checking on me. And if you needed to go back over there, I understand. I hate you had to run out on her on account of me. I realize now, when I called you earlier, I didn't even ask you what you were doing or anything. I shouldn't have assumed you were free. I'm sorry about that."

He frowns. "I didn't run out on her. And I am free. Do you really think I'd bail on you? You needed me and I was happy to be there for you. You scared me half to death, but I'm just glad you're okay, Ophelia."

"Well, thank you for coming to my rescue."

He gives me this great lopsided grin that makes my chest ache. "Not sure you've ever needed anyone to rescue you, but I'm glad I could help out."

His phone buzzes again and he ignores it and asks, "So, when we get done eating, you think you might feel up to watching a movie? Or would you prefer to read for a while?"

"A movie might be nice. But you'll probably have to go to bed halfway through it."

"I'll be fine. Tomorrow's Friday. I can sleep in this weekend."

His phone buzzes again and I tilt my chin in its direction. "Do you need to get that?"

"No." It buzzes again as he's speaking.

"Are you sure?"

His jaw clenches. "Yeah. It's just Brooklyn. She's pissed because I'm refusing to even read her texts. This is what she does."

My eyes go wide. "She's texting you? And you don't want to see what she has to say?"

Jess shakes his head and takes a sip of his wine. "No. I said everything I have to say to her. She thinks if she gives me some time to cool off, I'll forget she lied to me for months and we don't want the same things."

I can't help but ask, simply for my own peace of mind, "What if she's changed her mind about the things she wants?"

He huffs a sad laugh. "It doesn't matter. I don't think I could ever trust her again. So, she could come crawling back to me, begging me to marry her and give her six kids, and I couldn't do it."

I nod. "Okay."

He twirls some spaghetti on his fork. "What are some of the things you can't overlook in a relationship?"

"I doubt I'm the best person to ask since I've never really had a relationship. Definitely cheating is a hard no, of course. I think a lot of other things can be forgiven, provided there's not a pattern of bad behavior. Bad hygiene."

He laughs. "So, no morning breath for you?"

"Morning would imply they were there all night. I wouldn't know what that's like."

Well, except that morning I woke up with you. But since I

didn't see your face and pretended to be asleep, I can't come out and say that.

He blinks. "I thought you said you had a boyfriend in college. You never spent the night with him?"

I shake my head. "He lived in the dorms and I slept on Rosalind's couch the whole time I lived with her."

"That makes me sad for you."

I shrug. "It is what it is."

His eyes fall to my empty plate. "Do you want some more?"

"No thanks. It was great, as usual."

"Thank you. Go sit and pick a movie. I'll be over as soon as I get the dishes washed and leftovers put away."

I wave away his offer. "You cooked; the least I can do is wash the dishes."

"Ophelia, you were in a car wreck. The only thing you're gonna do is hobble your ass over to the couch. If you even pick up that plate, I will be forced to scoop you up and carry you myself. And then I'd feel bad because you're sore."

I roll my eyes. "Fine, I won't have you put your back out."

He snorts a laugh and rises, stacking our dishes. "You wouldn't put my back out."

"I'm not exactly small."

"*You* are exactly how you are supposed to be—perfect." I open my mouth to tell him there's no such thing, and he puts a finger to my lips and looks into my eyes. "If the words that are getting ready to come out of your mouth are anything other than 'you're right' or 'thank you for noticing', they better stay in there."

Currently, I'm not sure I know how to breathe, let alone speak. Because all I can see now are his green, green eyes and his five o'clock shadow and the way his throat bobs with a swallow when he examines my face. Those full lips and that straight nose and those arched brows. All I can feel is his finger on my lips and the thundering of my heart behind my ribs. I nod slowly as I hold his gaze and he gives me a slow smile. "Good girl. Now go relax."

Cheeks flaming and mouth agape, all I can do is watch his back in wonder as he turns away from me to ferry the dirty dishes over to the kitchen. What the fuck was that? I mean, other than something incredibly hot.

A few minutes later, I realize I'm still sitting and analyzing his words and how affected I was. I've known for a long time I had a praise kink. And *good girl* is my insta-horny button. Sweet lord, to hear Jess say it so nonchalantly? I'm gonna have to change my panties.

CHAPTER NINETEEN

JESS

I hadn't meant to say the words. Those aren't words I throw around outside of the bedroom. And granted, unless the person who hears them has a praise kink, they don't generally mean anything. It must be all the smut Ophelia's got me reading, because they just slipped out.

And I turned away, but not before seeing how quickly her pupils dilated or how flushed she was. Too bad I don't need to be thinking about whether or not Ophelia has a praise kink. Nope, don't need to think about that at all. I don't need to ponder all the other phrases she might enjoy hearing during sex. I don't need to think about sex with her at all. Even if she reacted to the words, it doesn't mean she'd want to hear them from me.

She finally rises from her chair to slowly make her way over to the sofa as I scrub the pots and pans after putting away the leftovers. A quick glance tells me she's not watching TV, even though it's on. She's just sitting, a contemplative look on her face. I hope I didn't fuck things up.

Even as I finish cleaning up, she's still sitting, a blank look on her face. Fuck, I did mess stuff up. I can get things back on track, though, right? Is it better to pretend it never happened or address it? It's not as though I propositioned her or said anything vulgar or blatantly sexual. Maybe it's better to not say anything.

Deciding to do exactly that, I grab both our glasses and refill them, along with my phone, and go to sit next to her. Garth must be able to sense something's wrong with Ophelia because he's not half on top of her as he usually is. He's laid his snout just on top of her thigh and I can't help but smile.

"What movie did you decide on, Birdie?"

She blinks, as if startled, and gives me her full attention. There's no trace of anything like I saw when she was at the table, and I know she's truly not affected by me. Not that I was going for that, but a guy can hope, right?

"Oh, um, *Labyrinth?*"

I nod, giving her a wide grin as I hand over her wineglass. "Perfect choice. David Bowie, catchy music, creepy puppets; what's not to love?"

"I guess we'll see."

As she starts the movie, I take a moment to check my phone and roll my eyes when I see the three texts from Brooklyn.

> Brooklyn: Call me when you get this.

> Brooklyn: Please, Jess. We need to talk.

> Brooklyn: I miss you, baby. Please.

I clear them off and I'm about to put my phone down again when it buzzes in my hand and I read the screen.

Josie: Ford and I have decided to turn our engagement party into a reception. We're eloping in Vegas on Saturday. Would you and Ophelia come be our witnesses? Your flight and hotel will be covered.

I nearly choke on my wine and Ophelia's brow pinches with concern. "What's wrong?"

I huff a laugh. "Wanna go to Vegas this weekend?"

Her eyes go wide. "What?"

"Josie and Ford are eloping. They need witnesses. You think you might feel up to it? She said they'd take care of our flight and hotel."

"What about Garth?"

I shoot off a quick text to Hensley to see if she could house and dog sit for us and when she confirms, I give Ophelia a smile. "Garth is covered. Come on, Birdie, wanna go to Sin City?"

She considers for a long moment. "I've never flown before. I've never really been anywhere before."

"Well, there's a first time for everything. And if I know Ford, we'll be flying first class and be in a five-star hotel. Josie said he doesn't mess around with travel." I gently nudge her with my elbow. "What do you say?"

"Can we go? Really?"

I nod. "Sounds like it to me. Neither of us works on the weekend, we have someone to watch our dog; we're good."

She grins. "Vegas? Really?"

"I'm gonna take that as a yes."

"What about their engagement party?"

I shrug. "From what Josie said, it's now gonna be a reception."

"Wow. Okay. Let's go to Vegas."

I send a text back to Josie to confirm we'll go and lay my phone down again so we can watch the movie.

By Saturday morning, when we get ready to leave for Vegas, most of Ophelia's soreness has subsided, and she's so excited for the trip, her good mood is contagious. She and Josie are talking about dresses and the plans for tonight and Ford and I are fetching coffee since we've made it through security.

He glances over his shoulder toward the girls. "So, what's the status?"

I shrug and shake my head. "Hell if I know, man."

"You like her, though, right?"

"Yeah. A lot."

"Okay, so what's the holdup?"

We take another step closer to the counter and I sigh. "I don't know if she feels the same way. We have to live together and I don't want it to be weird."

He shoots Josie a wink and a goofy smile, and I roll my eyes. "God, y'all are so disgustingly perfect it's not even funny."

Ford shrugs, not a bit apologetic. "Is that envy I hear, Jess?"

I keep my voice low. "Fuck yes, it's envy."

He laughs. "Man, you've got it bad, don't you?"

"Bad enough that if she ran away from home, I'd pester her roommate for weeks for any tidbit of information about her," I deadpan, reminding him of the lengths he went to before he and Josie reconciled.

His eyes widen and he sobers. "Okay, well, I can relate to that. So, you think it's the real deal?"

I nod. "I do. And I don't know, it's different with her than it was with Brooklyn and we're not even 'together'." I put the last word in air quotes and drag my hand down my face and take another step closer. "It was always a fight with Brooklyn. Trying to get her to cave to what I wanted. I thought because I loved her, I had to keep fighting to keep us together. And I can see now I wasn't the right guy for her. We don't want the same things."

"So, you're over Brooklyn?"

"I think so. I wouldn't take back the time we had together, because it was a lot of fun. But I don't want her. I don't want to be with her. I want to be with Ophelia."

He considers as we step up to the counter to place our order. After we pay and step to the side to wait, Ford looks back over at the girls. When he turns back to me, he wears a wide grin. "She was just looking at you."

I roll my eyes. "What is this, middle school?"

He shrugs. "I'm just saying, Josie is over there talking a mile a minute, and Ophelia's eyes were glued to you until I looked over at them. I've got exceptional peripheral vision. Trust me. Go for it." We pick up our coffees a few minutes later and as I'm adding cream and sugar to Ophelia's, he nudges me, a wicked grin on his face. "Shouldn't be too hard, considering."

I frown, unsure if I like his expression. "Considering what?" I ask and take a drink of my coffee as we make our way back over to Josie and Ophelia.

"Considering your room only has one bed."

I choke on my coffee and feel my eyes bug out of my head. "What?"

He shrugs. "Sorry, all they had was a suite—which Josie and I took—and a king on such short notice." He wiggles his eyebrows. "You can thank me later."

I'm nearly hyperventilating as I sit. It's one thing to accidentally fall asleep with Ophelia as I comfort her. It's a completely different thing altogether to intentionally sleep in the same bed. I remind myself it's only one night and chances are, it'll be really late when we turn in and we'll be so tired, we'll just fall into bed and crash. But I also remember how nice it was to wake up with her and I've thought about what it might be like to do it again.

"You okay?" Ophelia eyes my face as she takes her coffee from my hand and sips it.

I nod. "Yeah. Of course."

"Are you sure? You look pale."

"I'm good."

"Okay," she replies with a smile. "So, have you ever been to Vegas?"

"Yeah, during college, Flynn and I went with our dad. Lost our asses."

She laughs. "Nice. Will you do any gambling while we're there?"

Possibly the biggest gamble of my life.

"Not planning on it. We're not gonna be there that long and I'm sure Josie and Ford will have us run ragged by the time the wedding is scheduled to start."

She takes a long drink of her coffee. "This might be the most exciting thing I've ever done."

"Well, I hope you have a good time."

"You think Garth is gonna be okay?"

I nod, touched by her concern. "Definitely. Hensley will take good care of him."

She gives me a small smile. "Is there a reason you invited me instead of Hensley?"

I frown. "Besides the fact Josie asked for you? I would've invited you, regardless. It never would've crossed my mind to invite anyone but you. Why would you think that?"

She shrugs. "You and Hensley seem kinda close, so I was just curious."

"Hens and I are pretty close." I move my face to catch her eye. "Close friends. That's all."

"So y'all haven't dated before?"

I almost want to laugh because it's Hensley. And not that she's not great, but I've never felt that way about her. "No."

She fidgets with the flap on the lid of her cup and asks, "Is that because you're worried you won't be friends anymore if you dated and broke up?"

"No. I just don't have feelings for Hensley. She doesn't have feelings for me."

Ophelia considers my answer for a long moment. "Okay."

I try not to read too much into our conversation and get my hopes up that she's fishing for possible information about my relationship with Hensley. Changing the subject, I pull out my phone. "This is the first time you're gonna be flying, right?" She nods and I grin. "Well, it must be documented. We'll have to make a little album from this trip. Might as well start now."

"Alright. And you can tag me in them when you upload them to Instagram?"

I blink. "You mean you finally broke down and got an account? Well, hell yeah. How did I not know about that? What's your handle?"

"Just my name. Original, I know."

I hold my phone up and we lean in and smile and I snap the selfie. I navigate to Instagram and follow Ophelia's account and notice she has several photos of Garth on her feed. "Hey, I'm offended. I should be tagged in these. He's my dog, too."

She chuckles. "I don't know how to do that."

I have her follow my account and show her how to tag someone by uploading the photo I just took of us and tagging her with the caption, "Sin City Bound".

"See, easy. Now, normally, when I go on any trips, I don't

upload stuff until I get back, but since Hensley's at the house, I'm not worried."

Josie hollers from across the aisle. "Don't upload any photos of Ford and me. At least not until we do, got it?"

"Sure." I turn to Ophelia. "I guess it's gonna look like it's just the two of us until Josie and Ford make their announcement."

"Not a problem. I think what they're doing is romantic."

"Yeah. A little impulsive for my taste, but honestly, I think Ford would've married Josie the day they reconciled after she ran away."

"They're really cute."

"So are you."

She blushes and I enjoy seeing it. "You're not so bad yourself. Did you bring a suit to wear to the wedding?"

"Of course. Did you bring a dress?"

"Duh. Can't have you stealing my thunder. The only person who gets to do that is Josie."

"I'm not worried, Birdie. I'm sure you'll look beautiful. You always do."

"Thank you, Jess," she replies quietly, her cheeks turning pink again.

CHAPTER TWENTY

OPHELIA

It's a little after noon local time when we land in Las Vegas. And try as I might to appear unaffected by everything, I feel giddy. Having never traveled anywhere except Wilmington, flying across the country—in first class, no less—is a bit surreal.

After making our way to the rental car counter and picking up the SUV Ford's reserved, we decide to go get some lunch. Knowing we have a lot of errands to run to prepare for the wedding, we opt to grab a quick burger at a roadside diner with great online reviews.

While we wait for our burgers and shakes, Josie and I continue our chat from earlier while the men are occupied talking about hockey. "So," Josie starts, keeping her voice low, "What are you gonna do?"

I shrug. "I don't wanna mess things up between us. I love living with him and I love how easy things are. We talk all the time and have our routines. He's become such a good friend to me, I don't ever want to lose that."

She nods. "But do you *want* him?" She wiggles her eyebrows so I don't misunderstand her meaning and I blush.

"That's what I thought. Well, at least you'll get your shot tonight." Her grin turns wicked and I frown.

"Why do you say that, just because we're in the same city and you're getting married? It's definitely romantic, but I don't look for either of us to get swept up in the moment."

She rolls her eyes. "I was referring to the room situation."

"What about it?"

"Your room only has one bed."

My eyes go wide and my mouth falls open. "What?"

She shrugs. "They only had a suite and a king single. It was really short notice and Ford is very particular about the hotels he uses. And who am I to argue with him wanting to put us up at the Four Seasons? Our room has a dining room and everything. After the wedding, we're all gonna come back and order a huge supper and dessert before I kick y'all out so I can consummate my marriage," she says wickedly.

All I can think is that I'll be sharing a bed with Jess. I mean, unless the room has a sofa. I can take the sofa. It's one night. Do I want to take the sofa, though? No, I don't, if I'm being honest. I steal a glance at Jess as he gestures animatedly about some kind of hockey play. He's relaxed and smiling and I could look at him all day.

Josie nudges me. "Jess is a really good guy."

I return my attention to her. "I know. He's amazing."

"I love him almost as much as I love my own brother—our past relationship not withstanding—and I want him to be happy. I don't know what you want out of life, but I know he's ready for a future with someone." She looks at him for a beat with affection in her gaze before bringing her eyes back to mine. "If that's not something you're looking for, I get it. Trust me. Although I know he loved Brooklyn, she wasted his time. I don't want that for him again. I know he's a big boy and can very easily make his own decisions, but I also know he cares about you. I just don't want to watch him having to be put in standby mode for years again. He's one of the best people I know, and I hope you can see that."

Seeing how much Josie cares for him makes warmth spread through my chest. "I do know he's a wonderful man. I know the things he wants in his life. And I while I have complicated feelings about family, it doesn't stop me from wanting one. And I care about Jess, too."

Josie smiles. "I'm glad we're on the same page. Now, how do you think I should wear my hair for the wedding?"

Even though I knew it was only one bed, my heart still trips over in my chest when I see it. It's large and plush and screams, *I'm ready for whatever.* And there is no sofa; only a wingback chair and ottoman, a padded bench at the end of the bed, and a large desk by the massive windows that overlook the Vegas strip.

Jess and I both stand, staring at the bed without speaking for a moment. After what seems like hours, but is probably more like two minutes, he says, "You don't seem all that surprised to find out it's only the one bed."

I shake my head. "You, either. Josie told me when we were waiting on our burgers. When did you find out?"

"Before we left Knoxville."

I snap my head in his direction. "Why didn't you tell me?"

He shrugs. "I was processing the news. I thought there'd be a couch."

"Yeah," I agree as I attempt to shake off my nerves. "This is fine, right? We've fallen asleep together before. This is practically the same thing."

He smiles, but it appears a bit too bright. "Right. And

besides, this bed is huge. I'm pretty sure you could sleep side-ways and you'd still not be able to touch me."

I huff a laugh. "Care to test that theory?"

Jess arches one brow and gives me a lopsided grin. "Maybe later tonight. We've got a schedule to keep."

I try not to think too hard about his facial expressions or how carefree his tone sounds. If he's nervous or dismayed at all, he's not broadcasting it.

"Sure, we can do that," I reply just as nonchalantly, even though my insides are quaking. Needing something to do in this moment, I set my suitcase on the bench at the end of the bed and open it up to take out my dress and hang it. Jess seems to think this is a great idea, because he, too, decides to unpack.

For several moments, we're moving around each other in the room. As I'm coming out of the bathroom from putting my toiletries on the sink, he's coming in and we nearly collide. In my surprise, my steps falter and I bring my hands up, to prevent a full-on collision. Jess has his toiletry bag in one hand and grabs my arm to steady me.

Somehow, in this little milliseconds-long dance, my hands have landed squarely on his chest. His solid, warm, strong, chest. "Sorry, Birdie. Didn't mean to almost run you over." He's giving me that crooked smile again and he's still holding my arm, his thumb brushing softly across my skin.

"No problem," I reply, my voice breathy, even to my own ears. "I'm used to it. I've danced with you, remember?"

He laughs, but still makes no move to release my arm. I also make no move to take my hands off his chest. I can't stop myself from splaying my fingers wider, feeling more of his pecs.

My mouth suddenly going dry—from what, I can't say; his proximity, his hand on my skin, how good he feels under my fingers—I swallow and lick my lips. Jess's eyes drop to them for the briefest of seconds, but it's enough to make my pulse tic up.

His eyes slide back to mine and lock and his bag clatters to the floor as he grabs my face and crashes his lips to mine.

Surprised as I am, it only takes half a second for my mind to catch up, and I grip his shirt and pull him closer. He slides his hand to the back of my neck and tilts my head, deepening and controlling the kiss and I can't bite back a soft moan as heat, unlike anything I've ever known, floods my middle.

He huffs a ragged exhale and I feel his heart banging against his chest under my fists and can't help but smile, knowing he's as affected as I am. Having dreamt of this moment for months, I suddenly need to feel his skin under my fingers. Trailing my hands down his chest, I tug up the hem of his shirt and run my fingers over his stomach. His skin is coated in a dusting of coarse hairs and I bring my hands higher up and grip his ribs.

Jess breaks our kiss with a near gasp and I'm just as breathless as he is. He searches my eyes and breaths in deeply. "Fuck," is all he says.

"Yeah," I agree.

He licks his lips and continues to drag in lungfuls of air. His face and neck are flushed and his pupils are blown wide. He smiles again and begins to lean in again, but then freezes and sighs and I frown, thinking he's changed his mind. At least until he drops his hands and reaches into his pocket and pulls out his phone. After a brief second of hesitation, he holds up his index finger and I nod as he swipes the screen to answer. "Flynn, a little late for you, isn't it?" He's quiet while he listens to whatever his brother is saying and I take a moment to pick up his bag from the floor and deposit it on the bathroom sink. "Yeah, so?" As he listens, he walks over to the window and stares down at the strip. "Oh, really?"

He nods along with whatever Flynn is saying and, as much as I don't want to eavesdrop, I don't have anywhere else to go.

So, as to at least appear as though I'm not hovering, I drop onto the end of the bed and pull out my phone. Tapping the screen, I see several Instagram notifications.

I tap into the app and see there are several likes and comments on the photo Jess posted of us and of the ones I tagged him in of Garth.

Many names of the people who liked the photo of us I don't recognize. Some I do, though. Ada, Hensley, and Josie all hearted it. There are also a few comments and I click into those as well.

Your_Girl_Hens: *Have fun! Say hi to Elvis for me.*

Ada_Campbell: *Stay away from the craps table, Jess. You remember what happened last time.*

WanderingBrooklyn: *Didn't take y'all long. Nice to see you will travel when it matters. Guess I didn't.*

Brooklyn's comment gives me pause because, in spite of the fact her ex-boyfriend just kissed the hell out of me, she probably assumes we've been together for a while. Or, worse maybe, that we got together before they broke up. The thought doesn't sit well with me.

"Birdie?" I snap my head up to see Jess standing about a foot away, a look of concern on his face. "You okay?"

I nod. "Fine. Everything okay with Flynn?"

"Actually, he's in Vegas this weekend, believe it or not."

"Wow, really? Small world. Are you gonna try to see him while we're in town?"

He sits next to me on the bed. "Yeah. He said he saw the Instagram post when he got out of a meeting. And no, I doubt I'll have time to see him."

Unsure what to make of his not wanting to at least attempt to see his brother but not wanting to pry, I return the subject to the photos. "He's not the only one who's seen it."

He considers. "I'm sure. Lots of people see them."

"Brooklyn saw it," I supply.

He shrugs. "That was bound to happen. She pretty much lives on Instagram."

"I don't want her to get the wrong idea."

He frowns. "What idea?"

"That we might have done anything while you two were still together."

"What does her comment say? Is she trying to say I cheated on her?"

"I don't think so; it's just important to me that she knows that's not the case."

Jess pulls his phone out and navigates into the app and reads her comment. "She's just pissed. I'm not worried about her. It also makes all the texts she sent me make sense. She's been blowing up my phone since I turned it back on."

"I'm not a cheater, Jess. And I don't want anyone to think that."

"I'm not either. Like I said, she's just pissed." He takes my hand in his and turns it palm up and intertwines our fingers, and I can only stare at our joined hands. "I don't want to talk about Brooklyn, Ophelia."

He leans over and presses a kiss to the side of my neck and I let my eyes fall closed. "What do you want to talk about?" I ask, aware of how husky my voice sounds.

Running the tip of his nose along my jaw, his breath plays over my skin and I nearly shiver. "I want to talk about the kiss."

"What about it?"

"I—Son of a bitch." My eyes fly open as he pulls away and drops my hand. "What, Jos?" he growls into the phone and I don't know whether to smile at his frustration or be annoyed that we keep getting interrupted. He drags his hand down his face. "Okay, we'll be there in a minute." Disconnecting the call, he lets out a heavy sigh. "We've been summoned."

"Oh. Alright. Do we need to change clothes or anything?"

"No, they're just sending us on some errands. Josie and Ford have spa appointments or whatever."

"Fancy." We rise from the bed and Jess grabs the room key and I pick up my purse as we head out. Once we're on the elevator, Jess turns toward me and I look up at him, expectant. "What?"

"Just thinking." Except his expression is a bit mischievous and I give him a slow smile. "Are you thinking, Birdie?"

I pivot my body to face his and reach up to drag my index finger down his chest. "That's a pretty safe assumption."

He takes a step closer and I'm forced to step back, my shoulder blades colliding with the wall of the elevator. He braces his hands on either side of my head. "And what kinds of things are you thinking?"

"Lots of things."

He gives me that sexy crooked grin and leans until his mouth is next to my ear. "Are you thinking it might not be such a horrible thing that we only have the one bed?"

I huff a laugh. "How did you know?"

"Great minds and all that." And again, he brushes a kiss down the side of my neck and I let out a shuddery breath. "Ophelia, I—." His words are cut off by the elevator doors opening and I almost groan. "I guess this is our stop."

I don't respond and simply follow him out of the elevator. Josie and Ford's room is located only about twenty feet away, and before I know it, he's knocking on their door. She opens it a few seconds later and eyes us both with a knowing smile. Surely I don't look as though I've been kissed within an inch of my life or that I'm struggling to not pounce on Jess in the next ten seconds. She extends the rental car keys to Jess. "Oh, by the way, your brother is coming to the wedding."

He frowns. "Why?"

CHANGE MY LIFE 189

She huffs a laugh. "Well, when you told him you were in Vegas with me, he called to see if I was free for dinner because you blew him off and I didn't want to lie. So, I invited him. It's just the wedding and supper, Jess. You'll survive. And I haven't seen my second-favorite Tate brother in a long time, since he's sequestered himself in France for the last decade. He really only comes in for Christmas and then he's gone again. And you and your mom hog all his time. So forgive me if I want to take advantage of us being in the same city at the same time. Lord knows I'll probably never make it to France."

He sighs. "Fine. What all do you need us to get today?"

"I'll text you a list. We've ordered and paid for everything, they're just pick ups."

"All right. We'll be back."

When we're back on the elevator, his entire demeanor seems to have changed. "What's the deal with you and Flynn? You're not happy to see him?"

"It's complicated."

I huff a laugh. "I have no clue what complicated family relationships are like. At all," I remark sarcastically.

He laughs. "Yeah, I know." As the elevator descends, he reaches for my hand and I let him intertwine our fingers, loving the way his much larger one envelops mine. His thumb brushes mine and he sighs. "Flynn and I don't see eye to eye on a lot of things anymore. We were really close growing up. During college, we started drifting. He's actually a lot like Brooklyn. Even though he's lived in France full time, he travels some for work. He thrives on it. The thought alone of being in a new city every few weeks just makes me feel tired. He doesn't want to get married or have kids. He's content to just hook up for the rest of his life. He brags about all the women he sleeps with and to each their own, I guess, but it just seems like the older we get, I can't imagine going home with someone new every night. To not really know the person who shares my bed. That's not to say I haven't had my fair share of one-night stands, but I guess I've grown up and he's still playing the role of frat boy. Makes me feel like the only adult sometimes."

"What does your mother think of his playboy lifestyle?"

He's quiet for a moment and the elevator door opens and he leads me out toward the parking lot. After a bit, I think he's not gonna answer, but when we step out into the hot Vegas sun, he finally speaks. "My mom has always had a soft spot for Flynn. I don't think he's her favorite or anything, but he seemed to have a lot harder go of making friends and puberty hit him like a truck, so he struggled with some self-esteem issues. I guess I had it a little easier, so she never had to worry about me. She loves France. He flies her out once a year and she stays for a month. She fancies herself some sort of expat. It's cute, really. She wants grandkids, I'm sure, but she knows she's not gonna get them from him. He's never kept his life a secret, even from her."

"So, the continuation of the Tate name falls to you, huh?"

He clicks the fob to unlock the car doors and nods. "Pretty much. And it's not as if we have some big family legacy to uphold, but I don't relish Flynn and me being the last Tates in our family." He opens the passenger door for me and I climb inside.

He shuts my door and jogs around to the driver's side and slides behind the wheel. "Flynn's a lot of fun; we're just very different people. People look at us and assume because we're identical twins, we'd be a copy and paste of each other and we're not."

I blink. "Twins?"

"Yeah. I thought I'd mentioned that before."

I shake my head, even as I reel from this news. "No. You

just said y'all were brothers. And you don't have any pictures around the house, so I guess it never occurred to me."

He takes my hand in his over the console. "Well, try not to get us mixed up, because I'm the only one who gets to take you home tonight." Giving me a wink, he lifts my hand to his lips and brushes a kiss across my knuckle.

"I'll try my best."

CHAPTER TWENTY-ONE

JESS

"So, is it weird having a twin?"

I laugh. "It's all I've ever known, so not really. When we were kids, Mom and Dad sometimes couldn't tell us apart and we'd pretend to be each other. As we got older, it was easier for people to know which of us was which. Flynn had glasses and braces and acne for a few years. Now, he runs marathons, so he's a lot leaner than I am. He also wears his hair different than I do and our personalities are night and day."

"Wasn't Josie's brother a twin? Was that strange that she had twin brothers and dated a twin?"

"I don't know. I don't think so. She's never known any different since she's the youngest. And we only dated for a few months while we were in high school, so it's not like we were together for years."

As I weave in and out of the Vegas traffic trying to complete all the errands Josie's tasked us with, I try not to think about the fact that had we not been interrupted by Flynn's phone call and then Josie's, Ophelia and I might be naked and I'd be kissing every inch of her body. Fuck, that was some kiss.

Possibly the best kiss of my life; not gonna lie. And hearing her soft moan made me think about the night I stood outside her door and listened to her masturbate.

I shift in the driver's seat, needing to try to relieve the ache of my cock straining against my jeans. I've been hard since I kissed Ophelia that first time and thinking about doing it again only makes it worse. Tempted as I am to simply pull over and do it again, I resist the urge knowing we'll be in our room later and we'll hopefully get to pick up where we left off. I can't wait.

Four hours later, after flowers, a cake, and rings have been picked up and delivered to Josie and Ford, Ophelia and I are getting ready for the wedding. I've showered and shaved and am dressed once again in my one good suit. I'm only hoping wearing it this time will result in a good night and not a disastrous one.

Knowing I have to see Flynn, who will no doubt be dressed in a suit that costs more than three month's worth of my mortgage, I decide to raid the minibar. Stepping out to fill up the ice bucket, I'm not expecting to see Ophelia out of the bathroom when I return. She's leaning over the dresser and adjusting her earrings.

Between the sleek, knee-length, dusty blue satin dress she wears that seems to have been made for her, and the nude strappy stilettos making her ass look even better than it already does all the time, I'm regretting we don't have time for me to take this dress back off her right now.

She smiles when she sees my face and a slight blush colors her cheeks as she turns to face me. "I'm gonna choose to take that open-mouthed stare as approval."

I step closer and take her in more fully. The dress has a

scooped bodice with minuscule shoulder straps that would probably only take a slight tug to snap. It has some ruching at the waist that seems to exaggerate her gorgeous curves. "I think it's a good thing you haven't put on lipstick yet, because I'm about to kiss you again."

She huffs a laugh and lifts her chin in invitation. And unlike our earlier kiss, I take my time reaching up to cup her face. I run my thumb across her bottom lip and they part on an exhale. "God, you're beautiful, Ophelia." She flushes with my compliment and her pupils dilate and as I lower my mouth to hers, the only thought I have is, *I'm a lucky son of a bitch tonight.*

Ophelia slips her hands under my jacket and wraps her arms around my waist, her fingers splaying over the small of my back, pulling me closer. Conscious of our lack of time to really give a proper kiss its due, I keep the kiss light, even as I reluctantly pull back, ensuring I've not mussed her hair and makeup in my need to get a quick taste of her.

When I step back, she's still smiling and I drag the knuckle of my index finger down the side of her neck and over her shoulder before lifting my hand from her body. "You're beautiful, too." She returns her attention to the mirror and expertly applies some berry-colored lipstick and I simply watch. She drops the tube into a small clutch once she's finished and turn to me. "Ready?"

I stand up straight and offer her my arm. "Shall we?"

As we meet Josie and Ford in the lobby, Ophelia and Josie gush over each other's dresses and Ford and I just look at them with goofy grins on our faces. He nudges me as he sips a bottle of water and adjusts the tie of his simple, but expertly tailored, black suit. "So, things are going well? You no longer want to string me up by my toes for only getting the one bed?"

I shake my head. "I guess not. You and Jos clean up good, man."

He looks over at his soon-to-be wife. "She's always gorgeous. But that dress she's got on definitely doesn't hurt."

Josie's and my past physical relationship notwithstanding, I can appreciate how beautiful she looks. Of course, it could have a lot more to do with how happy she is. She's always been beautiful, even when we were kids, and as she's grown into a self-assured, take-no-shit ball-buster who only Ford seems to have been able to tame, she's radiant in a strapless, cream-colored, silk and lace sheath dress. "Thanks for making her so happy, Ford," I say, my tone serious.

He gives me a genuine smile and nods. "I'm just glad she finally let me."

"I'm sure."

A familiar voice behind me and Josie's subsequent squeal draws my attention away from the groom. Flynn and Josie embrace in a warm hug and Ford blinks. "I didn't know he was your *twin* brother."

I sigh. "Yep." Stepping up next to Ophelia, I see her examining Flynn with curiosity. I drape my arm around her waist and pull her closer and whisper in her ear. "Like I said, don't go getting us mixed up, Birdie. You're all mine."

She blushes and shakes her head. "No worries. I know what I've got," she says, her tone sweet, as she runs her fingers down my tie. My chest fills with warmth and I drop a kiss onto her bare shoulder.

After Josie introduces Flynn to Ford and pleasantries are exchanged, he finally turns toward me with a smile and extended hand. "Baby brother, good to see you."

I roll my eyes and take his hand for a shake. "Just because you're three minutes older doesn't make me the baby."

"Sure it does," he quips with a cocky grin before turning his gaze on Ophelia, his eyes dragging down her body in blatant appreciation, making me want to grind my molars. "Wow, bro, nice upgrade. Brooklyn said you two split. I can see why."

Ophelia stands up straighter and holds her head high, her eyes narrowing. She opens her mouth, but I'm speaking before she can. "If you think Ophelia had anything to do with our breakup, Brooklyn didn't tell you the whole story. Not that it's any of your business, but if you want to know, I'll tell you. Not right now, though. I don't want to ruin Josie's day with shit that doesn't matter anymore."

Flynn holds his hands up defensively. "Chill, bro. I was just saying you've got good taste. Damn." He returns his stare to Ophelia and extends his hand to her. "Ophelia, is it? Lovely to meet you. I meant no offense with what I said a moment ago, although I can see by Jess's reaction, I did offend. If that is the case, I apologize. You look beautiful and I'm sure my brother is a very lucky man, regardless of the circumstances of how you two kids ended up together."

Ophelia, to her credit, doesn't knee my brother in the balls for his syrupy tone or his lascivious stare. She simply shakes his hand and offers him a tight nod. "You're brother is a good man and I'm lucky to call him one of my best friends."

Again, her words make warmth flood my chest and I can't help but smile. "Aww, Birdie, you're gonna make me blush."

She lifts a brow. "Wouldn't be the first time today."

Apparently witnessing this entire exchange, Josie snorts a laugh behind Flynn and heat creeps up my neck. "Guess she really has come out of her shell," Ford says with an impressed chuckle. He checks his watch and gives Josie a winning smile. "It's time, Freckles. Last chance to jump ship."

Josie stares lovingly up into Ford's eyes. "Not a chance, Viking. You're stuck with me forever."

I spare a glance at Ophelia, who is looking on with nothing but happiness for our friends and I couldn't be more pleased to get to share this moment with them.

As weddings go, it was a beautiful affair; even as seemingly thrown together as it was. Apparently money talks, because I couldn't tell this thing hadn't been in the works for months. And by the time we get back to the hotel and up to Josie and Ford's suite, a huge spread of food has been laid out, along with the cake Ophelia and I picked up earlier in the day.

Soft music streams through the suite and Ford and Josie dance, oblivious to the presence of anyone else. I sip a beer and look out the window while Ophelia excuses herself to use the bathroom. Flynn steps up beside me with a tumbler of gin and doesn't look at me. He opens his mouth but I honestly don't want to hear what he has to say, so I ask, "You remember the last time we were here together?"

"Yes," he says flatly.

"Good weekend, right? Dad had a good time. One of his last good times, if memory serves. I think he especially loved seeing Brighten when we came in for dinner that first night. He always had such a soft spot for her. What's she up to these days? Are y'all still close?" I try to remember the last thing I heard about her. "Is she still married to that guy? That was, what, ten, twelve years ago?"

The grip on his glass tightens at the mention of his child-hood best friend, and his spine straightens. "So, what happened between you and Brooklyn? From what she said, she's been trying to get you to call her for days."

I sigh and side-eye my brother for his abrupt change in subject. I really shouldn't be surprised, though. Talking about Dad is still hard; even after over a decade since he died. So I just roll with it. "What's it matter? We're not together anymore. We're not getting back together."

"Because of the roommate? Which, I gotta say, Jess, good job. Pique the interest of one while you flame out with the other? Maybe we really are brothers."

I feel my jaw clench and I grip my beer bottle tighter. "You and I are nothing alike, and you know it. And what did you do, talk to Brooklyn today? Otherwise, you wouldn't have even known Ophelia was my roommate since I just posted that picture this morning. And nothing happened between Ophelia and me while I was still with Brooklyn. Not that I owe you any sort of explanation."

"So you haven't been playing house with that hot piece of ass for months and you never once stepped a toe out of line while you were with Brooklyn?"

"Just because you would, doesn't mean I'd do the same thing. Again, I'll ask, what's it matter?"

He shrugs and sips his drink. "Brooklyn seems really upset that you're flaunting this new relationship so quickly after you two split. She and I are friendly. We talk."

"I'm not flaunting anything. Again, not that it's any of your business since you've not given a shit about my life since you moved to France, but I tried to make it work with Brooklyn. I was willing to move to be with her and she bought a fucking house without telling me. She kept saying she needed travel and adventure and wasn't ever gonna be ready to settle down. At least, until they threw a shit ton of money at her, and then she grew roots faster than you can blink. She lied to me for months. She came to visit me and pretended to be jetting off to parts unknown every week when she was really in Asheville continuing to lie to me. So spare me the speech about how tore up she is when she's not sorry she did it; she's only sorry she got caught."

Flynn nods thoughtfully and looks out the window. "You've got to admit, having Ophelia on the back burner can't hurt, right? Door number two, ready and waiting for you."

"Fuck you, Flynn. Just because you like to use people and don't want to wake up with the same woman more than once doesn't mean that some of us don't wanna settle down. And Ophelia isn't a consolation prize or some afterthought. She's amazing and strong and has overcome more in the last ten years than a lot of people face their whole lives. And I want to build something with her. And I'll be damned if I'm given a lecture by someone who probably hasn't ever loved anyone to begin with."

He rolls his eyes. "Whatever, I didn't need the whole fairy-tale. I just wanted to know why Brooklyn was so upset. Jesus. And for the record, I have been in love before, so fuck you very much."

Caught off guard by his statement, I don't see Josie approach. It's not until she inserts herself between us, a mischievous gleam in her eyes, that I snap out of the trance my brother's words put me in. When the fuck did he ever fall in love?

"If y'all are done gossiping like a couple of biddies at the salon, you're welcome to join us at the table. It's time to eat. And drink. And thank God, because I need one. I'm a married woman, fellas. Come celebrate with me."

I can't help but smile at one of my best friends and let her tug me away from the window. Flynn seems to be of the same mind, an almost identical smile pasted on his own face. "Fine, let's go, Campbell. The least I can do is drink all this booze your new husband is buying," my brother quips.

"Such a gracious answer," she says with a roll of her brown eyes.

CHAPTER TWENTY-TWO

OPHELIA

My mind is pulled in so many directions while we eat. What if it wasn't Jess in the park all those years ago? If it wasn't, does that mean the attraction I have for him isn't real? I quickly dismiss the last thought because yes, I am very much attracted to Jess. And judging by the lack of anything except annoyance I feel toward his brother, it wouldn't matter who I saw in the park back then. And either way, whoever's dick I saw when I was fifteen planted a seed in my mind that over the years has made me who I am now. For that, I can only be thankful.

For this to be the nicest place I've ever visited, I'm pleased to see the food is all totally recognizable. Cornish game hens and roasted sweet potatoes, lobster macaroni and cheese, along with salad and a glass of white wine to round out the meal. Following supper is a delicious red velvet cake.

Jess and Flynn tell stories of their childhood and Ford and I laugh at their recounting of Flynn coming to pick Jess up as he was attempting to sneak out of Josie's room when they were in high school. It should feel strange to hear about their past, but it's actually a great story.

After someone comes to take away the dishes and we're left with an empty table, Josie hops up and returns a moment later with a pitcher. Flynn's eyes go wide. "Josie, please tell me that is what I think it is."

She grins at Jess's brother. "If you think it's Pap's apple pie moonshine, you'd be correct."

"How did you even get that here?"

"I checked my bag. I had it packed into soda bottles. I just poured it up once we got here. I'm thinking it's time for a little Never Have I Ever."

Jess and Flynn groan. "Jos, you already know everything we've done," Jess says with a wince.

"That is true, but Ford and Ophelia don't. And we don't know everything they've done, either."

"Freckles, I'm pretty sure you do know everything I've done."

She shrugs. "This is what I want. It's my party. Pass over your cups."

"What's Never Have I Ever?" I ask.

Flynn blinks. "You grow up under rock? They didn't play it where you went to college?"

"Flynn, don't be a prick," Josie scolds and turns her attention to me as she returns everyone's glasses filled about halfway. "It's a drinking game. You go around and everyone takes turns saying something they haven't done. If you've done it, you have to drink. It can get really dirty and you learn a lot about your friends." She winks at Ford. "Or new spouses. I'll go first." She thinks for a beat. "Never have I ever had married sex."

"Lame," Flynn calls.

Ford takes a sip and levels Josie with a gaze. "After tonight you can't say that, wife."

She grins wickedly. "I know."

"Excuse me while I gag," Jess retorts with a laugh.

Ford clears his throat. "Never have I ever done drugs." After a beat he amends, "Not even pot."

Everyone but Ford drinks, including me. Ford and Josie both eye me with surprise and I shrug. "I've smoked pot, so I get to drink, right? Or did I misunderstand?"

Jess snorts a laugh and leans over to me. "I think they're just shocked, Birdie. They know how sheltered you were."

I nod knowingly. "Gotcha."

Jess perks up with a wicked grin and looks between Josie and Ford. "Never have I ever had sex in a bar."

Josie and Ford share a glance and drink and so does Flynn. Jess and I are the only ones who abstain. It's apparently my turn and I rack my brain thinking of stuff I've never done. It's a lot to choose from and I decide to keep my answer innocuous. "Never have I ever stayed in a hotel before."

They all blink at me in shock. I glare at Flynn. "I grew up under a rock." To his credit, he laughs and gives me a nod as everyone drinks.

Flynn sits up straighter and looks at me, seeming to challenge me in particular. "Never have I ever slept with Jess."

Ford scoffs. "Well, I'd hope not, that'd be sick."

The only one who drinks is Josie and I don't drop my gaze from Flynn's. I'm not sure what his problem is with me, but I don't like the way he's looking at me. Like I'm some sort of bad guy in this situation. He must be team Brooklyn or something. Jess's voice cuts through whatever this stare down is between Flynn and me. "So, since I regularly sleep with myself, do I get to drink?"

Josie tosses a balled up napkin at him and laughs and I can't help but join in. She holds her glass up. "Never have I ever had sex in public."

Ford holds his hand up, seeking clarification. "What constitutes sex in this situation? Is it only full-blown intercourse, or do oral and handies count, too?"

Flynn nods. "Yeah, I need to know, too."

Josie sighs. "Anything past heavy petting over the clothes. If your bare junk or someone else's has ever touched any other bare part of your body or theirs and it resulted in a happy ending, then that is sex."

"And what is considered public?" Jess asks.

She thinks for a beat. "Jesus, I didn't think this would be that complicated. Not a bar bathroom since you can usually lock the door. Anywhere someone could've readily witnessed you getting it on to whatever degree you got it on."

Ford, Flynn, and Jess all drink and I'm not sure if I should be relieved or alarmed that Jess could still be Park Blowjob Guy, but I remind myself again it doesn't matter.

As the game continues, I'm not afforded very many opportunities to drink, as I truly haven't done a lot of things in my life. My cup still has plenty of moonshine, while everyone else has had to refill theirs. Ford clears his throat. "Last round, because I'm not getting any drunker since I plan on throwing Josie over my shoulder in about thirty seconds. Everyone come up with one last 'never' and let's call it a night. After, you ain't gotta go home, but you can't stay here. Never have I ever made a sex tape."

Flynn and Josie both drink and Josie shrugs when Ford's eyes widen as he looks at his wife. "What? It was college and I had the only copy. It has long since been destroyed."

Jess raises his cup. "Never have I ever had a threesome."

Flynn drinks and we all stare at him. He shrugs. "I live in France."

I blink at his explanation and try to come up with my own

"never". I toss out the first thing that comes to mind. "Never have I ever had sex in a car."

Everyone but Ford and I drink and Josie raises her brows at her new husband. He laughs. "What, I'm six-foot-six. I've been six-foot-six since the tenth grade. You try finding anything other than a minivan with the seats removed where I could comfortably get it on."

Jess snorts. "Oh, come on. Half the fun is figuring out how to make it work. That, and not getting caught."

Flynn and Josie laugh and Ford just shakes his head. "Not happening. I survived my entire career without scandal. I'm not about to tarnish my record by twisting myself into some sort of pretzel just to bust a nut. I've got way too nice a bed at home for that."

Flynn thinks for a long moment. "Never have I ever joined the mile high club."

Jess is the only one who drinks and I raise a brow and he shrugs. "Happens sometimes."

I huff a laugh and Josie stands. "Last one and then your asses are out. Never have I ever been out of the country." Ford and Flynn are the only ones to partake in the last "never", and she nods. "All right, bitches. I need y'all to go so I can remedy the married sex 'never'." She shoots Jess and me a wicked smile. "Don't do anything I wouldn't do, you two."

Ford is practically dragging Josie to the bedroom. "That's not a lot, Freckles."

She laughs. "I know." He finally bends and pulls her over his shoulder as she squeals. Flynn, Jess, and I are halfway to the door when she points at us and hollers, "Wrap it before you tap it, boys."

Flynn laughs and opens the door for us. "God, I forgot how much fun Josie is when she's tipsy."

The three of us walk toward the elevator, and Jess takes my hand in his with a smile. "Josie's fun all the time."

As we climb aboard the elevator, Flynn asks, "When do you guys go home?"

"We have a flight in the morning. You?"

"Monday."

The elevator dings as it stops on our floor and Jess drops my hand to extend it toward his brother. "Have a safe trip. I'm glad you got to see me."

Flynn smiles and shakes Jess's hand. "Me, too, bro." He turns his gaze on me. "Good to meet you, Ophelia. Good to know you can hang and not let a little ribbing get to you."

I shrug. "I'm used to assholes, Flynn. Good to know you know how to not be one sometimes."

He laughs and looks at Jess. "I like her. She can stay."

Jess rolls his eyes. "That wasn't your decision, but whatever. See you at Christmas." We step off the elevator and I wave to Flynn as the doors close. Once we're alone, he wraps his arms around me and pulls me to him and gives me a deep kiss as he shuffles me back toward our room door. I grip his shoulders and barely have time to register the kiss before he's pulling back. "Sorry, I just couldn't go another minute without kissing you."

I grin. "You don't have to apologize for wanting to kiss me."

He continues shuffling me backward, and I let him, not caring that I can't see where we're going. All I care about is that I can look at him. "Have you really never stayed in a hotel before?"

I shake my head. "Nope. So, that means no hotel sex, either."

He blinks and blows out a breath, his cheeks turning pink. "Well, I kinda figured that."

With my heels on, we're nearly the same height and I lean

forward and kiss a trail up his jaw. "Would you like to remedy that for me?" His steps falter for a beat and I nearly fall, but he manages to keep us both upright and I can't help but laugh. I pull my face back to look into his eyes and his are dark and our steps slow. His throat bobs with a swallow and he searches my face, his chest rising and falling with his quickened breath. His arms tighten around my waist and I try to stifle the nerves threatening to bubble up as he doesn't say anything.

"Are you drunk, Birdie?"

I frown and snort. "No. Why?"

"Because I don't have sex with women who are inebriated."

"Oh," I reply, my voice breathy. "No. I'm not drunk." My back hits the wood of what I assume is the door to our room. "Are you too drunk to get it up?"

He gives me a cocky grin. "Never been that drunk before."

"So that's a no?"

He bends to brush a kiss across my bare shoulder and moves his hands to my hips. "That's a hell no, Ophelia." His words and the huffs of his breath skim my skin and my breath catches. He brings his eyes back to mine. "But there's something you need to know."

I drag my hands down his chest to grip his waist and pull him closer. Nope, he's definitely not too drunk to get it up if the bulge currently pressing into my thigh is to be believed. "And what's that?"

"If we do this, I don't want it to be for just tonight. I don't give a shit about what happening in Vegas staying here. I know there would be a lot of stuff to talk through when we get home, but I'm not interested in this being a one-night stand. I care about you, Ophelia. A lot."

I huff a laugh. "That was sufficiently cheesy." I press a soft kiss to his lips, touched by his words. "I care about you, too, Jess. And I don't want it only for tonight, either." Reaching into the inside pocket of his jacket, I pull out the room key and swipe it over the reader and push down on the handle, tugging Jess with me as I enter the room.

Bringing his hands up to cup my face, he gives me a wicked smile as we continue into the room. "Now that we've got that squared away, what shall we do with the rest of our night?"

I bite my bottom lip and drag my teeth over it until it pops free. "I can think of a few things."

"Do any of them require us to be clothed?" Giving my head a slow shake, I push his jacket off his shoulders, forcing him to drop his hands to let it fall to the floor. "Thank God," he breathes before giving me a wide grin and grabbing my face and kissing me soundly, making me smile into our kiss.

My knees hit the edge of the bed and I drop and he looks down at me, that same dark, hungry look in his eyes. Without taking his gaze from mine, he lowers himself to his knees and lifts my foot by the ankle, making quick work of the fastening on my shoes and pulls the stiletto from my foot before repeating the process with the other foot. His movements aren't hurried or frantic. He takes his time and lowers each foot gently back to the floor.

As he looks up at me from his position on his knees, need and heat sear through every fiber of my being, and I lean forward and run my fingers through his hair before settling my hands along his jaw. I simply take in the sight of him and how perfect he looks. "You like seeing me on my knees for you, Birdie?" He slides his hands up my calves before wrapping them around the outsides of my knees and yanking me closer to the edge of the bed. The movement forces my dress to hike up to nearly my hips and my thighs part, my knees coming to rest under his armpits.

"Yes," I answer honestly.

"Good." He lets his eyes trail down my face and chest, stopping at my breasts for a second longer than would be considered polite before continuing to drop his gaze lower, his nostrils flaring when he sees how high my dress has ridden up my legs. "Do you know what seeing you in this dress does for me?"

I plant my hands behind my hips and attempt to look relaxed, even though my insides are practically humming with pent-up want for this man. "Did you like what you saw?"

He inches has hands higher up the outsides of my thighs. "I immediately wanted to rip it off you."

I blush at the mental image that conjures. "Good, then it did what I wanted it to."

His hands continue their ascent and I nearly shiver when his fingers skim under the bunched up fabric of my dress. "Did you buy this dress with the intention of torturing me?"

I shake my head. "No, that was just a perk."

"What did you imagine I'd do to you while you wore this dress?"

Giving him a half-shrug, I smirk. "I think part of me hoped I wouldn't be wearing it very long after everything was said and done."

His thumbs brush over my hips and slide under the sides of my panties and my heart lurches. "Did you think about this?"

"Think about it? Yes. Really considered it might happen? Not until today."

He nods. "Me, too."

I lean forward and rest my hands on my knees. "I didn't think you liked me like that, and I didn't want to make things weird." I swallow and fight through the tightness in my chest. "Yours is the only place I've ever lived that actually felt like home, and I didn't want to mess that up if I made things awkward. I didn't want to possibly lose the best friends I've ever had if I told you how I felt and you didn't feel the same way. "

He blinks, his brows drawing down in consideration before his expression softens. "It is your home, Ophelia. For as long as you want it."

Unexpected tears burn my eyes and I blink rapidly, trying to keep them held back, but I'm unsuccessful and they roll down my face. Jess pulls his hands away from my body and for a second, I think I've totally made this weird and he's changed his mind. But then, he's sitting next to me on the bed and scooping me into his arms and depositing me on his lap. He wraps one arm around my waist and grips my jaw with the other.

"Look at me, Ophelia." His voice is soft and pleading and despite my shame from letting him see me cry at a time when all I want to do is be seen as sexy and desirable, I raise my eyes to his. He swipes my cheek with the pad of his thumb and presses a soft kiss to my lips. "Regardless of what might happen between the two of us, you're not gonna lose your friends. I know they were my friends first, but they love you. You're a lot better dancer than me and pretty soon, you'll probably outpace me in the pop culture department."

I huff a laugh and shake my head. "Not possible. You've taught me almost everything I know."

He grins and pushes a stray hair off my forehead. "There's that smile. Do you know what I've enjoyed most about living with you these past few months?" I shake my head again. "When I met you, you were this quiet little mouse who wouldn't even cook in a house where she paid rent. You seemed to be afraid of your own shadow. Watching you blossom and grow and become comfortable in your own skin and seeing you stand up to your father have been the most amazing things to witness.

"And I thought you were cute when you came to look at the house. Some might say you cutting your hair or changing the way you dress or wearing makeup has made you beautiful and I'd say they're full of shit. Your beautiful started here." He lays his hand over my heart. "Getting to know yourself and being able to have somewhere you were comfortable and able to thrive. *That* made you beautiful. Your personal growth has been astounding and I've loved seeing it."

CHAPTER TWENTY-THREE

OPHELIA

I let his words sink in and for a long moment, I'm unable to speak. Once I feel as though I can talk without blubbering, I bring my hand up to Jess's cheek. "Thank you for providing me a safe place to finally be myself; even when I didn't know who I was."

"I was so happy to do it. I'm happy to keep doing it. I can't wait to see who you become. Who *we* become." The last sentence comes out more quietly and is tinged in vulnerability and something in my heart twists.

"I can't wait either." I shift in his lap until I'm straddling him and am forced to drag my dress farther up my thighs to allow myself enough space to settle as comfortably as possible. He's hard beneath me and I can't resist rocking my hips ever so slightly, smiling when Jess lets out a soft groan. He grabs my hips to still my movements and I give him a knowing smile as I reach to loosen his tie. He swallows, his Adam's apple moving as his throat rolls. I work the silk free from his shirt and once it's loose, drop it to the floor.

Running my hands down his arms, I don't take my eyes

from his as I lift his wrist to unbutton the cuff of his shirt. I repeat the process on the other cuff and his legs shift as he toes off his shoes. Tugging the tail of his shirt free from his pants, he plants his hands behind his hips to recline and provide me more room to work.

He watches with barely concealed hunger as I take my time loosening the buttons of his shirt. When the last one is freed, he sits up straight again and allows me to push the shirt off his shoulders and down his arms. Next comes his undershirt as I run my hands up the shirt and yank it over his head.

Happy to finally have him bare chested, I trace the tattoo on the left side of his chest, loving the way his coarse hairs feel under my fingertips. "You're beautiful, Jess."

Blushing from my compliment, he takes my face in his hands and presses soft kisses to my lips. And again, his movements aren't hurried. It's as if he's content to draw this out all night. I'm not sure I'd mind.

Letting my eyes fall closed, I melt into him, loving the way his lips are both soft and yet, unyielding, as if to communicate he controls even these sedate kisses. His hands leave my face and slide down the sides of my neck and down my back, the zipper of my dress descending seconds later. Cool air plays on my skin and goosebumps scatter down my arms.

Jess kisses a trail over to my cheek and down my jaw and neck, and I inhale sharply when his tongue skates over a sensitive spot at the base of my throat. He continues kissing lower and lower until he reaches the trim of my dress. Pulling back, he brings his hands up to my shoulders and slips his index fingers under the flimsy straps of my dress. He drags them down my arms until the front of my dress falls down my chest, revealing my strapless bra.

"Stand up." I obey without a word and Jess reclines on his hands again. "Take your dress off."

I shimmy the dress down my hips and let it fall to the floor, not taking my eyes off his. "Do you like telling women what to do?"

"Only in bed."

I huff a laugh. "Well, I guess it's a good thing I don't mind."

He lifts a brow before reaching down to give his dick a squeeze through the front of his pants and need pools low in my belly to see him do it. "Is that because you like hearing you're a good girl, Ophelia?"

His words make my skin prickle and I can't hide the way my breath hitches when he says them. I swallow, my chest heaving. "Do you like good girls, Jess?"

"I liked what happened to you the other day when I said it." His eyes drag down my body slowly and I stand still and allow his appraisal. "Lose the bra." I reach behind my back and work the hook-and-eye closures loose until it falls to the floor.

I let him continue to look at me and a slow smile pulls at the corners of his mouth. "Fucking perfect." I blush and hook my thumbs in the waistband of my panties and when Jess only looks on, I shove them down my hips and let them fall to the floor.

His hand returns to his dick and squeezes again and I smile as his chest rises and falls faster with his increased respiration. "Do you like what you see, Jess?" I take a step closer to the bed and plant my knee between his spread legs and kneel on the mattress. When I run my hands up his thighs, Jess exhales loudly. "Do you like my hands on your body?" I continue letting my fingers wander higher and higher until my thumb grazes the bulge straining against the fly of his slacks. His breath hitches and satisfaction and warmth flood my middle, making me want to press my thighs together.

He still doesn't say anything as I stand again and work the buckle of his belt loose and simply watches me with hooded eyes and parted lips. I bend down and press a kiss to his stomach and relish the way his muscles twitch beneath my lips. His eyes fall closed, and he lets his head fall back and I smile. "Cat got your tongue?" I ask, my tone playful. "I thought you liked telling women what to do."

He returns his eyes to mine, one brow lifting. "Why would I need to tell you what to do when you're already doing exactly what I want? But to answer your earlier questions, I fucking love your hands on my body and there's no word in the English language to describe exactly how much I like what I see." His eyes drop to his pants. "Now finish what you started."

Wordlessly, I keep my eyes on his as I loose the button and zipper of his slacks. He lifts his hips to allow me to pull them down his legs and I take in the sight of him in only a pair of black boxer briefs. My heart slams against my ribs at the knowledge that this is actually happening. That all my fantasizing for months will no longer be just fantasies.

Dropping his pants on the floor, I watch as he takes a beat to pull off his socks and toss them as well. I let my eyes roam, starting at his toes. He has nice feet, the soles visibly soft and nails neatly trimmed. There's just something about a guy with nice feet. Don't ask me what it is. My gaze travels up his calves, shins, knees, defined and thick quads, stopping at his underwear. His legs are dusted in coarse, dark hair and I can't wait to feel it against my own smooth skin. The thought alone makes my skin tingle in anticipation.

"Do you like what you see, Ophelia?"

I give him a slow smile. "I think I asked you that when I was naked. You are not naked."

He chuckles, his abs flexing as he huffs a breath. "Touché. I suppose we should remedy that." He stands from the bed but makes no immediate move to take them off. He does, however, turn down the covers and pats the center of the bed. "Lie down for me."

I climb into the bed, but shoot him a curious glance as I lie on my side, facing him. "I thought you were getting naked."

He laughs. "I will. But once I am, I'm not getting back up from this bed until both of us are nearly comatose." He steps to the end of the bed and opens a pocket in his suitcase, pulling out a strip of condoms. "No sense in stopping the party right when it's getting good."

"You're so wise," I say with a chuckle.

He drops the condoms onto the bedside table and shoves his thumbs into the waistband of his underwear and pushes them down his hips, his cock bobbing free. My mouth nearly waters at the sight of it and heat floods my belly. He climbs into the bed and lies beside me, his body mirroring my own. Dragging his fingertips down my arm, he takes my hand in his and lifts it to his mouth, pressing a kiss to my palm. "No, I just know that once I get my hands on you, I'm not gonna want to stop for anything, so I'm just trying to be prepared."

"Good answer."

"The truth always is." He lets go of my hand and I drop it to his ribs, allowing myself the freedom to feel every inch of his skin under my fingers as I slide my hand over his back and down toward his ass. Jess tucks a stray hair behind my ear and drags a knuckle along my jaw. "Can I confess something to you?"

I nod and turn my face to kiss his palm. He scoots his body closer to mine and presses a soft kiss to my lips. "The other night, I couldn't sleep. I laid in bed for an hour and all I could think about was the group scene from the book you lent me. And then, of course, it made me think of you, because I'd been thinking about you for weeks." I blush with pleasure at the knowledge that he had been thinking of me.

He drags the tip of his index finger down my side, just barely grazing the outside of my breast, and I press my thighs together.

"But I couldn't sleep, and I got up to go have a drink in the hopes it'd make me sleepy. I didn't want to wake you up, so I tried to be extra quiet, but when I passed your door, I heard something."

His eyes come back to mine and he lifts a brow and for a terrifying moment, I'm afraid he's gonna say he heard me talking and ask me why I'd be talking about my fantasies out loud.

"You were talking, but I couldn't make it out and at first, I thought you might've had someone with you, but I knew you wouldn't have snuck someone in because that's stupid. And then, you moaned, and I thought for a second you were watching porn, but something just told me it was you."

Relief slams into me that he didn't hear what I was saying, quickly followed by satisfaction that he heard me—I do have an exhibition kink, after all. I bite my lip. "Did you stay and listen?"

He grins. "Like a big 'ol perv." Bending to drop a kiss onto my chest, I arch my back, encouraging his direction and he grips my hip, his large hand splaying over the entire width. "You sounded so fucking sexy, Ophelia. And all I could think was, how were you getting yourself off; what did you look like when you came?"

I slide my hand up his back and neck and thread my fingers through his hair. "Did it make you hard?"

"Fuck, I was dripping."

His tongue flicks over my nipple and I gasp. "What did you do? Did you touch yourself while you listened to me?"

"Yes."

Smiling, I crook my leg around his hip to pull him closer,

his dick nestling between us, and he lets out a soft groan. "Did you get off?"

"Not until after you did," he admits.

"Did you like what you heard?"

He circles my nipple with the tip of his nose and runs his hand around to my ass, giving it a possessive squeeze. "I wished I'd been with you." He glances back up at me with a grin. "I didn't need a drink to feel sleepy after that. I slept like the dead."

I laugh and lean in to press a kiss to his lips. "Can I confess something to you?" He nods. "It was you I was thinking of when I came."

Satisfaction flashes in his eyes and in the next second, I'm flat on my back, Jess's face hovering inches above mine, his torso between my knees. His hair hangs down and even when I reach up to push it off his face, it falls back to where it was. He braces his hands on either side of my head and searches my face. "Can you show me?"

I lift a brow and bite my lip, fire seeming to lick over every inch of my skin at the thought of having an actual audience. "You want to watch me get myself off?"

He gives me a slow smile. "Judging by the look on your face, you like the idea of being watched."

I nod. "I do."

He lifts a brow. "And yet, you've never had sex in public?"

I shrug. "Never had anyone willing to possibly get caught for the sake of satisfying my kink."

His nostrils flare and his chest heaves. "We might have to remedy that as well." Dragging his eyes down my torso, he shakes his head. "But not tonight. You want to be watched? Tonight, I'll be the only one who watches you."

I look over to the wingback chair by the window. "Go sit in that chair."

He grips my chin and gives me a deep kiss. For a moment, I want to say fuck it to having him watch me getting myself off in favor of letting him get me off, but I can't deny the pleasure it will give me to actually watch him watch me, so I let him go when he pulls back. He hops off the bed, not bothering to redress and moves the chair into a position that would provide him the best view. He sits, knees spread, his cock jutting proudly away from his body.

Jess braces his hands on his thighs and gives me a nod, as if to say, *you may proceed.* Normally, I close my eyes and imagine someone looking on. Tonight, I don't have to imagine it and the knowledge that someone is actually watching makes me feel so alive; I'm not sure I've ever experienced this heightened level of awareness before.

As always, I start by simply skimming my hands over my body. Down my throat and over my breasts; not even teasing really, just feeling. My nipples draw tight with the barest touch, and I watch Jess's eyes fall to my breasts as the flesh hardens with my arousal. Dragging one fingertip over my stomach and around my belly button, he shifts in his chair, the lower my hand goes, his own fingers seeming to twitch with the need to touch.

"Is this difficult for you, Jess? To look but not touch?"

He licks his lips and shakes his head. "I'll have my turn, but I want this more right now."

I pull my knee up and let my thighs fall open and trail my hand back up my leg. "Do you have a voyeurism kink?"

He huffs a laugh. "I didn't think so, but now I'm not so sure."

I let my eyes fall to his groin. "Are you going to touch yourself while I get myself off for you?"

Color rises to his cheeks. "Would you like that?"

I nod. "Yes. Because I do, in fact, have a voyeurism kink."

His throat bobs with a swallow. "Have you watched people having sex before?"

"Yes," I admit, thinking back to the night at the park all those years ago.

"And it made you horny?"

I sweep my fingers up my pussy, and when they brush my clit, I gasp. "At the time, I didn't know what it was, but yes."

His eyes darken as he watches the slow movements of my hand as I work my fingers in slow circles. "So it was before college? Before you left home?"

"Yeah," I reply, breathless. Jolts of electric sensation shoot through my body. I'm so close already, even after only a moment, and I know it's because Jess is watching.

"How old were you?"

"Fifteen."

"And how did it make you feel?"

I huff a ragged breath and Jess's hand closes around his dick, his fist pumping slowly, making my need ratchet even higher. "Confused. Dirty. Aroused. It was the night everything changed for me, I think." I whine as my pleasure builds and almost close my eyes, but I like seeing Jess too much to do that. "I began to question what I'd been told my whole life. I think— fuck," I breathe as I get closer, "I think it was what began my journey toward escape."

Jess's chest heaves. "What was the couple doing?"

"Engaging in oral sex. I'd always been told sex was simply a duty for women, something you do to satisfy your husband's needs. But the woman looked like she was very much enjoying giving head." A whimper falls from my lips."And the man looked at her with such adoration, I knew it was more than simply the sating of some primal urge. I knew there had to be more to it than that."

His fist pumps faster, as if he can sense how close I am. "So, would you say that was your first moment of desire?"

"Yes. After I got home, I locked myself in the bathroom and took a shower."

"Did you touch yourself?"

"Yes," I admit. "I had this...ache." I moan, and Jess stills his hand.

"Did you get off?"

"No."

"Why not?"

"Guilt, shame, fear; pick the negative emotion and I probably felt it."

"But you don't feel that now?"

I huff a laugh. "No. I only feel good and alive and the need to get off. You want to see?"

"Yes."

"Will you come fuck me once I do?"

"If you do a good job." He rises from the chair and I watch him walk back over to the bed, a thick pearl of precum leaking from the tip of his cock. I continue strumming my clit, even as he kneels between my thighs. "You're close, aren't you?"

"Uh-huh."

He bends to swirl his tongue over one of my hardened nipples, his eyes never leaving mine, and I gasp. "Are you gonna come for me? I want to hear you."

"Yes. Oh, fuck."

"Jesus, you're sexy." He reaches over to the nightstand and rips off a condom and, after opening it, rolls it down. "You want my cock? You want me to fill you up, Birdie?"

I huff a ragged breath. "Yeah. Shit."

He leans down, bringing his mouth close to my ear. "Come for me, Ophelia."

Hearing my name on Jess's lips, along with his command, is

enough to push me over the edge and my orgasm explodes, my body shuddering with the intensity, a raspy cry falling from my lips. My heart is still thundering in my chest when Jess hooks his arms under my thighs and yanks me down the bed. He claims my mouth in a greedy kiss and slams himself to the hilt and I scream with the sudden, fierce pleasure.

He jerks his head back, his expression concerned, to examine my face and check in and I smile. "Fuck, you feel good." Gripping his waist, I rock my hips, encouraging. "Don't stop. Please."

Relief evident in his face, he slows his movements and runs his hand up the outside of my thigh to settle on my hip, gripping firmly as he sets a pounding, but measured, rhythm. "I won't. Jesus, you feel so fucking perfect."

I pull his mouth back to mine and kiss him, needing this extra point of contact as he seems content to wreck my body with pleasure. He breaks his lips from mine and drags his mouth to my ear. "Have you thought about this? What my cock would feel like?"

"Yes. Fuck."

"Me, too. God, it's even better than I imagined."

"Yeah," I agree.

He drops his chin in concentration and I thread my fingers through his hair. "Fuck, Ophelia. You're gonna make me come." I huff a laugh and he looks up at me, his expression wicked. "But don't worry, not before you do."

I smile. "I'm not worried. I already got off once, remember?"

He shakes his head, shifting to brace the back of my thigh on his bicep and going up on his toes as his thrusts increase in power, making me gasp. "But once is not enough. I want to feel you come on my cock. You gonna do that for me?"

I grip his shoulders as he slams into me, another stronger climax building. "Fuck, Jess. Shit."

His eyes close briefly and his nostrils flare. "Jesus, I didn't know I needed to hear you say my name. Fucking hell."

I let out a long moan, and he groans through gritted teeth. "Please, Jess, I'm so close."

"I know. Fuck, you feel so good. I need you to come. Shit."

I drag his mouth to mine and kiss him deeply as I reach between us and work my clit, feeling myself let go once more with a whimper.

"Fuck, Ophelia," he gasps, his hips bucking twice more as his own release crashes into him, his body going rigid above me before he lets out a low, guttural grunt and heaves a ragged breath.

CHAPTER TWENTY-FOUR

JESS

I. Am. Wrecked. Yeah, wrecked is an apt description. I suspected it would be good—great, even. I didn't expect to feel as though my world has slid completely off its axis and I'm a totally transformed person. I've had a lot of sex I would classify as "great". This wasn't that. This was something else entirely.

Ophelia feels like a part of me that I never knew I was missing until the moment our bodies came together. Watching her face and feeling her body against mine and hearing the sounds she utters during sex are things I never knew would shatter my perception of what it means to "make love". And at this moment, that's exactly what it felt like. I am gone for her. I love Ophelia.

For a long moment after I come, I can only try to breathe as the realization washes over me. Ophelia lifts her head and presses soft kisses along my cheek and jaw, and I turn my face to capture her lips with my own for a tender kiss. She smiles into our kiss and my heart squeezes.

Even knowing I need to get up and take care of the not so glamorous part of "after", I can't bring myself to even pull out, let alone leave this bed. But when she pulls back and yawns deeply, I can't help but chuckle and take that as my cue to get ready for bed.

"Tired?"

She nods sleepily and yawns again. "Yeah. Sorry."

I shake my head and check my watch as I stand from the bed. "Don't be; it's after two AM at home. It's way past our bedtime." I head into the bathroom and dispose of the condom and pee and wash my hands before brushing my teeth.

Passing Ophelia on her way to the bathroom, I give her ass a playful slap and she laughs. "Now, where was that earlier?"

"Maybe next time."

She grins. "I'll hold you to that."

I slip on my boxer briefs and crawl under the covers and plug my phone up, annoyed when I see three more texts from Brooklyn. Clearing them off without reading, I settle under the covers. Although I'm nearly dozing when Ophelia climbs into bed next to me, I wake fully when she curls up beside me, dressed in a short nightgown.

Her face is bare and she smells of moisturizer and toothpaste and I wrap my arm around her and pull her closer and press a kiss to her forehead. "Can I ask you something?" she inquires with a yawn.

"Sure."

"Did you pack condoms because you thought we might have sex? Because I know you didn't run out and get them. Or did you and I'm just not aware?"

I shake my head. "I already had them in my bag. It's the same bag I always took to Brooklyn's. I just never took them out. Kinda glad now, if I'm honest."

She nods. "Me, too." Struck with a thought, she pushes up on her arm to look at me more fully. "Y'all were together for three years and still used condoms? Did she have issues with birth control?"

I shake my head again. "No. She had an IUD. She just always liked that extra layer of protection."

She considers my answer. "Gotcha. I have one, too, and I've always used condoms, but only because I wasn't in a committed relationship. I always thought if I was, I wouldn't."

I nod. "Me, too."

Rushing to press forward, she adds, "And I don't say that in the hopes we'll have some sort of label. I didn't mean to imply that, I was just curious."

I swallow and search her face, my expression serious. "Does that mean you don't want a label? What if I do?"

Color rises to her cheeks. "I didn't want to assume," she says quietly.

I shift on the bed until she's flat on her back and I'm between her legs. And tired as I am, I can already feeling my need for her stirring again. "I don't sleep around, Ophelia. You know that. I meant what I told you earlier; I care about you. I wouldn't have said I didn't care if other people know if I didn't want them to. So, yes, I want a fucking label." Her eyes flash with satisfaction and I give her a deep kiss before breaking my lips from hers.

"I want you in my bed every night. I want to wake up beside you and fuck you every chance I get. But make no mistake, I want this—us. I want to build a relationship with you. And if we both go get tested and you're comfortable with it, I want to ditch the condoms. Because I'll be honest, there is nothing more sexy to me than the thought of fucking you raw."

Her breath hitches with my words and she huffs a breath. "Okay," she says with a small smile. "I want that, too."

I give her a slow smile. "You want what? The label, or for me to fuck you without a condom?"

"Both."

I nod. "Good." I give Ophelia one last kiss before I roll off of her and shut off the light, confirming before I pull her into my arms that my alarm is set. As I curl my body around hers, she covers my hand with her own and in the dark, she scoots her back closer to me. I bury my nose in her hair and inhale deeply, committing the scent once again to my memory, thankful I don't have to try to avoid it any longer. "Can I confess something else to you?" I ask as I press a kiss under her ear.

"Okay."

"That morning after we fell asleep together?" She makes a sound of acknowledgment and I continue. "I kissed you under your ear. I couldn't stop myself."

She huffs a soft laugh. "Can I confess something?"

"Okay."

"I know. I was awake when you did it."

I can't help but laugh. "Even after that, you didn't think I had feelings for you?"

She shrugs. "You didn't act any different after that, so I didn't want to have a whole conversation if I didn't know for sure. I thought it might have just been, like, a friendly sort of kiss. I thought if I brought it up, after everything that had happened the day before with my dad and Jax, you might tell me what I wanted to hear out of pity. Not that I think you'd actually do that, but that's where my mind went."

I press another kiss to her neck. "I get it. But no, it wasn't a friendly kiss."

"I'm glad."

As we join Ford and Josie in their suite for breakfast, we all seem to be dragging ass. It's quiet except for the sound of silverware skittering across china and sips of coffee being drunk. Josie has on sunglasses and Ophelia is nearly falling asleep in her omelet. "Well, Jos, you can't say you haven't had married sex anymore," I say with a laugh.

She shakes her head. "Nope. And I'm guessing I can't say I'm the only one at this table who's slept with Jess."

Ophelia's cheeks turn bright pink and Ford snorts. "Aww, now I'm feeling left out." He jerks his thumb toward the direction of the bedroom. "Come on, Jess; I've got time for a quickie."

Josie laughs. "Listen, pal, if you can still get it up after last night, I still have more work to do."

Ophelia shoves the last bite of her food into her mouth and rises from the table. "I'm gonna go finish packing and take a shower."

I look up at her. "Give me a second and I'll go with you."

She eyes my plate. "I know you; you're nowhere close to being done and haven't even touched your coffee. Stay."

I dig the room key out of my pocket and extend it to her. When she takes it, I grab her hand and pull her down for a kiss. "I'll be there soon."

"Okay," she says with a smile.

I watch her go, and once the door closes behind her, Josie cackles. "Good lord, you're so gone."

I sigh. "Yep."

"Does she know?"

"I haven't told her; if that's what you're asking. I told her I wanted labels, and that I wanted to build something with her."

She nods. "Good. You look happy, Jess. And so does she."

"I hope she is."

Ford's phone rings and he steps away from the table as he

answers a call from his daughter. Josie returns her attention to me. "Brooklyn's been calling me."

I scrub my hand down my face. "Me, too. And texts. She even spilled her version of events to Flynn yesterday after she saw the Instagram post of Ophelia and me."

"What are you gonna do?"

I snort. "I'm not gonna *do* shit. I have nothing to say to her. She wanted her big, exciting life without being tied down; she has it. I'm happy. I'm in love with Ophelia."

She raises her eyebrows in surprise. "That must be some good pussy."

I laugh. "It is, but that's not why I'm in love with her. I can see being with her for the long-term. It's easy with her. And not that my time with Brooklyn wasn't exciting and shit, because it was, but I felt like I had to sacrifice every single thing I wanted to keep her. I don't have to do that with Ophelia. Watching her come into her own these past few months has been amazing to witness. She's...home," I admit.

Josie's smile softens. "I'm happy for you, Jess." Her expression morphs into one decidedly more mischievous. "You know, there's time to swing by one of those drive-thru wedding chapels on the way to the airport."

We do not, in fact, get married via drive-thru chapel. We fall asleep almost the instant we take off from Vegas and jar awake when we land in Atlanta for our layover four hours later. Ophelia is yawning sleepily as we make our way to the gate for the last leg of our trip. I pull her into my side and press a kiss to her temple. "When we get settled, I'll get you some coffee."

"Bless you," she says with another yawn. "That would be

—." She freezes, her words and steps halting mid-sentence when we're nearly to the terminal.

I almost stumble and give her a puzzled look. "What's wrong?" I follow her gaze and a woman, nearly identical to Ophelia, except blonder and a bit taller, stands at the counter at our assigned gate. "You know her?"

She swallows and nods. "It's Rosalind."

I smile. "That's a good thing, right? You haven't seen her in years. Weren't y'all close?" I glance back toward the woman and it's clear she's spotted Ophelia and her expression hardens. I turn back to her. "What happened?"

Having moved on ahead of us, Josie and Ford get settled in some chairs before noticing we've stopped. She catches my eye and her expression is concerned and she darts her gaze between Ophelia and me and I shrug to tell her I'm not sure what's wrong.

Josie says something to Ford and walks back over to where we stand. "You guys okay?" She gently squeezes Ophelia's shoulder. "You alright, honey?"

Ophelia still doesn't say anything and I take her face in my hands, forcing her to look at me. "Birdie, what is it?"

Tears well in her eyes and my heart squeezes for her. "She still hates me."

I pull her into my arms and she buries her face in my neck and I look over at Rosalind, who stares back with a look of blatant disdain on her face. Returning my attention to Josie, I ask, "Will you take our bags and watch them? I'm gonna take her on a walk." Josie nods, a worried look on her face, and takes my backpack and Ophelia's suitcase and walks back over to her husband.

Turning us in the direction of a nearby coffee shop, I put my arm around her shoulder and begin to walk. She sniffles and wipes her eyes and when we reach the cafe, I deposit her at a table and place our order.

She's composed herself by the time I get back to the table and sips the cup I hand her. "You want to talk about it?" I ask as I drop into my chair. "You don't have to, you know that, but obviously, whatever it is still bothers you all these years later."

Nodding, she looks down into her cup. "When I moved in with Rosalind, she had a boyfriend. They broke up about two years after I started school. She was single for a long time after that because she was really torn up about the breakup. We became a lot closer, almost like sisters.

"My senior year, I started seeing this guy. It was after my first boyfriend had moved away after graduation. Oz was this guy from my psychology class and we hit it off. We hung out and studied together and started hooking up. It was totally casual, no strings or anything, just after we'd study together. I liked him. We had fun.

"Around the same time, Rosalind started seeing this guy she worked with named Wally. And because I had a job at night working at a diner, I never saw them together. Either, she'd stay at his place or I'd be up and gone to class before they ever got up when he stayed at ours."

I nod, getting the feeling I know where this story is headed as she continues. "Oz and I hooked up pretty much the entire semester. I mean, I hooked up with other guys, too, but Oz and I were pretty steady. I didn't want a relationship, and neither did he. It was just fun.

"Rosalind fell hard for Wally. They started talking about moving in together and I was happy for her. She'd heard me talk about Oz, of course, because we were so close, but she'd never met him and I hadn't met Wally because my schedule and hers never lined up to where we could get together."

She sighs. "Spoiler alert: Oz and Wally were one in the same, in case you haven't figured it out yet."

I nod. "I assumed. So, how did he get found out?"

"I was sick with a stomach bug and didn't go to work one night. I'd gone to class and Oz and I had studied and I even felt well enough to have sex, but as I was getting ready to go to work, I started throwing up. Rosalind was getting ready to go meet Wally's parents for the first time and there was a knock on the door and because I was on the couch, I got up to answer it since Rosalind was still getting dressed. When I opened the door, it was Oz. I was surprised since I'd never brought him home because we lived off campus and it was way out of the way.

"He looked just as surprised to see me when he stepped inside. She called from the bedroom and asked if it was Wally and I said that it was Oz and she got all excited. I guess she thought if he was there, it meant that I was getting serious with a guy and she was all for that. He looked panicked when he heard the name Wally and I still didn't put things together until she came running out and saw Oz.

"She said, 'I thought you said Oz was here.' I pointed to Oz and said, 'He is'. She looked at me like I was crazy and said, 'This is Wally'." She looks down at her coffee cup. "The rest was kind of a blur. She assumed I knew, and that I was a home wrecker, even though he'd given us both different names and never told me he had a girlfriend. She blamed me and called me a whore and gave me five minutes to pack my shit and get out. It only took me three since I'd been living out of a suitcase the entire time I lived with her. My name wasn't on the lease, so I couldn't fight the eviction and Oz, Wally—Oswald, actually—just acted like he was the injured party. I lived in my car for a couple of weeks and showered in the school fitness center before a guy I worked with let me crash with him and his boyfriend until graduation."

Tears well in her eyes again, and I take her hand across the table. "I kept trying to talk to Rosalind and explain things; even going so far as to show up at her work. She slapped me across the face and told me I was dead to her. I lost the only person in my life and after that, I was in a pretty bad place. I went through the motions and did my student teaching and graduated and moved back home.

"I'd realized before I'd even graduated that I didn't want to be a teacher anymore and after I came back to Knoxville—because where else was I gonna go—I tried to visit my family. And we know what happened there."

"I'm so sorry, Ophelia. You know none of that was your fault, right?"

She nods slowly. "I know. I never would've willingly hurt Rosalind. But after that, 'do you have a girlfriend or wife or significant other' became my first question when someone flirted with me. I never want to be complicit in someone's heartbreak ever again."

"That wasn't on you. That was on him. And the fact that she didn't stand beside you proves you were the better person in that situation. You're a good person, Birdie; you didn't do anything wrong."

She nods. "It still doesn't take away the guilt. I hurt Rosalind; even inadvertently."

I drain my coffee and give her hand a squeeze. "Again, that makes you the better person in this situation. You can't make someone listen who doesn't want to hear what you have to say." Checking my watch, I give her an apologetic smile.

"I know, we have to go."

"We do, but I'll be right there beside you."

We stand and I wrap my arm around her as we walk back toward the terminal.

CHAPTER TWENTY-FIVE

OPHELIA

When we make it home, I'm still reflecting on the way Rosalind looked at me as though I was shit on her shoe. She barely glanced at me as she checked my boarding pass and had it not been for Jess holding my hand and tugging me along, I probably would've fallen apart.

As we walk through the laundry room and into the kitchen and Garth catches sight of us from his place on the couch, he bounds off the sofa like a dog half his age and jogs over to us, barking with excitement. I bend to greet him and he wags his entire body, instantly putting me in a better mood.

"So, how was the wedding?" Hensley asks, joining us in the kitchen.

"Great," Jess says. "Flynn showed up."

She rolls her eyes. "How is our favorite asshole?"

I snort a laugh and he shakes his head. "Still an asshole."

"Figures." She narrows her eyes and looks from Jess to me. "Oh my God, you guys fucked." My cheeks flame and my mouth falls open, and she grins wickedly. "And it was good," she says with an approving nod.

"Okay, Hens. I think that's your cue to go. I love you and we appreciate you watching Garth, but you've officially worn out your welcome." Jess nudges her toward the door.

"Wait, so does that mean you did? Are y'all together? I need details. I'm a dry well, dude."

"Yes, we're together. No, you don't get details."

She huffs and picks up her bag. "Fine. For the record, I'm happy for you both. If y'all decide to elope, I want to go to Vegas this time."

"Goodbye, Hensley." He shuts the front door and drags his hand down his face and I can't help but laugh. "You've gotta love her," he says with a sigh.

"I do. She's great. Sad, but great."

He frowns. "You think she looks sad?"

I nod. "Takes one to know one. She tries to hide it, but she's sad. Soul sad."

"She'll get there," he replies, his tone confident. Garth, tiring of my affection, trots back over to the sofa and climbs up to his normal spot. I rise and sigh, happy to be back home. "I'm gonna go unpack."

"Okay. Are you hungry? I can throw something together for supper."

"Alright." As I pass him, pulling my bag behind me, I press a kiss to his cheek. "I'll be back soon." When I walk into my room, it only takes me ten minutes to unpack and put away my suitcase. Music streams from the kitchen and I smile. It's joyous and upbeat and I hope it's a reflection of how Jess feels, because it certainly matches the way I'm feeling.

I can't recall a time in my life when I've been happier than I am now. Knowing Jess wants not only my body, but also a future with me, I'm nearly giddy.

Walking back toward the kitchen, I stop when I see Jess chopping what looks like garlic on a cutting board. When the music begins to build in intensity, I simply lean against the wall just out of his peripheral vision and watch as lifts the knife from the board and conducts an imaginary orchestra for a moment before continuing his task. The music changes to what I recognize as "No Diggity" and he moves his body with the rhythm of the music, and sings along.

I don't take my eyes off of him. I no longer have to. I don't have to disguise my desire for him or even keep my hands off of him. He's all mine. The knowledge spreads a pleasant warmth through my middle, only for it to settle somewhere below my navel.

Walking up behind him, I wrap my arms around his waist and give him a hug, my cheek resting perfectly between his shoulder blades. He pats my clasped hands with one of his. "Did you enjoy the show?"

I snort a laugh. "Very much. How long did you know I was there?"

"About the time I started conducting."

"You make it look really sexy. And you say you can't dance, but it looked like you were getting it pretty good."

He lays the knife on the counter and turns in my arms, his own wrapping around my shoulders as he looks down at me. "I like you a lot, you know that?" he asks with a sweet smile.

"You're alright," I say with a shrug.

A bark of laughter falls from his mouth, and his fingers dig into my ribs as he tickles me. I immediately convulse and giggle. "Alright? *Alright?*"

I try to get out of his grasp, but he's has me in an iron grip and I'm at his mercy as I squeal and wriggle. "Okay. Okay," I plead, nearly breathless.

He stops tickling me and instead pulls me tight against him and drops a kiss onto the top of my head. "Now, what do you say?"

I take the opportunity to bring my hands up and return the tickling favor. His arms instinctively drop and I run away. "I say you're too slow," I reply with a laugh. He gives chase and for a brief moment, we're running around the kitchen island and living room like a couple of kids and laughing. He eventually corners me in the living room and I hold my hands up in surrender, my breathing heavy. "Okay, I surrender. You win."

Walking toward me, he reaches up to grip my face with a triumphant grin. "You just remember that." His smile turns wicked as he examines my features. "However will I celebrate my win?"

"Oh, no," I say dramatically and clutch my chest, my voice coming out in a terrible monotone. "I hope you will not steal me away and ravage me. For I am but an innocent."

He snorts a laugh. "That is a terrible acting job. Remind me to never let you do any community theater."

"Rude," I reply with a chuckle and lift one brow. "Fine, how about this," I wrap my arms around his waist and begin tugging him toward my room, "you come and take your win out in pussy?"

He grins. "Now that, I can do." He claims my mouth in a punishing kiss and turns us into my room and slams the door with his foot. I yank up the hem of his shirt, needing it off of him. He hurriedly sheds it, followed by his socks, and I shuck the thin cardigan I have on over a camisole, letting it fall to the floor.

Our lips crashing together again, I make quick work of his belt and the button and fly of his jeans and dip my fingers inside his underwear and give his dick a long stroke, loving the feel of him in my hand. He lets out a soft groan, his mouth trailing down my jaw and neck. He nips at my shoulder, shoving the strap of my tank top and bra down my arm until my breast pops free. He cups my breast, his thumb sliding over the nipple and I huff a breath into our kiss as my heart begins to pound.

My knees hit the mattress, and I sit, my grip on his dick loosening. We both scramble to finish shedding our clothes and I reach into my nightstand and pull out a condom, dropping it on top before Jess joins me on the bed. I lie back and he cages me in with his hand and knees and I simply look at him, the man who has become my best friend and now, so much more.

"Getting a little ahead of yourself there, aren't you?"

I chuckle and drag a fingertip down his chest. "What, are you saying you won't need one?"

"Let's see how you feel after I'm done *celebrating*." He gives me a wicked grin as he drops a kiss on my lips. I attempt to deepen it, and he pulls back and slowly shakes his head. He trails kisses down my cheek and jaw and I tilt my head, allowing him access to my neck and I gasp as his teeth scrape over a sensitive spot near my shoulder.

He trails his mouth lower, employing his lips and teeth and tongue to make my body hum with awareness. Jess flicks his tongue over one of my nipples and I bury my fingers in his hair. "Shit," I breathe, my back arching. He grins against my breast, his hand coming to tease my other nipple, rolling it between his fingers. "Oh, God, Jess."

He groans against my skin, his cock jerking against my inner thigh, and my need grows more and more insistent. His mouth pulls off my nipple with an audible *pop* before he blows cool air over the sensitive flesh. I can't bite back a low moan as I press my thighs together, needing friction more than anything in this moment.

"Is that pussy needy, Birdie? You want me to make it all better?"

"Fuck, Jess."

His mouth moves lower and lower over my stomach. "Is

that what you want?" He nips at the skin just below my belly button, and I shiver as his tongue skates over the same spot, soothing the sting of his bite. "God, I can smell your sweetness. I'm gonna bury my face in your pussy." He presses soft kisses into the top of my thigh. "You gonna let me get my fill of you?"

I'm nearly trembling with need and can barely think straight. I'm not sure I've ever been this turned on in my whole life. "Yes. Please, Jess."

Jess plants his palms on my inner thighs. "Open up for me, Ophelia. Let me see what's mine." *His.* God, yes, I'm his. Maybe for forever. I immediately comply with his words and drop my knees wide, allowing him access to every part of me.

"Jesus, that's pretty." He drags his nose up my center and groans. "Fuck, you smell good." Licking a slow line up my folds, he groans again, this time louder, making me gasp as the vibrations travel through me. "Christ, you taste even better." He hooks his arms around my thighs and holds me in place as he explores with his mouth.

I'm utterly at his mercy, only able to sink my fingers into his hair and give in to the pleasure as his lips and teeth and tongue conduct a symphony to rival that of any composer. My breaths —what even is breathing at this point—come in short, raspy pants, and I nearly scream when Jess sucks my clit into his mouth.

"Oh, fuck. Jess, I'm so close. Please." Still holding my legs in place, I'm forced to simply hang on as sensation after sensation begins to wash over me. "Jesus. Oh, shit. I'm coming. Fuck. Fuck. *Fuuuuuuuccccckkkk.*" My words come out like a plea or a prayer or some sort of chant of worship, followed by a choked sob as I come hard enough to see stars.

I am spent and lie limp on the bed as Jess kisses his way back up my body. I grab his face and look him in the eye. "Holy shit. Who are you?"

He chuckles, a smug smile pulling at the corners of his lips, and lowers his mouth to mine. After a brief kiss, he pulls back. "You just remember this when you're reminded that I can't dance."

I huff a laugh. "Who the fuck needs dancing when you can do *that?*"

He nods. "I'm glad you can see I have some valuable assets."

I reach down to wrap my fingers around his cock and squeeze the tip, making him groan. "Don't go selling yourself short. You've got a lot of *assets.*"

Huffing a breath, he pulls my hand away from his body. "You're gonna have to quit that." Settling back onto his knees, he reaches over to pluck the condom off the nightstand. He takes a moment to tear the wrapper and roll it down, his eyes hungrily scanning my body as he gives me a wicked grin. "Get on your hands and knees for me."

I scramble to obey and after I'm in place, one of Jess's hand skims up my spine while the other grips my hip. His fingers drag down my back as my heart rate tics up. "God, you're gorgeous, Birdie. Look at this ass." The sharp sting of his hand on my ass cheek makes me gasp as warmth spreads through the area as rubs his palm over the spot he's just struck.

I shift my ass from side to side, rubbing against his dick, and he delivers another smack to the other cheek. "Fuck," I breathe, my eyes falling closed.

"Do you like that? If I touch your pussy, will it be even wetter?"

"Only one way to find out," I quip.

Instead, he delivers strike after strike and I grunt. "Fuck, that looks pretty; my handprints all over you. Jesus. And you took it so well. You're so good for me." I whimper with his words and he chuckles. "Looks like I can add praise kink to the list."

He drags the tip of his cock up and down my pussy and I moan, my head falling forward. "So fucking drenched for me. Fuck. You want my cock, Ophelia?"

It's still such a shock to my senses to hear my name on his lips in this context, and my heart lurches. "Yes."

"Ask me for it."

Too far gone with need, I don't hesitate. "Please, Jess. Please fuck me."

He huffs a breath through gritted teeth. All the while, he still teases me with the blunt head of his dick. "You want me?"

"More than anything," I admit. He slams inside me and I cry out. "Oh, Fuck."

"Jesus, Birdie." He drops a kiss onto my shoulder blade and reaches around to grip my breast as he pistons his hips and I let out a long moan. "So fucking good."

"Jess. Oh, God. Baby, shit. So good," I whine.

He lowers his mouth next to my ear. "You take my cock so fucking well. You're gonna make me come," he groans. "Fuck."

Jess raises up and grips my hips, his fingers digging in as he continues to pound into me, before he slides one hand over the curve of my ass, the flesh still stinging and sending jolts of heat down my legs, and making me gasp. He slides his thumb down the cleft of my ass, brushing against my back entrance, and I inhale sharply. As he adds just a bit of pressure, my climax explodes within me and I scream his name, my legs shaking, and my breaths coming in ragged sighs. "Fuck, yes. Jesus Christ, Ophelia. Shit, I'm coming, baby." He lets out a low grunt as his hips buck one last time.

I nearly collapse onto the mattress, but Jess holds me tight and lowers me gently to the bed. As he pulls out, my body mourns the loss and I whimper. Brushing a kiss below my ear, he rises from the bed. "Be right back."

For several boneless moments, I don't move. Not until Garth comes to lick my hand as it hangs over the edge of the bed. I sit up, my body heavy from what might be the best sex of my life, and rise from the bed, slipping on Jess's tee shirt, not bothering to pull on my underwear, and walk across the hall to pee.

When I walk into the kitchen a moment later, Jess is standing at the kitchen counter, his back to me. I step up behind him and wrap my arms around his waist and he startles. "You okay?"

He clears his throat. "Oh, yeah. Fine." He shoves his phone in his pocket and resumes chopping garlic. "I'm thinking meatloaf for supper. How's that sound?"

"Sure. Need any help?"

"No, I'm good."

He seems off and I'm not sure what to make of it. "Are you okay? Did I do something...wrong?" Realistically, I know I didn't, but his whole body language has shifted and I'm not sure what to think.

He turns to me and his brows are drawn down. He takes my face in his hands and presses a kiss to my lips, and I immediately relax. "No, why would you think that?"

I shrug and answer honestly. "We just had really, *really* good sex and now you seem tense. I would think you'd be more relaxed, is all. So I thought I'd maybe done something."

His expression softens. "No, you were perfect, Ophelia." He swallows. "Brooklyn keeps texting me and it's just got me annoyed. Not something I wanted to see after what we just did." He smiles. "Which, yes, was excellent."

I breathe a sigh of relief. "Okay. I just wanted to make sure."

CHAPTER TWENTY-SIX

JESS

> Brooklyn: I told you something about her was familiar. Google Ivy Sinn. She's a fucking porn star, Jess.

I've been sitting on it for weeks. For a lot of reasons, really. Part of me says it could just be Brooklyn being a spiteful and vengeful person; that she simply wants to drive a wedge between Ophelia and me. Another part of me doesn't want to know. Because who am I to judge the things she did before she met me? And if it is true, I sure as hell don't want to watch her fucking other guys.

Besides, things between Ophelia and me are good. We are solid. I'm so in love with her it's unreal. Although technically, we both still have our own rooms, we always sleep together; sometimes in her bed, sometimes in mine. We're essentially playing house these days and it's great. I'm starting to picture this—us—years in the future. We've fallen into this routine that I can't get enough of and I am happy.

Even so, Brooklyn's text still nags at me and I'm a naturally curious person. I don't necessarily want to bring it up to Ophe-lia, since if it's part of her past, I don't care. The past is the past, right? She doesn't need to know about all the shit I've done, either. But I can't deny it's still eating at me. And today, I give in. Prepared for whatever, I type "Ivy Sinn" into my search engine. Ophelia is still at work, so I have to time to put this to bed.

The first result that pops up is *The Confessions of Ivy Sinn*. My leg jiggles under the kitchen table and Garth stares up at me accusatorially, his muzzle sitting on the leg not currently burning a thousand calories. "What?" I ask him? "I'm not doing anything wrong. Don't I deserve to satisfy my curiosity?" He huffs a breath, and it nearly sounds indignant, but I continue to hover the cursor over the link. Taking a deep breath, I click it.

I'm no stranger to porn. I'm a man, after all. But this doesn't look like any porn site I've ever seen. For starters, there are no videos. There is simply the page banner at the top of the site with a link below it titled, "Episode 10: The Awakening"

Unsure what I'm about to find, I click the link again.

THE CONFESSIONS OF IVY SINN
EPISODE 10: THE AWAKENING

Do you mind if I tell you a story? I think you should know where I come from; my motivation. And while I tell this story, as usual, I will be naked and running my hands over my body. Because in reality, this story is a memory.

I grew up sheltered; insulated from the world and all its evils. I was allowed one activity outside of the home and I chose running. Even in a long skirt and long sleeves, I enjoyed the outlet the physical exertion provided. Now, I realize it was the endorphins I was after.

When you grow up as I did—ultra-religious and without even a television or radio for entertainment—you don't know anything about the ways of the world. And because one of the only books we were allowed to read was the Bible, I wasn't exposed to things like romance books or Cosmopolitan *magazine.*

The farm where we lived butted up against a park and one of my brothers, who was a few years younger than me, would walk with me to the park so I could run on the track. He would sit at a picnic table with a pocket knife and stick and whittle. Because that was the type of entertainment we had.

As usual, I was on my run and was rounding a bend. This bend happened to be in a more secluded portion of the park, and there was a bench. That day, I came to understand why the bench was usually occupied.

You see, normally, when I ran, it was earlier in the day. But on this day, it was closer to dusk because chores had taken longer. And in the waning light of early evening, the bench only illuminated by an amber street light, I had my sexual awakening.

Even now, thinking about it makes my pussy wet. The way the couple looked together, it shattered everything I'd been taught about sex. My mother had "the talk" with me when I started my period and informed me that I was now a woman. And with the aid of an ancient science textbook, she explained reproduction.

A lot of things I knew, of course. We lived on a farm. But to hear my mother describe sex—since someday I would have a husband—it was a duty and something to be tolerated. That my sole purpose was to grow a family and to bring my husband pleasure.

And that day in the park, there was no doubt the man was experiencing pleasure. How could he not be with the sounds he was making? Although, at the time, I was confused about why a young woman would put her mouth around a man's penis, since that's not how babies are made.

But that wasn't what truly struck me that day. It was the way the woman who, by all accounts, was enjoying the act just as much as the man. The look they shared was enough to make me question everything I'd been told about "duty".

And that day, as I watched the man's head fall back in

ecstasy and the woman seemingly relish the experience, I experienced desire for the first time.

Ensconced as I was in purity culture, I didn't know that's what it was. I only knew I felt heat and a sort of tightening in my lower abdomen and when I got home and went to take a shower, my panties were wet. I also had this...ache I didn't understand.

As I climbed in the shower, my body hummed with awareness. I couldn't get the image of the couple out of my mind and my nipples hardened. I washed my body and as my hands roamed over my breasts, just like now, my breath caught.

Again, I knew breasts had a purpose since I have several younger siblings and watched my mother feed them. But the idea they could also cause these stirrings? I was floored.

Thinking of the couple made me throb with need. I didn't even know what a clit was at that time. But like any soreness or ache, I thought if I rubbed it, it would go away. So, I did. It didn't make it go away; it made it grow.

Right now, it's growing, too. This ache I need to soothe. Can I touch myself for you? Would you like to hear me do that?

That day, in my shower, when I touched myself for the first time, I was immediately bombarded with feelings of guilt and shame and as if I'd done something terribly wrong that required repentance. I didn't even let myself continue to touch myself because I was so ashamed. I had sinned. At least, that's what I thought at the time.

I know better now. I'm not here to debate religion, so don't worry about that. I know that's not what you're here for.

Now, I have no issues bringing myself pleasure and I think about the man I've dubbed "Park Blowjob Guy" even now. Especially now. I imagine myself as the woman on her knees for him as he looked at her with appreciation, adoration; dare I say love? I credit him—them—with knocking over the first domino that led me to where I am today.

Today—oh, fuck—I'm a woman who is in touch with her body and its needs. Today, I know sex is natural and good and if you think it's a "duty", you're doing it wrong or you're with the wrong person.

I'm so close—oh, Jesus—I'm telling you, Park Blowjob Guy does it for me every time. Just thinking about his cock and how he fucked that woman's mouth; I wish it had been mine. I'm not sure what it was about his dick, but it was beautiful—if there is such a thing. I'm not sure. It was the first one I ever saw in person and even fifty feet away, I could see the blunt crown and the veins down the thick shaft. It was...something, let me tell you.

Oh, God. Fuck, that's it.

Thank you listening to my confession and joining me on my journey to heal.

CHAPTER TWENTY-SEVEN

JESS

I slam the laptop shut, my heart racing. That's Ophelia's voice; her moans and curses. I've become so accustomed to those sounds over the past few weeks, I know exactly what she sounds like as she seeks her pleasure. What does this mean? Did she make these audios and upload them? Why would she do it? How long has she done this?

Needing to satisfy yet another curiosity, I open my laptop again and clicking on a link marked "All Confessions", I'm shocked to see a list of audios going back almost three years. My eyes widen when I see that the links for all but the one I listened to are available only to subscribers. *People pay for this? Ophelia makes money off of people listening to her get off?* I suppose I shouldn't be surprised. With the invention of things like OnlyFans and Patreon and other creator-driven platforms, it only makes sense, right?

I could rationalize and say it's not really porn, per se, even though it is. There're no video, but just her voice with its natural rasp is sexy as fuck and is plenty enough to get off to. Especially if she's getting herself off.

Are they all only of herself? Or did she ever record her having sex with other people? Do I even want to know? What good does it do me to know any of this? I should delete Brooklyn's text and close out my browser and be done with it. I already know I won't.

The thought of other people listening to the woman I love this way makes jealousy burn in my guts. I know Ophelia likes to be watched—she told me so herself. Maybe this is her outlet for that?

Looking closer, my stomach drops when I see the most recent date is from only a few days ago. *She's been uploading since we got together? What the hell?* And I'm not sure it's the knowledge that she's done it, but that she's *still* doing it. That she's been doing it since we got together. When does she ever have the time? We're together every night. Maybe after I leave for work? Is her sex drive so high that despite us having sex almost every single night, she still needs more?

Rationally, I know this isn't about me. But I can't help but feel somehow like this is cheating. She's bringing other people pleasure while we're in a committed relationship. We don't even wear fucking condoms anymore. I'm so confused.

For two weeks, I struggle with indecision. Part of me wants to listen to all of them. But I can't bring myself to pay to listen to what might possibly be sex with other people or worse, possibly videos. I'd be lying if I said I haven't been tempted, though. She's still uploading, too, as of yesterday, and it makes me feel even more like this is cheating somehow.

The thing is, she doesn't act any different. She's still sweet and attentive and we still watch movies and play with Garth. She goes to work; I go to work. We cook together and go to the grocery store. We're still "Jess and Ophelia". But do I even know her? I think I do, but I find myself questioning things.

I've known for as long as I've known her there was more than meets the eye. And she told me she wasn't a virgin, and I didn't expect her to be. But with her upbringing and everything she's revealed of herself, I wouldn't have imagined *this*.

Even now, as she lies beside me in bed, I have no clue how to even broach the subject with her. I have to do something, though. I'm losing sleep and I'm pretty sure I have an ulcer. I'm distracted at work and I can't stop myself from wondering, does she record us having sex and upload it? That thought makes me feel incredibly violated. It's one thing to engage in sex in a car or something. That would be with consent. I haven't consent to anything.

And that, more than anything, bothers me. It's what finally prompts me to get up and sit at the kitchen table and wait for her to get out of bed.

CHAPTER TWENTY-EIGHT

OPHELIA

The sun is hardly up, but I already smell coffee. And not that this isn't a normal occurrence, but usually not on Saturdays. If neither of us has to set an alarm, we usually wake lazily. And some of our best sex happens in the morning. I love waking up next to him and falling asleep with him. I just love...him.

Is this what contentment is? This feeling of completion and hope for things to come? Or am I dreaming, because this is exactly what I imagine when I think about my perfect relationship. I know no relationship is perfect, and I'm sure Jess and I will have our differences, but considering we lived together before we started our relationship as a couple, I think it actually has helped us to be more compatible. We already know each other's worst habits, I'd say. And none of his are any I can't live with.

He seems a bit changed since we got back from Vegas and maybe that's just how he is in a relationship? Not that either of us has ever talked just to fill the silence, but he's quieter these past several weeks. Or maybe he's got stuff on his mind he's working through; I don't know.

Hoping he'll come back to bed, I wait a few minutes before I finally rise and make the bed and pull on my jogging shorts, sports bra, and tank top, socks and sneakers. Heading across the hall to the bathroom, I note Jess's presence at the kitchen table with his laptop, his fingers tented under his chin in contemplation.

I make quick work of my morning bathroom routine and hum one of the songs from *Practical Magic*, which might be one of the best movies Jess and I have watched yet. Walking into the kitchen, Jess's eyes follow me as I pour my coffee and add creamer, but he doesn't say anything. I give him a smile. "Did you already take Garth out, or do I need to? I can do it before my jog."

"I already took him out. Can you come sit down?"

I huff a laugh. "Why do you sound so serious? Everything okay?" My eyes widen, worry setting in. "Did your stocks crash or something? Did something happen in France? Are Flynn and your mom alright? Is it Ada and the baby?"

He blinks. "No, everyone is fine. I need to talk to you."

Even as I take my seat, I can already feel anxiety creeping in. He's not smiling. He hasn't smiled since I walked into the kitchen. He's not happy. He's not happy, and he's got apartments pulled up and he's going to ask me to move out because despite what he told me in Vegas, if we break up, he's not gonna want to keep living with me.

I rack my brain for why he'd want to *talk*. Nothing good can come from this. Whatever this is, he's past the point of emotion, meaning he's given it thought. He's weighed options and has come to whatever conclusion all on his own. And yet, when I speak, my voice is calm. "Okay. What do you want to talk about?"

He swallows and looks at his laptop screen before bringing his eyes back to mine. "Let's talk about Ivy."

Thank God I wasn't mid-sip, I would've choked on my coffee. I blink. "What?"

"Ivy Sinn. I want to talk about Ivy, Ophelia."

I suppose I always knew there was a possibility that he might find out. And I suppose I could've told him. I guess now I know why he's been different. I examine his face. "You've known for a while, I take it?"

It's his turn to blink. Probably not the response he was expecting. I fold my arms. "How long have you known? The whole time I've lived here?" He opens his mouth and realization washes over me. "After Vegas, right? How? Or maybe, did us having sex trigger some memory of something you'd heard before and you put the pieces together?"

"It's not important how I found out."

I snort. "Okay. I guess that true. What do you want to know?"

"So you don't deny it's you?"

I splay my hands on the table. "You already know it is; why would I deny it? I don't lie. How long have you known?"

"A few weeks."

"Did you stumble across the audios or what?"

"No."

"So, you were already a listener before we slept together and put it together?"

He kneads his palm with the thumb of his other hand as if trying to dispel some nervous energy. "No, and that's not what I want to talk about, anyway."

"Okay, so what do you want to talk about?"

"Are there any of me on there?"

I frown. "Why would there be any of you?"

His jaw clenches. "I don't know; maybe because you're still fucking uploading shit even though we've been together for weeks. Every week. I don't give a shit about the stuff from before us. What you did before *us* is irrelevant. But if you've recorded us having sex and put it online, that's a huge violation of my privacy."

I'm shocked by the vehemence in his voice and a weight drops into my stomach. "There aren't any of us," I confirm quickly. "It's only me. All the audios are only me. I would never record someone without their permission. I'm not a predator." I can't help but ask my next question, even though I don't really want to have this conversation to begin with. "Can you tell me how you found out?"

"What's it matter how? What matters is that I found out my girlfriend is a—."

I cut him off, my eyes narrowing. "Be real careful how you finish that statement, Jess Tate."

Color rises in his cheeks. "You don't get to be indignant, Ophelia. You're a fucking porn star."

I shake my head. "No, I'm not. And even if I were, you're going to sit there and try to tell me you've never watched porn?"

He scoffs. "Of course, but that's not the issue. Stop deflecting."

I fold my arms again. "Deflecting? You're the one who won't even tell me how you found out. What, you just *happen* to be trolling the internet for erotic audios?"

He's quiet for a long moment and for a while, I think he won't say anything. Finally, he sighs. "Brooklyn sent me a text that night we got home from Vegas."

I try not to react to her name. I know they have history and he's never hidden the fact that she still calls and texts him. I just thought he'd told me everything she'd said to him. I guess not. "That was almost two months ago. You've been sitting on this that whole time?"

He opens his mouth to speak and I hold up my hand. "Let's

just skate past the fact that the source of this revelation is your ex-girlfriend. The same ex-girlfriend who is still calling and texting you and has not been quiet about the fact she's unhappy you're with me. She even tried to turn your brother against me before he even met me. But sure, we can forget *she's* the reason you know. I'm sure she's just looking out for you, right? I'm sure she has no ulterior motives."

"You don't get to act like the injured party here, Ophelia. You—not an angry ex or someone with a vendetta against you—uploaded recordings of you masturbating online. People pay you for this shit."

I level him with gaze, one brow lifted. "I don't see you complaining about taking the money I pay you."

"You have a full-time job. How the hell was I supposed to know you were selling yourself to pay rent? How could you do this to yourself? Do you not have any self-respect?"

"*Selling myself?* That's what you really think?" I can't stop the hurt in my voice. "You act like I'm standing on a street corner giving blowjobs for ten bucks a pop. And even if I were, who are you to judge me for things I did before we even got together? You stayed with Brooklyn for weeks while you were unhappy and knew things were already over. How's that any different? You broke up with her, she comes over here and gets on her back for you and all is forgiven?"

He stands and his chair falls back and he pounds his fist on the table. "That's not the same fucking thing and you know it."

I look up at him, unimpressed by his temper. "No, I guess it's not. But for you to say I have no self-respect is a little hypo-critical, don't you think? At least I didn't lie to myself for months about a relationship I knew was over. You knew that night you came home from her apartment you should've ended it and you did. But she comes crawling to you and begs you take her back and you did. And then, had she not lied to you, you would still be with her. You would be settling for someone who doesn't want the same things you do. You would've kept putting your dreams on hold. And she would have let you."

"Brooklyn doesn't have anything to do with you and me. She's not the one who's got a whole website of her getting herself off for people to listen to and pay for."

I give him a sad laugh. "For it to not have anything to do with her, you're awful quick to compare me to her."

"Fuck, Ophelia. Stop turning this around."

"How am I turning this around? I think you're just pissed I'm not crying and snotting and remorseful for doing something that is one, completely legal and two, before we got together. Would you be as up in arms if I was a romance author and wrote scenes like the that? How's that any different?"

"It's different because it wouldn't be you getting off for other people to hear and them getting themselves off to your voice. Fuck, it's not that hard to understand."

"Oh, so you're jealous, is that what this is?"

Anger flashes in his eyes. "You're damn right, I'm jealous. You think I want anyone but me knowing what sounds you make when you come? You think I want other people to hear your fantasies? No."

"No one but you does since we got together."

Jess spins his laptop around to face me and points at the screen, his tone indignant. "Then explain why there are uploads since we went to Vegas? I'm not stupid, Ophelia." He closes the distance between us and yanks my chair out and drops to his knees in front of me. "This is tantamount to cheating. You getting off for other people since we got together; I don't even have words to tell you how much this hurts."

I blink rapidly, my breaths coming short. "Cheating? Are you fucking kidding me?"

"What would you call it?"

"Healing my trauma."

He snorts, his face a mask of barely concealed disgust. "Oh, you're gonna play that card? You think because the way you were raised gave you some fucked up sense of what sex was supposed to be like, you making audio porn is some kind of therapy? Don't kid yourself, Ophelia. You enjoy it. You said so yourself you like the idea of people watching you."

"I've never kept that a secret. Last I checked, you liked watching me."

"In our home. In the hotel room we shared. Not on the fucking internet where other people can listen to the woman I love orgasm," he spits out.

My mouth falls open. We haven't said that we loved each other, even if I felt it. And for him to drag it out right now just feels cheap.

I push him away and stand. "Not that I should have to justify my healing process, but yes, it did heal my trauma. And yes, I enjoy it. My hope is, some other girl who was raised to be ashamed of her body and the entirely natural reactions it has will find my audios and break her own cycle of shame."

Walking to my room, I pack a bag with a few days' worth of clothes and pull my laptop off my desk and bring it to the kitchen and set it on the table. "Password is on the bottom of the laptop. Folder on the desktop titled 'Self Care.' You don't even have to buy a subscription. If you feel like talking, you know how to find me."

I pull my bag over my shoulder and he grabs my hand. "Where are you going? We're not done here."

I yank it away. "I can't do this right now. You only see what you want to see and probably, no matter what I tell you, you're not gonna understand." I gesture to the laptop, my voice even. "And for the record, I haven't cheated. I didn't lie. I've answered your questions calmly and rationally. I'm not ashamed of what I've done or who I am. I know what it cost me to get here, so I'm not gonna be made to feel guilty for what took to heal."

He swallows and for the first time since we started talking, he looks unsure. "Where will you go?"

"Don't worry about it, Jess. I have lots of *dirty porn money* to get a hotel room." Knowing even if he's mad at me, he's not gonna take it out on Garth, I give our dog a quick hug before walking out toward the garage.

I'm not even backed out of the driveway before the tears start. Even though I know I haven't done anything wrong, the look of revulsion on his face when he talked about how I was kidding myself when I said Ivy was how I healed was too close to the look my father gave me all those years ago and when I stood up to him that day in the feed store.

CHAPTER TWENTY-NINE

JESS

For a solid twenty minutes, I don't move. I stand in the same exact spot I was in when Ophelia walked out. It's not until Garth comes over to where I stand and plants his massive paw on my thigh do I snap out of my daze. The dog circles, signaling he needs to go out and I walk over and let him out the back door, all the while the only thing I can see is Ophelia's face when I said, *the woman I love.*

I didn't mean to tell her like that and judging by the look on her face when I said, it felt more like a slap than an endearment. And fuck, I do love her. That's why this hurts so bad.

Following Garth back in the house, I shut the door and my eyes fall on the laptops on the kitchen table. Mine sits there, still open to the website like some flashing marquee. Dropping into a chair at the table, I put my head in my hands, my whole conversation with Ophelia replaying in my mind.

In spite of my ire and up to the point where I basically accused her of being a sex worker—did I actually fucking do that—she was entirely calm. Yeah, I totally did try to shame her.

I'm an asshole. My gaze lands on her laptop. She even gave me permission to go through it. I'm a fucking tool.

Her words play over in my mind. *My hope is, some other girl who was raised to be ashamed of her body and the entirely natural reactions it has will find my audios and break her own cycle of shame.*

Picking up my phone, I call Josie. "Wow, I'm popular today."

I frown. "What do you mean?"

"I just got off the phone with your girlfriend a little bit ago. What did you do?"

I sit up straighter. "Is she okay?"

"Yeah. She just wanted to let someone know where she was staying in case there was an emergency. Why would she be staying somewhere else, Jess?"

"We got in a fight and she left. It was my fault," I admit.

She sighs. "Well, good."

"Why is th—." A knock at the door cuts me off.

"Open the door, Jess." I disconnect the call with a sigh and walk over to the door. Josie stands with her arms folded, a jar of what I know has to be moonshine cradled in her arm. "Glad to know me coming here was the right call. You're not usually the one to instigate a fight. What happened?" she asks as she walks past me into the kitchen and pulls down two lowball glasses.

"Little early for that, isn't it?"

She eyes me over her shoulder. "You tell me. I figured you'd want to be at least a little numb before you get your ass handed to you."

I heave a sigh and sit back down. "Better make it a double, then."

Josie nods, and a moment later, brings the glasses to the table. Eyeing my laptop and Ophelia's, she frowns. "What's with this?" She scans the screen on my open one. *"The Confes-*

sions of Ivy Sinn. What's that? Ophelia catch you trolling for porn and y'all get in a fight?"

I shake my head. "Did she tell you anything about our fight?"

"No, just that y'all had one, and she didn't want you to be alone," she explains.

I snap my head up to look at her. "What?"

Josie levels me with a gaze. "She said you were angry and knows you like to verbalize about whatever the situation is. And since she knows you don't want to talk to her right now, since she's said everything she has to say about the situation, she figured, who better for you to talk to than me? She said she gave you permission to speak freely about anything you wanted; that she wasn't ashamed. What would Ophelia have to be ashamed about?"

I down a gulp of the moonshine and cough as the liquor burns all the way down. "Fully leaded? Damn."

She shrugs. "Figured this was a doozy. Spill."

So I do. I tell her about how great everything was in Vegas and after we got back, but that I received a text from Brooklyn that same night and couldn't get it off my mind. I tell her about finally giving into my curiosity and what I found. I even let her listen to the sample audio on Ophelia's website. With headphones, because I'm not a glutton for punishment and already miss Ophelia more than my next breath. Although she doesn't say anything as she listens, her eyes widen several times and her mouth falls open at intervals.

When I relay our conversation, her nostrils flare and she folds her arms and clenches her jaw. By the end and hearing myself repeat everything I said, I feel even worse than I did when I let her leave.

Josie drains her glass and rises to retrieve the jar and refill both our tumblers. "Okay, how brutal do you want me to be?"

"I'm the asshole," I supply.

"You are the grand champion of assholes, Jess. Jesus. You realize you can't police other people's trauma or the things they have to do to heal, right? Did you even listen to that recording?" She points to the screen and I nod. "I know you heard it, Jess, but did you listen to more than what sounds she was making and stuff? Which, damn, your girlfriend has a sexy voice. But did you hear what she was saying? About what her upbringing was like?"

"Yeah, I know about how she was raised."

"You think you do, but you haven't lived the life she has. You and I had parents who were real with us about sex. Hell, you and I had great sex, even as young as we were. We fooled around and we had fun. We had rom-coms and high school movies where sex was a huge plot. She had none of that. She got told her whole life that her entire purpose in life was to be subservient to a man. She got told her only use was to birth children. Hell, her parents disowned her when she wanted to seek an education. Jesus, do you know how strong she would have had to be to decide to leave the only life she's ever known to even try?

"Could you do it? Be thrown into a completely different country where, even though you might speak the same language, you don't understand the references or the slang or anything except that there's more to life than what your parents told you. And then, on top of that, she was expected to know how to kiss and date and all before she even understood her own body? You don't get to judge her for exploring ways to take ownership of her body. Her whole life, she was told it didn't belong to her. She had no choice in anything until she stood up for herself and demanded it. God, I admire her strength of will. To know she'll probably never be accepted by her family and be willing to sacrifice that to live her truth? We should all be so bold."

Bombarded with thoughts of everything Ophelia has shared with me—the lack of even a birth certificate and sleeping on couches and in her car and doing all her undergrad work on a school library computer—reminds me how incredible she truly is. And I'm the asshole judging her.

When I look back at Josie, she's tapping her index finger on the top of Ophelia's laptop. "What are you gonna do?"

I scrub my hands down my face. "I can get past the audios. But I can't handle lies. She said she hasn't done any since we got together, but dates don't lie, Jos. She uploaded one last week. We've been together for two months."

She considers my statement. "You ever listen to any podcasts?"

Frowning, I shrug. "What's that got to do with anything?"

"Do you think the people who do the podcasts actually upload them immediately after they record? Like, if they upload on a Saturday, do you assume they were recorded that same day?"

I shake my head. "No, most of that stuff has post-production; editing and stuff." She blinks and gives me a patronizing grin and waits. She waits way longer than she should for me to get it. My eyes widen and I slam my palm against my forehead. "Fuck. I fucked up. Shit. Fuck. I'm such a fucking asshole."

I groan and hang my head. Josie just sighs and pats my shoulder. "Glad you get it." Tapping Ophelia's laptop, she stands. "My work here is done. It's up to you whether or not you listen to all of them, but if she told you she hasn't done any since y'all got together, I don't think the dates on her laptop will prove her wrong."

After a beat, she retakes her seat and I give her a confused frown. "I thought you said your work was done?"

"I changed my mind."

Her voice is chilly and I lean back, afraid of whatever she's about to say. "Okay," I reply, unsure I want to hear it.

"I love you, Jess. You are one of my best friends and one of the best men I know. And I'm glad you know how badly you fucked this up. But Ophelia would be well within her rights to not forgive you. You know that, right?" I nod. "Good. I hope she does because you're happy with her. Y'all are good together. But the fact you let *Brooklyn* be the thing that caused this issue in the first place makes me want to punch you in the nose.

"Ophelia was nothing but supportive when you were with Brooklyn. She encouraged you to try to work it out and when she broke your heart, she was a good friend to you. She was better to you as a friend than Brooklyn ever was a girlfriend. And honestly, she might be too good for you. She's loyal and she's honest and she's been through more than either of us can ever comprehend. Even now, when you've essentially labeled her a whore and sex worker, she calls your best friend to make sure you're okay."

My chest grows tight as I think about exactly how badly I've fucked up here. And Josie's right, Ophelia is way better than I deserve in this moment.

"Where is she?"

Josie snorts. "Why should I tell you? I'm pissed at you. You've hurt someone I care about."

"I know. Please, Jos. I promise I will make this right. Have you ever known me to break a promise?"

She sighs and after a moment where I know she's wrestling with what she should do, she pulls out her phone and taps on the screen. "Don't make me regret this, Jess Tate." My phone vibrates on the table and I breathe a sigh of relief and nod.

Josie rises from her chair. "Want me to take Garth for the night?" After a moment to consider, I shake my head. She seems surprised, but simply nods. "Alright. If you change your mind, let me know. You know how Emerson feels about dogs. We'd have about ten if we were home more."

She squeezes my shoulder and I cover her hand with mine and give it a squeeze. "Thanks for coming to kick my ass, Jos."

Huffing a laugh, she drops a kiss onto the top of my head. "Least I could do. Si doesn't mess up so much anymore, so I'm usually itching to put someone in their place. Might as well be you."

"You're a good friend."

Giving me one last squeeze, she lifts her hand. "So are you most of the time."

CHAPTER THIRTY

OPHELIA

I could have left Jess to stew. But knowing him the way I do, he needs to talk things through. I knew Josie would listen to his side, but also not sugarcoat. She's a good friend to him.

Even after I check in, which, thankfully, the hotel let me do an early check in. I wasn't thinking when I left that it would be way before traditional check-in hours. Although the room is a double, it feels suffocating and small and too quiet. And with the speed in which I left, I forgot to even bring my e-reader. I read for a bit on my phone, but it gives me a headache, so I abandon the endeavor.

TV bores me after only a couple of episodes of some home improvement show and when I try to simply lie down and sleep through this ache in my chest and my heart, I'm reminded of the way Jess looked at me. Even thinking about the ways he's looked at me in the past don't negate the look of disdain. That one's all I see.

After a healthy dose of tears—not out of shame, because I haven't done anything wrong. Simply for feeling once again like some man is telling me the things I've done are sinful or unacceptable.

That train of thought leads me to thinking about my parents and the way I was raised. And how, if they'd just been open and communicative with me, I wouldn't have had trauma that I needed to sort through. I might have never needed to heal myself that way. And then, I'm just plain old angry. Angry that my past has yet again ruined something in my present. That I can't simply be like everyone else.

I'm halfway to my parents' farm before I even register that I've climbed into my SUV and driven this direction. In for a penny, in for a pound, I guess. And besides, I'm so fucking tired of needing to justify who I am as a person.

Pulling into the driveway, I try to imagine who all might still be living at home. Most likely, Edgar, Lavinia, and Ajax would be the only ones who haven't been married off yet. The rest are probably on their third or fourth kids, raising them the exact same way we were raised. I can only hope I'm not the only one who escaped.

Even knowing I'm wearing shorts and a tank top and I'll likely be looked upon like the whore of Babylon for showing some thigh and arms, I climb the stairs and knock on the door. Taking a few steps back, I wait. It seems as though I never stop waiting. The curtain next to the door flutters and still, I wait. I wait so long, I imagine this is futile. But then the lock clicks and the door opens.

Lavinia, my youngest sister, who should be about eighteen if I'm remembering correctly, stands at the door, dressed in a long denim skirt and long-sleeved, button-down blouse. She eyes me wearily, as if I look familiar, but she's unsure why. "Can I help you?"

My heart lurches. She looks and sounds so much like our mother—and me, I suppose—I immediately want to know if she can sing and does she sound like Mom. Her hair is darker than mine, but her eyes are the same color blue. We're practically the same height, but her curves are a lot more generous than mine. We could almost be twins, except for her having our father's chin, with its slight cleft. Not wanting to get emotional, I clear my throat. "Lavinia, it's me, Ophelia."

Her eyes widen. "You can't be here. Daddy won't like it."

I hold up my hands to assure her I mean no harm. Fucking hell, what am I, the devil herself? "I know. He's not home?"

She shakes her head. "No. He and Edgar went to look at some cattle."

"And Ajax?" I ask, hopeful.

"In the barn. One of the dogs is whelping, and she's having a tough go of it. He's with her."

I nod. "Can I come in?"

She shakes her head, but steps out onto the porch and folds her arms, her posture wary. "Why are you here?"

"Well, I'm not sure, to be honest. I wanted to talk to Dad, but since he's not here, I can talk to you." I gesture to the swing. "May I?"

She shrugs. "Okay."

"Will you sit with me? I know you're probably doing chores and what, making bread? Is that still a Saturday thing?"

She nods. "It's rising. I have a few minutes. I don't know when they'll be back."

"Sure." We each take a seat on the swing and for a long moment, I'm unsure what to say, but then I ask, "Are you eighteen now?"

"Yeah, this past December."

"That's good. And what do you do these days?"

She shrugs. "Mainly cook and clean. I'm reading *Taming of the Shrew*. I think I have it memorized at this point, though."

"I always liked that one."

"Momma did, too."

I nod. "I know. Can I ask what happened to her? I ran into Dad and Jax, and they told me she passed." I blink back tears and exhale a steadying breath.

Lavinia looks down at her hands. They're chafed and calloused and her nails are short, nearly to the quick, and naked. My own are now soft, and unfamiliar with the intense physical labor of farm work any longer. My nails are a dark, almost black, red. "She was pregnant."

My head snaps in her direction. "What?"

"She was pregnant and had gone into early labor and I tried to help her, like with the others, but something went wrong. I'm not sure what."

I blink, trying to comprehend. "Do we have other siblings? Ones younger than Jax?"

She looks back down at her hands and shakes her head. "No. She was pregnant several more times, but they never took. The last one did, but in her seventh or so month, she started bleeding and I couldn't get it stopped. She went to sleep and never woke up."

"Jesus Christ," I breathe, anger and sadness and pity washing over me.

My sister's inhalation of breath is sharp. "You can't say that."

I snort a sad laugh. "Livie, I say a lot of things now you wouldn't agree with."

"Because you're backslid," she says, as if this is simply a fact. "Daddy still prays for you, you know. We all do."

"Thank you." Because what else am I supposed to say? I don't want to upset my sister.

"Would you like for me to pray for you right now?"

I shake my head. "That's okay. Thank you, though. What are your plans?"

"Plans?"

I nod. "Plans. You know, for your future?"

She huffs a laugh, as though it's a ridiculous question. "I'm getting married. Viola's making my dress. She was always the best with the sewing."

My eyes fall closed in resignation. "Who are you marrying?" I ask, returning my gaze to her.

"Gabriel Thomas."

"Is he nice? Do you like him? Is he handsome?"

She shrugs, as if these questions aren't valid. "He's tall. His father is a carpenter. He's an apprentice."

"You're only eighteen, Lavinia. Surely, you have more to do before you're ready to marry and have children."

"What else is there to do? Our entire purpose is to accept as many blessings as the Lord sees fit for us to have."

My chest aches knowing Lavinia is probably never gonna be more than she is at this moment. I swallow. "Does this Gabriel make you want to do nothing but kiss him forever?"

Her eyes widen. "We don't kiss, you know that."

"Right," I agree. "How silly of me. So, I take it you won't kiss him until the wedding?"

"Of course."

"That's not normal, Livie."

"We're called to be abnormal, Ophelia," she counters.

"Do you know what will happen after you get married? The wedding night? Has anyone told you about that?"

She blushes. "I will lie with my husband. We will hopefully make a baby."

An involuntary groan falls from my mouth, tears welling in my eyes. "But you know it should feel good, right? Have you and Gabriel talked about that? What it will be like?"

Again, her cheeks flame and I want so badly to be blunt with her; to tell her the honest truth about what sex—making love—should be. That it should be with someone who looks at you as though you are the most precious thing they've ever laid eyes on. That when she goes to bed with a man, it should be her choice and not simply to fulfill a duty. But she won't understand. Not without more context that she also won't understand.

Instead, I turn the subject toward our other siblings. "I take it everyone else is married?"

"Edgar is scheduled to marry a few months after me. Juliet is married and has seven children." I'm unable to hold back an audible gasp.

"How old was she when she married?"

"Twenty," Lavinia says, her tone matter-of-fact.

I do some quick mental math. Juliet is twenty-eight. That's seven children in eight years. God, I can't even imagine. "Angelo?" I ask.

"Sure. He was twenty also and has five children." She thinks for a moment and counts off on her hand. "Bianca has five. Viola and Duncan both have three."

I blink. "What about Marina?"

Her eyes drop to her lap. "I'm not sure."

Frowning, I ask, "What do you mean? Where's Marina?"

"I'm not sure. She was caught with...someone in the barn loft and Daddy told her she had to leave."

My stomach drops. "What? What do you mean, *someone*?"

Her cheeks turn pink again and she licks her lips. After a moment, she mutters, "It was right after Momma died. She was with another girl. They were indecent."

My mouth falls open and a bark of shocked laughter works its way up my throat, but I quickly sober. "So, he kicked her out, just like that? Because she was with a girl? You don't know where she went?"

She shakes her head and I want to rail and scream. I want

to burn this fucking house to the ground. I want to murder my father. I want to talk to my mother and hear her sing one last time. I want to shake some sense into my baby sister, but I have no clue how. I swipe away a tear just before it rolls down my face. "I take it you don't have a cell phone?"

"Of course not."

I nod, not expecting a different answer than I received. "Do you have a piece of paper?"

She pulls a small spiral-bound notebook and a pen from her pocket and extends it in my direction with a curious frown. I open it to a few pages from the back and write down my number. When she goes to take it from me, I wrap my hands around hers and hold them tight as I look into her eyes. "I gave you my number. If you ever need anything, anything at all, you call me. Memorize it so Dad doesn't find it. Do you hear me, Livie?"

She searches my eyes and finally nods. I pull her hands to my chest. "No questions asked. I will come and get you. I will help you however I can. What *he* tells you—what they taught us—it's not everything. I know you think I'm this horrible, evil person who chose the world. I get that. But please know, there are good people outside the ones they tell us are who we should associate with. Or, you could go with me. Right now, I could get you out of here. I promise, it's not a bad life."

After a beat, she pulls her hands from mine. "I should get back to the bread. I'll pray for you, Ophelia."

I nod as she rises from the swing and walks back into the house and for the span of several heartbeats, I don't move. I should, but I don't. Emotionally drained after the conversations with Jess and my sister, I suddenly feel like I could sleep for years. And yet, I can't bring myself to rise from my spot on the swing.

Taking in the expanse of the farm—twenty-five acres, if I

recall—I have vivid flashes of my childhood. Running barefoot through the fields with Juliet and Angelo. Dad mounting the tire swing down by the creek and us spending hours playing on it and flinging ourselves into the water. Snuggling with Ajax when he was cranky or sick and smelling his little boy scent. My mother's laugh.

Closing my eyes, I try to hear it. The only one that comes to mind is that first memory I have of her with the chicken pot pie and her singing, laughing as she swipes the flour off my face with a towel. Please, God, don't let that be the last time she laughed.

Surely, this can't be what she imagined for her children's lives—her own life. Surely she had ambitions, aspirations, dreams. Please tell me they included more than simply staying pregnant until she died. Did she suspect she'd be going? Did the idea scare her, or was she relieved to finally be rid of this prison?

"You can't be here."

I whip my head up, brought out of my thoughts by the sound of a male voice. Ajax's voice. I nod. "I know. I was just leaving." Although his words were harsh, his tone wasn't and I can't help but examine my baby brother. "You've gotten so big, Jax."

He shrugs and folds his arms across his chest. Even though he's still young, he's lost all the softness that comes with youth. His shoulders are broad and his forearms are sinewy, his legs are long and his torso lean. He's handsome in the way lumber-jacks and fireman are handsome and he's got this rugged quality that says he could break as many hearts as he wanted. I know from photos, he looks like our father. My father's hard-ness stripped away a lot of his appeal for me. Now, I only see an icy stare and that snarl when he said he was happy my mother couldn't see my life.

"Are you happy in this life, Ajax?"

"What kind of question is that?"

I sigh and attempt to be more succinct. "Do you have joy in your daily life? Is there anything you do that's only for you—outside of farm work or Bible study or anything else Dad requires of you—is there something that's only yours?"

He shrugs again and leans against one of the porch posts. "I play guitar."

I nod. "That's really good. What's your favorite song to play?"

He scratches his chin, as if he's unsure where my line of questioning is going, but answers. "That song you used to sing to me; the one Momma sang in the mornings. 'Walking After Midnight', I think it's called. Is that right?"

Tears burn my eyes. "You remember that?"

He nods. "Yeah. After you left, I'd sing it to myself when I went to bed. I thought if I kept singing it, you'd come back."

My chest aches and I swipe the tear just beginning to creep past my lashes. "I did. Five years ago."

He frowns. "No, you didn't."

I blink. "Yes, I did. I came back after I graduated from college. I banged on the door and Dad was standing in the kitchen. I saw him. He saw it was me and wouldn't even come to the door, Jax."

He blinks. "But he prays for you to come home. Every day."

I blow out a breath. "He prays for me to come home and be obedient to him, Ajax. That's the only way he'd ever let me come home. If you're not someone he can control, he has no use for you."

"Children are supposed to obey their parents."

I nod. "Yes, and we're also called to love like Jesus. You think disowning your children is embodying that love? Last I checked, Jesus ate with the tax collectors and sex workers the same as he did with the religious people. He loved them; he didn't condemn them and write them off. Like when he kicked Marina out. If Dad loved like Jesus, he wouldn't have done that."

Ajax's frown deepens. "He didn't kick her out. She ran away. Like you."

"Is that what he told you? Did she leave a note?"

"No, he just said she'd gone, but that we'd pray for her to come home, like we do for you."

I rub my chest, trying to relieve the ache and pressure from not exploding at this moment. I can't lose it on Jax. He has no clue what things are really like. I simply say, "The truth isn't always as it appears. And his truth isn't the only one there is."

Standing from the swing, knowing I can't stay around here and this house still be standing if I do, I walk toward the steps. "That man you were with the day we saw you." I stop and pivot to face him. "Your roommate; isn't that what you called him?"

"He was my roommate, yes."

"He's not anymore?"

"He's the man I love. He's more than my roommate now."

"He was nice to you that day," he offers.

I nod. "Yeah. Jess is very kind."

"Will you marry him?"

"I'm not sure. I'm not in a big hurry, but I want to get married someday and have children. He wants the same things I do. Why do you want to know about Jess, Jax?"

"Where is he today? He didn't come with you? He wouldn't worry about you getting in another fight with Dad?"

"If he knew I was here he might. We got in an argument this morning. I needed some space."

Ajax gestures to my clothes. "And he just lets you show off your body like this? For other people to see?"

Indignation burns my chest. "First of all, Jess has never *let* me do anything. Outside of this tiny sliver of reality Dad has constructed, it's not like this a lot of places. I wear what I want; I do what I want. I read and watch what I want. I have a full-time job. Jess had no say in any of it. We respect each other and communicate. Good relationships are built on trust and respect and friendship. We were friends before we were ever more. He's my best friend. That's the way it should be."

And despite the argument Jess and I had, I still believe all the things I've just said. I know we have shit to sort out, but we will sort it out. I truly believe we will. Because that's what people who love each other do. I truly believe that, as well.

"And you're happy living in the world?"

I take a step closer to my brother. He's taller than I am and I'm not sure how to feel about that fact. And yet, I look up into his eyes. They're brown, like our father's, and curious. "I wasn't for a lot of years. The life our parents conditioned us for is nothing like the real world. It's like being transported to another place entirely. It took a long time for me to find myself and figure out where I fit. I am now, yes. I had to unlearn a lot of the things our father taught me."

"Like what?"

"Things about relationships, mostly. Romantic ones. That I should expect more from a relationship than simply fulfilling a role. That things should be equal. That I should have a say in how many children I have and when. That I should want my husband's affections, not just tolerate them. That sex isn't a duty. That it's amazing and beautiful and fun. That our bodies aren't dirty or shameful simply because we experience desire. That if you don't know what you like for your own body, how can you expect someone else to?"

Movement down the road catches my eye and I recognize the beat up Ford my dad has driven almost my entire life. I look back to Ajax. "I have to go. Think about what I've said. Lavinia knows how to reach me. I'll tell you like I told her. You call me, I'll come. No matter what, okay? I will help you any way I can." Tears burn my eyes. "I've never stopped thinking about you; any of you."

Reaching up to touch his face, I try to memorize his features. I know I'll never come back here, although it's only fifteen minutes from home. I wouldn't be able to resist setting the house on fire. "I love you, Jax."

His eyes soften and he nods, but doesn't say anything. I jog down the steps and slide behind the wheel of my car, not willing to have a confrontation with my father right now. Unfortunately, he seems to want to the fight since he pulls his truck in, blocking my SUV.

Climbing back out, I slam the door. A few feet away, Edgar exits the truck and blinks at me. "Ophelia? Is that you?" His voice is a mix of wonder and surprise and my heart squeezes.

"Hey, Eddie. I hear you're getting married. Congratulations."

He nods. "Thanks." He looks at our father, who is still behind the wheel of his truck. "Dad, you okay?"

"Just fine, Edgar. Go on in the house now."

He darts a glance between the two of us and nods. "Yes, sir."

As he passes me, he shoots me a smile and says quietly, "Hey, Opie. Freedom looks good on you."

I almost grab him to me and hug his neck. Maybe there is hope for my siblings yet. Maybe some of them play the part but still have some spirit. "Thanks," I reply, my voice thick with emotion. "You take care, okay?"

He winks at me, reaching to give my hand a squeeze. "You've got it." It's in that moment, I'm reminded of Edgar when he was young. My sweet, funny, daredevil. God, please let him still be that same way. Please don't let my father have driven that out of him.

My father waits until the door closes, Edgar and the others safely inside, before slithering out of the truck. No doubt, so they won't be privy to whatever vitriol he's about to spew. "You know you're not welcome in my house." He stares down at me in disgust and I try not to remember Jess looking at me that same way.

I square my shoulders and hold my head high. "I was just leaving actually."

"Why are you here, Ophelia?"

Instead of answering his question, I ask him one of my own. "How many times did you get Mom pregnant after I left? How many babies did she lose before the last one killed her?"

Color rises in his cheeks. "You don't get to ask about your mother."

"Fine, I'll ask about your wife. Are you proud of yourself? For how well you were able to keep her chained to you? For how your *love* killed her?"

He closes the distance between us until his nose is only inches from mine. I nearly flinch, but I'm not about to give him the satisfaction. "You shut your whore mouth talking about my wife."

"Nice. Let's pull out the name calling. How about 'slut'? Does that work for me, too, Dad? Or, what about 'dirty', 'filthy', 'worldly', 'sinful'. Any of those you want to call me? The thing is, those words only have power if the person you hurl them at gives a shit. I don't. You can take your smug self-righteousness and shove it up your ass."

He folds his arms and I'm forced to take a step back. "You don't get to come to *my* house and treat me this way. This isn't how I raised you."

"No, you're right," I say with a snort. "You sure as hell

didn't. I raised myself. I raised most of your kids. While you were trying to build some sort of twisted community of people who believe the same way you do, I remember you keeping your wife pregnant the entire time I was home. I remember her being so depressed after Ajax was born, *I* was the only mother he had. I also remember her being pregnant again three months later. You ruined her. You ruined me. You ruined all of us. You've insulated them to the point that they wouldn't even be able to survive in the real world. You've brainwashed them to the point that they are nothing but robots, parroting back the bullshit you've shoved down their throats their whole lives.

"You claim to pray for your wayward children to return; hiding behind some great mask of piety. All the while, you won't even come to the door when they come knocking. You stare down your nose in disgust when we don't do exactly as you want. You claim to be a loving Christian, and in the same breath, disown your children. That's not very Christlike, Dad. Pretty sure Jesus frowns on hypocrites. Pretty sure he'd rather have the humble offering of a tax collector than the boastful worship of a Pharisee. I'll let you sort out which one you are."

I step past him. "Now, if you'll kindly move your vehicle so I can go home, I'd appreciate it."

He grabs my arm and yanks me to him, his voice a low hiss in my ear. "Why, so you can go back to your *roommate?* Do you play the whore for him, Ophelia? Is that how you pay your rent; on your back? I can see your sin on you plain as day, little girl. You are wicked and God will not be mocked."

I yank my arm away. "Your words don't hurt me, Dad. I know who I am." I give him a smirk. "I can be very wicked and I enjoy every minute of it. And you know, I feel closer to God when I make love to Jess than I ever did under your roof. Because sex isn't sinful. Sex is good and natural and one of God's best gifts to his children.

"Just because you're a sick individual who's twisted what it should be to match your own system of beliefs doesn't mean it's right. And you like to cherry pick your verses to match your mindset. The Bible also teaches that if you have iniquity in your heart, the Lord won't hear you. Iniquity, evil, malice; pick your synonym, they're all interchangeable.

"The fact that you rail against sin while you yourself don't show love *is* iniquity, Dad. You think God hears the prayers you pray when you have hate in your heart for your own children? When you judge them and disown them because they aren't perfect little followers? You are the reason people have such a negative reaction to the church. Because of believers like you who twist things to suit their opinions. And I thank God every day I got away from you.

"Now, I'll politely request one last time that you move your truck so I can leave. Otherwise, I will call the police to inform them that I'm being held against my will. You think they'd be upset if I also showed them the graveyard when they got here? How many babies are buried back there now, fifteen? More? You are the worst sort of man. You use and you manipulate and you take and take and take until all that's left is dust. You killed my mother as surely as if you'd shot her in the head. But you killed her spirit long before her body gave out."

His jaw clenches and I jerk my chin in the direction of the vehicles. And yet, none of my words seem to have any sort of impact on him. I told Jess once that he wasn't cruel. I see now I was wrong. Very, very wrong.

He walks over to his truck and climbs inside and pulls up just enough that I can back out of the driveway. Passing him as I make my way to my vehicle, he stops. "This is the last time you'll ever come back to my home. You're not welcome here."

I huff a sad sigh. "You don't have to worry about that. Although, I hope someday, you have a change of heart. I hope someday, you wake up and realize every hurtful thing you've done and all the years you wasted being so filled with hate that you lost your family and you're filled with the same kind of shame and guilt you chained to all of us. I hope that shame eats at you and you can't sleep until you make it right. I hope at least some of my siblings can see through your bullshit and think for themselves."

CHAPTER THIRTY-ONE

OPHELIA

Although, I'd love nothing more than to go home and curl up with Garth on the couch and cry into his big, wrinkly body, I drive past the turn off for the house and continue on to the hotel. And even though my room is only on the second floor and the stairs are right there, I'm not sure I can drag myself up them.

Once I'm in my room, I fall onto the bed, wishing Jess was here to pull me into his arms like he did the day I found out about my mother's death. I know there's a chance that might never happen again. There's a possibility he packs up all my stuff and tosses it on the lawn. Okay, that might be a bit dramatic, but I'm not exactly in the most serene headspace at the moment.

Instead, I pull my knees up to my chest and roll myself into a ball and hope some seed of *something* will have been planted in my youngest siblings today. I can only hope I'll someday get a call.

At first, I think it's the room next door; the banging. But then, I hear it again and realize it's my door. I rub the sleep from my eyes and squint at the bedside clock and see it's nearly nine. AM or PM? I'm not sure what time I got back from my dad's, but this must be what it feels like to wake up from a coma. My body feels heavy and I must have slept like the dead. I suppose I should be thankful for the escape sleep provided me for a time since I didn't have to remember my fight with Jess or my confrontation with my father.

Was all that today—or possibly yesterday, depending on whether it's still today or it's rolled over to tomorrow. I have no clue. A knock sounds again and I jerk to attention. There're only two people it could be. I know who I hope it is, but I still steel myself to the reality that it might be Josie telling me Jess wants me to come get my shit.

"Birdie?"

My heart gives a lurch at the sound of Jess's voice. And despite how hurt I was by the things he said and the way he looked at me, I still love him and I want us to move past this. I want to build a future with him. I want to wake up next to him for the rest of my life. Is that something he wants now? Only one way to find out, I guess.

I blow out a deep breath and after checking the peephole, I open the door. Jess looks tired and unshaved. Definitely AM, right? "Hey," I offer.

He nods. "Hey. Can I come in?"

I stand aside and allow him to enter and when I see my laptop tucked under his arm, I'm even more unsure how this will play out. I allow the door to close and return to the main space, taking a seat on the bed I just left. Reaching to turn on a bedside lamp, Jess takes a seat on the opposite bed, facing me.

"I've been trying to call you."

I blink, surprised. "I'm sorry. I didn't know." I grab my

purse from the nightstand and search through it before looking up at him as I fish it out. "I turned it on silent and forgot to plug it up before I crashed."

"I came by yesterday afternoon."

"Is this Sunday?"

He frowns at my question. "Yeah. Are you okay?"

"I'm fine. I—." I'm about to tell him about going to see my family, but I don't want to spill things to my best friend if he's not that anymore. I don't want to have the expectation that he will comfort me if he can no longer be that to me. "What are you doing here, Jess?"

He extends my laptop to me. "Here." Confused, I accept it and place it on the bed next to me. I open my mouth and he presses forward. "I didn't do anything with it."

"What? Did you have issues trying to login? I told you the password was written on the bottom."

He shakes his head. "I don't need to. I won't say I wasn't tempted, simply because I missed your voice more than anything. You've only been gone a day and I feel like someone cut off one of my arms, Ophelia."

I bite my lip and try to guard my reaction. I attempt to keep my emotions in check and not get my hopes up. "You didn't listen? To any of them?"

Jess shakes his head again. "No. You tell me there aren't any since we got together, I believe you."

I lift a brow. "You sure about that?"

He nods. "And even if there were, that's your business because I don't have any right to tell you what you can or can't do with your body. And nor do I have a right to tell you how to heal your trauma. I was an asshole for the things I said to you and I'm really sorry. I'm sorry I didn't bring it up when Brooklyn originally texted. I'm sorry I let her drive a wedge between us."

Dropping to his knees on the floor in front of me, he takes my hands in his. "I'm so sorry I presumed to know anything about what life was like for you growing up and what kind of herculean feat it is that you're as well-adjusted as you are. I'm sorry I hurt you. I don't deserve your forgiveness, but I'm going to ask for it anyway. Please? Will you forgive me? I love you."

"I love you, too." He heaves a sigh of obvious relief and lifts my hands to his mouth. "There are things you should know, though."

Uncertainty flashes in his eyes and he nods and retakes his seat on the bed. "Okay."

"I think it's important for you to know where Ivy originates from."

He holds up his hands. "You don't have to tell me. It doesn't matter. Really. You don't owe me any kind of explanation."

I lick my lips, a bit nervous since I've never shared all of it with anyone. But I want Jess to know. Since he knows about Ivy and has come here to make amends, I want him to know me. "I know, but I want you to understand. I told you I didn't kiss someone until I was twenty, right?" He nods again but remains silent. "Well, after I moved in with Rosalind, her boyfriend set me up on a date with this guy; one of his friends. We all went out and I don't even remember his name anymore, but after the date, we were riding in the backseat of Rosalind's car and he kissed me. I'd been drinking, so I was relaxed. It was nice. But when he tried to do more, I froze up and had a panic attack. Because all I could hear was my father's voice saying how dirty and sinful I was.

"The guy was an asshole and called me a prude and made me feel bad. Rosalind's boyfriend told him he was being a tool and that night, I realized I knew nothing and after we got home, I made Rosalind tell me what it was really like. She did her best, but she wasn't much better off than me, I don't think. Her boyfriend was sweet but I'm not sure there was a lot of chemistry, so she had a hard time explaining things to me. And so, I felt like there was something wrong with me; like I was a freak."

"You're not a freak," he interjects, indignation in his tone.

I sigh. "I know that, but that's how I felt. A few months later, I met this guy. Abel. We were paired up for a biology lab. He was easy to talk to; he was sweet and cute. He was graduating, so honestly, I'm not sure why he was in a sophomore level science class, but whatever. We hit it off, and he asked me out. I hadn't told him everything about the way I was raised, but he knew enough to know that I was sheltered. We'd made out and stuff, but he wasn't pushy and didn't pressure me or anything. Like I said, he was nice.

"One night, we'd been drinking and I wasn't drunk, but I was pretty buzzed—enough to make me chatty. He knew I was a virgin, of course, and I asked him about his first time, so I could try to understand things, and he told me. At that point, we hadn't done more than kiss or him putting his hand up my shirt. I'll give him this, he was patient.

"That night, after we talked, I wanted to do more but when he put his hand up my skirt, I froze again and panicked. He respected my boundaries and asked me if I felt comfortable sharing why I'd freaked out. I was embarrassed and felt like I'd done something wrong, but Abel was calm and reassuring and made it easy for me to open up to him.

"So I did. I told him everything about how I was raised and even about the time in the park when I began to question things. He asked me if I'd touched myself since then and I said no, of course not. I couldn't do that. He asked me why.

"I realized I couldn't tell him why. I didn't have a good reason. And it wasn't because I didn't get horny. I did. I got aroused when Abel and I made out or when I thought about the couple in the park, but I never did anything.

"Abel asked me how could I expect to know what sex is supposed to be like, how good it can be, if I didn't even know my own body. If I'd never explored myself and knew what brought myself pleasure, how could I expect to know how to direct my partner when the time came?

"It had never occurred to me that I would ever *direct* anyone during sex. Wasn't that the man's place? He said that good sex has give and take and you should be able to listen to your partner so it can be a pleasurable experience for both parties.

"And I was still so repressed; I wasn't sure I could do it. He offered to help me. And because I felt so safe with him, I agreed. He kept all his clothes on, I think to ensure me he didn't have any ulterior motives or anything, and he told me to strip down to whatever level I felt comfortable. I remember I was wearing some leggings under the skirt I had on, so I took off the skirt and left on the leggings. I also had on a camisole and cardigan, so I took off the sweater. I know it sounds lame, but it was the first time I'd ever been in front of a man in anything remotely tight or revealing, and I felt scandalous.

"He sat on his bed and leaned against the headboard and he had me sit between his knees with my back against his chest. He kept his voice low and told me to close my eyes. He told me if at any time, I got uncomfortable, we could stop and to say the word and we'd go back to just kissing.

"But his whispers in my ear and the way his breath was warm on my skin, I was already getting turned on, so I told him I was okay. He covered my hands with his and for a long time, he just had me feel my body. Not even, like, my breasts or anything, just my body. My arms and legs and throat, my stomach and hips and thighs. It was enough that it made my whole body feel awake, if that makes sense.

"He said, 'This is *your* body, Ophelia. You're the only one who knows what it needs. It is yours to explore by yourself or with someone else. It is yours to share with someone who will show it the respect it deserves. This body is beautiful and yours. No one else can make you feel shame for something that is all yours.'

"And as things progressed, I forgot his hands were on mine. Even though he was the one who guided my hands, it was still my hands that touched me and brought myself pleasure for the first time.

"By the time I got close, I felt myself starting to tense up and he must have, too, because he reminded me that it was *my* body. I owned it and I owned that moment. He reminded me that I was a beautiful woman and there was no shame in pleasure. Not like this. And then I came. I had my first orgasm at twenty-one. One I gave myself. I immediately burst into tears because it was so intense and I still felt that shame I'd been trying to keep tamped down rise up.

"And he was still patient and kind and reassuring. Honestly, he could've been some kind of sexual surrogate in training for all I know. And for days after that, he continued to guide me, with less and less assistance until it was all me and that was the night I finally felt like I truly had ownership of my body. That it didn't belong to my father to marry off to some guy who expected me to pop out five kids in as many years. It was mine.

"And when Abel and I finally had sex, it wasn't scary, it was beautiful. It was perfect—well, as perfect as first times can be. After that, he continued to help me work through my issues and encouraged me to touch myself even when we weren't together. I did and got more confident and one night, we were on the phone and our conversation turned a bit flirty and one thing led to another and we had phone sex.

"He told me how sexy I sounded and asked if I'd ever

recorded myself. Of course, I hadn't, but Abel made me feel empowered, so I did and surprised him with a recording for his birthday. I guess that helped me discover my exhibition kink, because it made me feel sexy to know he was listening to me and it gave him pleasure.

"We went our separate ways; which was bittersweet, to be honest. He was the best first boyfriend ever and reminded me the day he left that my body was my own and it was beautiful. But he also told me I had a sexy voice and the recordings I made for him would hold him over until he found someone as great as me.

"Those few months I had with Abel were the most confidence-building of my life. I still hadn't figured out my sense of style or anything like that, but I knew my body. From then on, I've never been ashamed of it.

"So when I tell you I'm also not ashamed of Ivy, I mean that, too. And no, it's not something I go around blasting, simply because it's one thing for a stranger on the internet who's never seen my face to listen. It's a completely different thing for people I know. I mean, I guess it doesn't matter since Brooklyn will probably out me.

"But I still wouldn't be ashamed of Ivy if that happens. Over the past few years, I've shared my story and yes, they are recordings of me masturbating. But they're also a record of the transformation of a scared, unsure, naive young girl into a confident woman who knows who she is and what she's overcome. And for that, I could never be ashamed.

"So, I won't take them down and I won't be made to feel as if I've done something wrong when I haven't. Not when I get emails from other people who grew up just like I did and are finding their way with Ivy's help. If you can't accept that Ivy will always be out there, I'm not sure we'll make it.

"I didn't lie to you when I said I hadn't done any since we

got together. I haven't. But it has nothing to do with you. I don't need Ivy anymore. Moving in with you, making real friends, finally standing up to my father, Ivy has served her purpose for me. She was always an outlet for me to find myself. I have and I feel complete and ready to close that chapter of my life. But to be clear, I'd already made my last recording and a goodbye of sorts before we even went to Vegas. So, as much as I love you and want a future with you, you are not the reason I'm putting Ivy to bed."

CHAPTER THIRTY-TWO

JESS

For a long moment, I don't say anything. I simply stare at this beautiful, intelligent, resilient, proud woman. And she's mine? Jesus, how did I get so lucky. "You're amazing."

Ophelia blinks, as if she thinks she may have misheard me. I drop back to the floor on my knees and clutch her hands to my chest. "You're amazing and brave and a hell of a storyteller. You're incredible and as long as I'm the only one who gets Ophelia, I don't care who has Ivy."

She huffs a laugh and pulls her hands from my grip to bring them to my face and look into my eyes. "You are the only one who gets Ophelia. For as long as you want her. Although, can we stop referring to me in the third person?"

"Sure," I reply with a grin before I sober. "I'm sorry, Birdie."

She nods. "I know." Pushing the laptop to the other side of the bed, she pats the mattress next to her. I take a seat and she intertwines her fingers with mine. "I went to my dad's yesterday." I raise my eyebrows in surprise and she nods. "I was so pissed and I'm not sure what I wanted from him, but I needed to put things to bed with him, too, I guess."

"Are you okay? What happened?"

"I saw my baby sister," she says with a sad smile. "And Ajax and Edgar. But I spoke with Lavinia for a bit. She looks so much like our mother. And me, I guess, since I look like her, too. She just turned eighteen. She's getting married in a few months. She's never even been alone with the boy or man she's planning to marry. They've never held hands or kissed. She has no clue what her wedding night will be like except that she will 'lie with her husband and hope to make a baby'."

Tears well in her eyes and I give her hand a supportive squeeze. "I tried to explain that's not what her entire purpose should be but she only knows what she's been told. It breaks my heart. All of my siblings that have married, except Marina, have a slew of kids. Between the five of them, they have twenty-three kids. Juliet had seven kids in eight years, Jess. She is twenty-eight and has seven kids."

My mouth falls open in shock. "Holy shit. That's—."

She nods. "I know. And Lavinia's next."

I blink, catching up with what she said. "What about Marina? She doesn't have kids?"

Ophelia's jaw clenches. "My father kicked her out. Found her and another girl in the barn. 'Indecent' is the word Livie used. He told Ajax she ran away. Just like me. And that my father prays for Marina and me to come home every day."

"Does he not know you went home?"

"Apparently not." She chews her bottom lip and gets this faraway look in her eyes. "I also found out how my mother died."

"And?"

"Childbirth. Lavinia said she'd gone into early labor and

started hemorrhaging and they couldn't get it stopped. Said she'd been pregnant several times before that, but had lost them all. She was about seven months along and Livie tried to help her, but she must've lost too much blood because she went to sleep and never woke up."

Her eyes fill with tears. "My mother was forty-nine and was still having babies. I don't doubt she should have stopped after Edgar or Lavinia. Even though I love Jax dearly, she was never right again after he was born. But all my father saw was that his wife had a duty to fulfill. And she did. I told him it was his fault she died and he might as well have shot her in the head. It would have been more merciful, that's for sure."

"God, baby, I'm so sorry. That's terrible."

She nods. "Yeah, it is. And if my sisters have married men anything like my father, they might suffer the same fates. Hell, my brothers may end up being husbands like my father. Part of me wishes I could pretend to be the obedient, repentant daughter simply to get my remaining siblings out. But I think I kinda killed that chance with everything I said to my father. I did give Lavinia my number. For all I know, she'll tell my father I gave it to her, but I hope she doesn't. I hope she or Jax memorizes it like I told them to."

She slumps against me and I press a kiss to the top of her head. "Sounds like yesterday was pretty eventful."

"No shit," she says, sounding tired.

"You tired?"

Nodding against me, she sighs. "I shouldn't be. I came here after I left the farm and crashed. I'm not even sure what time it was, except before dark." Her stomach rumbles loudly. "I haven't eaten anything since a drive-thru biscuit yesterday."

"God, you must be starving. Let's go home. I'll fix you breakfast."

"Okay."

After a shower and change of clothes, Ophelia lounges on the sofa with her e-reader in one hand, Garth's ear in the other as she absentmindedly rubs her fingers over the softness as he rests his head in her lap. Looking over at my two favorite beings on the planet, I can't help but feel as though all is right in my world again. Not having Ophelia in my bed because of a rift isn't something I want to ever experience again.

"Over medium, Birdie?"

"Yes, please." She looks over at me. "You sure you don't want any help?"

"Nope. You are exactly where you're supposed to be. How can I woo you with my sensuous culinary capabilities if I'm not employing them all by myself?"

She laughs. "Pretty sure it's not your cooking that woos me, mister."

I shoot her a wicked grin. "Don't worry; that's next. Gotta get you some energy first. Can't have you losing steam before I've even gotten started."

Returning her attention to her book, she says, "We'll just have to see who loses steam first."

Smiling, I flip the eggs in the skillet and cut the heat as I assemble our plates. I'm just dropping the last slice of buttered toast onto mine when there's a knock at the door. Ophelia sets her reader down, but Garth seems pretty content where he is and won't budge. I jog around the counter. "I got it."

Opening the door, my mouth falls open in surprise. "Brooklyn? Um, hi?"

She throws herself at me and bursts into tears. I'm so

shocked, I don't even know how to react. "Jess, I messed up so bad, baby. Please. I'm so sorry."

I pry her off me, and watch as Ophelia is finally able to work herself out from under Garth's bulk. I hold Brooklyn at arm's length as she continues to sob. "What are you doing here?"

"I missed you so much. I was in town and just had to stop by. I wanted to see if—." Her words and tears stop as Ophelia comes to stand beside me and slips her hand in mine. Her expression hardens as her eyes drop to our joined hands. "What's she doing here?"

I snort a shocked laugh. "Why wouldn't she be here? She lives here. Ophelia and I are together. You know this."

Her face morphs into one of disgust. "You mean, even after you found out who she was, what she does, you still want to be with her? God, I knew you were desperate to get married and have kids. I didn't think you'd stoop to doing it with a hooker."

I open my mouth, rage, hot and sudden, bubbling up in my chest. Ophelia drops my hand and steps forward. "We all sell ourselves for something, Brooklyn. For accuracy's sake, let's clarify something. I sell my *voice,* not my body. Not that there's anything wrong with the people who *choose* to do that. Also, I'm really good at what I do. You must have thought it was pretty memorable from whenever or wherever you heard it. Actually, come to think of it, I believe I recall a wandering_brooklyn@ymail.com on a subscription report several months back. Is that you?"

I blink in shock as Brooklyn's face turns bright red. But apparently, Ophelia's not done. "And if my memory serves— I've got a great memory, have I ever told you that—that specific email listened to all of my audios numerous times. Did you get what you needed from them? I've been told women enjoy them just as much as men; go figure. Glad I can provide some quality entertainment for you.

"Like I said, we all sell ourselves. Mine was to heal my personal trauma. I make no apologies for making a buck in the process. Student loans and all that, you know. You, on the other hand, sold yourself for some big corporate dream after all signs pointed to you *needing* to be free. You sold out a relationship with a fantastic guy to have said freedom. Looks to me like you got exactly what you wanted. Sorry your gamble didn't pay off.

"And I'm sure you thought you were doing Jess a favor by outing me. It actually did *me* a big favor. Jess and I had a really productive conversation, and I got to confront the source of a lot of my trauma directly. So, in reality, I should be thanking you." Ophelia folds her arms across her chest. "Anything else you need clarification about today?"

Brooklyn fumes, her chest rising and falling in quick succession. A considerable weight presses against the outside of my leg and her eyes fall to Garth, where he's come to investigate.

"Wow, you've really jumped in the deep end, huh, Jess? You've got someone willing to be your baby factory. You've even got a dog. What's next, a minivan and soccer games? Baby strollers and trips to the zoo?"

I smile. "I should be so lucky." I lift a brow and cool my expression. "What's the matter, Brooklyn? Upset that I'm not still broken and waiting for you to get your shit together? Upset that after three years of expecting you to choose me, I moved on to someone who wants the same things I do?"

Her eyes narrow. "You know, I think the hospital would love to know that one of their employees is peddling porn."

Ophelia stands up straighter. "Brooklyn, I'm sorry your life is shit right now. I'm sorry you feel the need to try to make other people's lives miserable so you can feel better about your own.

But if you think I give one flying fuck about my job at the hospital, you're delusional. I could've given that job up after six months of starting my website. I work at the hospital because it gives me something to do. I don't need it. I could survive solely off of Ivy Sinn subscriptions for three years and never have to work."

Brooklyn sputters and I have to admit, my heart lurches with her revelation. Ophelia smirks. "Like I said, I'm really good." She puts her hand on the edge of the door. "Now, if there's nothing else, I'd like to eat my breakfast before it gets too cold."

My ex-girlfriend backs up. "You know, the dick wasn't even that good to begin with."

Ophelia snorts and gives her a sympathetic smile. "Oh, honey. I know it's dire, but don't go lying to yourself. We both know the dick is excellent." She slams the door and blows out a breath. Turning to me, she points to the door. "I'm sorry; did you want to do the honors?"

I grab her face and give her a sound kiss. "God, you're something else."

She laughs and wraps her arms around my neck. "I'm glad you think so."

Shuffling us toward the kitchen, I set her in a chair at the table. "I think you should eat so I can take you to bed."

Although we go to bed, we don't have sex. Despite our blatant need for one another, we both seem content to simply lie facing one another and talk. More about her past, my father's long battle with multiple sclerosis and his death, our hopes for the future. For hours, we hold each other and share ourselves; our souls.

Shortly before sunset, with the sunlight streaming orange through the blinds, she raises onto her elbow to look at me. "Come on a drive with me?"

I look into her beautiful blue eyes and smile. "Anywhere. Let me get ready."

She shakes her head. "What you have on is fine. I don't want to go anywhere that requires a dress code. We'll only be in the car or outside. Shorts and a tee shirt are good."

"Alright. Do you want me to drive?"

"Okay if I do?"

"Of course." After grabbing our phones and her purse, we lock up the house and head out to the garage and climb into her Explorer. "Gotta say; this is definitely a step up from the clown car."

She rolls her eyes as she backs out of the driveway. "I will admit, Garth does seem to like it."

"True."

For about ten minutes, she seems to have a specific location in mind, but it's a part of town I've not been to in years, even though it's only a few miles from where I currently live. A few minutes later, she turns onto an unfamiliar road and pulls under a tree.

Knowing she probably has a reason she's come here, I simply wait. She peers out the windshield and points at something in the distance. "You see that house?" I squint in the distance and sure enough, about five hundred yards off, there's a white farmhouse. It reminds me a lot of Josie's grandfather's place, except much larger.

The house sits against a backdrop of pastures and a stand of evergreen trees. Farther in the distance, I can make out a red barn. Lights shine from several of the windows and a large pickup truck sits in the driveway.

Even though I know where we probably are, I simply answer, "Yeah, I see it. You don't want to get any closer?"

"No. This is the property line. If I ever park any closer, it will be to burn the house down." Her tone isn't angry, just matter-of-fact. I take her hand across the console and give it a squeeze. She jerks her chin in the direction of the woods behind the house. "My mother is probably buried back there. Along with who knows how many babies."

She turns her gaze on me. "I know you want kids. And despite my...complicated feelings about family, I want them, too. But I will not be my mother, Jess."

I shake my head, prepared to tell her I'd never want that for her, but she holds up her free hand. "I know you'd probably never want ten kids, and I know you're nothing like my father. I only mean, I don't *only* want to be a mother. I don't know if I'll work in the records department forever. I don't know what I'll do, honestly. But I refuse to lose myself simply because I have a family. And I don't say this because I think that's something you'd expect of me. I think it's more a promise I'm trying to make to myself. One I hope you'll help me keep?"

I lift our joined hands to my face and kiss her palm. "I promise I will never let you lose yourself. I know simply from what you've overcome, you have the biggest spirit of anyone I know. Your perseverance is a wonder to behold, Ophelia. I know whatever you decide to do, you will crush it."

I point at the house. "You are so much more than that place ever offered you. Despite your circumstances and a million reasons you should've never made it, you did. That place isn't your cage anymore. You've been free for a long time. You're the only one who gets to determine what happens to you.

"I'm not your keeper. I'm sure as hell not your father. I will never tell you what you can or can't do. I don't ever expect you to simply agree with me. I love how quick you are to stand up for yourself and demand the respect you deserve. I expect our children—whenever and however many *we* decide to have—will be just as spirited as their mother."

Ophelia blushes and nods. "As long as they can be as kind and loyal as their father." Leaning over, she presses a kiss to my cheek and sighs before starting the car and pulling out onto the road. When she drives closer to the house, I tense and she laughs. "No worries, I don't have a molotov and I'm not parking. I'm just driving past."

CHAPTER THIRTY-THREE

OPHELIA

For all the animosity I have regarding the place I was raised, as I drive past, not slowing down, I simply feel nothing. Nothing except the dull ache of knowing my siblings are in there. Other than that, though, I feel absolutely nothing when I look at that house. It no longer holds anything for me.

Taking another familiar road just past the farm, the landscape turns a bit more urban and another half-mile has me almost to a park. *The* park. Jess looks around. "I know where we are."

"Oh?"

"Yeah. Pull in?"

"Okay." I obey and park in a spot. Over the years, they've added volleyball courts, more playground equipment, nicer bathrooms, and even a splash pad.

He climbs down from the Explorer, and I follow suit. I lock up and drop the keys in my pocket and without speaking, we join hands and head in the direction of the walking track. As it's nearly dark, the park is mostly deserted save the last few stragglers playing on the playground.

Our way is lit by short street lamps that cast an amber glow every thirty feet or so. As we walk, I think about how my entire life changed at this park. Passing a pavilion with picnic tables, I remember Angelo sitting there, whittling, while I ran. Could he see it the day things changed for me? Was it as visible to him as it felt to me? Probably not.

Walking around a bend a few minutes later with a very memorable bench, Jess halts in his steps. Unsure if it means what I think it means, I simply turn to him. "What is it?"

He blinks, recognition hitting him. "I used to come here in college."

"Really?"

Nodding, he gestures in the direction opposite of my family's farm, where the woods butt right up against the property line to the park. "I used to see this girl from class. We'd come here to study. On that bench, actually."

I nod, my heart rate picking up. "You ever do anything else on that bench?"

He huffs a laugh. "Yeah, actually. One time she—." His head snaps to me, his eyes wide.

"One time she what?" I ask, still not giving anything away, since I'm not entirely sure, even if everything points to me being right that it was Jess that night.

He swallows and searches my eyes. "It was only the once. It was late. We made out after we finished our statistics homework. Things got heated and there was no one around. She gave me head."

I lift a brow. "You thought no one was around. My chores ran late that day, so I was late to do my run."

His breath catches. "Your story. *I* was the guy? What are the fucking odds?"

I let out a light laugh. "Truthfully, I'm just glad it wasn't Flynn."

A bark of surprise laughter bursts from his mouth. "So, this whole time, you knew it was me? Did you know who I was when we met?"

I guide him over to the bench and we sit. "I mean, I didn't know who you were that night or anything, so until I showed up to look at the house, I'd only ever seen you that one time. But it was a memorable experience."

He laughs. "I guess it was. I can't believe this."

I nod. "I know. That night changed the whole trajectory of my life. Had I not seen you that night and what you were doing, I might have never begun to question things. I might have ended up exactly like my mother. And then, for weeks after we moved in together, I keep flashing back to that night. Except now, I lived with you? It was so surreal." I blush. "I'll be real honest; yours was the dick I compared all other dicks to. It's beautiful. I thought it that night and still think it."

Jess laughs. "Well, I guess it's a good thing it's not hideous; you might've had a completely different path altogether."

I sober and take his face in my hands, turning my body to face his. "Thank you for that night. I know it had nothing to do with me, but it changed my life. *You* changed my life, Jess. You still change my life; even now. You have been the best friend I could've ever asked for and I can never repay all the friendship and kindness you've shown me. I'm even more thankful for your love."

He lets his forehead fall to mine. "Thank you for being there for me. You are the best person I know, Ophelia. I'm in awe of you daily and I'm so fucking in love with you."

Tilting my head, I press my lips to his, letting my hands slide down the sides of his neck to grip his shoulders. He deepens the kiss, his arms coming to band around my waist seconds before he hauls me into his lap. Although I'm taken by surprise, I don't bother breaking the kiss and instead shift my body until I'm straddling him.

The rational part of my brain says we're in public and someone could see—the same way I saw all those years ago. But that other, more primal part of my being is more turned on than anything, especially as Jess begins to grow hard under me. And the thought of anyone walking up to see us like this; his hands skimming under the hem of my sundress, my fingers sinking into his hair as I roll my hips, has me growing wetter by the second. He groans into my mouth and digs his fingertips into my thighs and breaks our kiss.

We're both breathing hard and he blinks, as if the reality of what we're doing has begun to sink in for him. He looks around and I grip his chin to keep his eyes on mine. "Don't overthink it. You want to help me knock out another 'never'?"

His eyes go wide. "Here? Now?"

I nod and place my hand on top of his and slide it the rest of the way up my thigh and slip his fingers under the crotch of my panties. "You feel how wet I am for you already?"

He's unable to stop himself from dragging his knuckle down my pussy and I shudder with need. He closes his eyes and blows out a breath. "Jesus, Birdie. You're fucking soaked."

I nod and shift to a kneeling position on the bench. "You're not going to make me suffer like this, are you?"

He drags his top teeth over his bottom lip and examines my face, a slow smile beginning to pull at the corners of his mouth. "Does it ache?" I nod and feign a pained expression and after a final glance around, he works his shorts and boxers down just far enough to free his cock. "Well, we can't have that now. Let's see if I can't make it feel better."

I pull my panties to the side and slowly lower myself onto his dick and I moan when I'm sunk all the way down his length.

Jess's jaw clenches and he blows out a steadying breath. "Fuck, your pussy is pulsing around me."

I huff a laugh. "Sorry; this is really hot."

He grips the back of my neck and drags my mouth to his and shifts his hips, making me gasp. "Get yourself off for me, Ophelia. Right here where anyone could see." The thought makes my pussy clench, and he chuckles. "You'd love that, wouldn't you?" I roll my hips and he groans. "Fuck. I bet you'd come so hard if someone saw us like this, with my cock buried balls deep in your sweet pussy."

He thrusts up into me and I grab his shoulders for support and can't bite back a long moan. "Someone could hear you. But we both know you get off on that, too. You're close already, aren't you?"

I don't have words in this moment, because I am so very close. So close it shocks me and I can only nod. He nips at my bottom lip as he pulls one of my hands off his shoulder and guides it to my clit. "Get off. I want to feel it. I want to see it. I want anyone around to be able to hear it. You sound so fucking sexy when you come, Birdie."

As I circle my clit, it only takes another moment before I'm crying out and my body goes rigid as my orgasm slams into me. He grins. "So fucking perfect." He grips my hips and drives up into me a few final times before he groans through gritted teeth as he comes. He presses his forehead to mine as our breaths come in great huffs. Neither of us makes any effort to move. "Marry me," he says after a beat.

I blink in surprise and pull back. "What?"

"Marry me, Ophelia."

I huff a shocked laugh. "You're asking me this now? When you're still inside me?"

He grins. "Seemed like a good idea."

"We've just gotten past this huge thing with Ivy and faced

down your ex. I finally confronted my father, and we had sex in public. Don't you think that's enough for one day?" I ask, rising from his lap and righting my dress as I return to my original position on the bench.

"Exactly," he says, pulling up his shorts. "We've gone through more in the last two days than most people do in a year. We've already proven that we don't let things fester and sit." He seems to think better of his answer. "Well, that's not entirely true. I know I let myself dwell on the Ivy stuff before bringing it up to you, and I shouldn't have done that. I won't do it again."

He takes my hand in his. "I love you. I know we only just told each other that, but I've loved you since Vegas. Probably before that, if I'm honest with myself. Your strength and spirit and your compassion. Everything you've been through should've made you jaded and cynical, but you're not. And I love that about you. I want to love it about you forever. When you left, I knew before you were even out of the driveway I never wanted to experience that again. It gutted me. And not that I didn't deserve it for the way I treated you, because I did. I was terrible."

I squeeze his hand. "I forgave you for that."

He nods. "I know. But it still shouldn't have happened. Let me spend the rest of our lives making it up to you. I want to marry you and grow old with you and watch you be a wife and mother. I know your feelings are complicated about that. I will never let you forget you are more than just a wife and mother. I promise.

"This amazing body of yours belongs to no one but you, and every time you share it with me, I'm in awe. But it's still yours alone. And when *we* decide our family is complete, I'm more than happy to get a vasectomy so it's not something we have to worry about anymore. I mean, really, it's the least I can do."

I let out a soft laugh. "You're something else, you know that?"

One of his brows tics up. "That's not a no."

I shake my head. "No, it's not a no. It's a take-me-home-and-convince-me."

He grins. "Oh. Well then, I'll have you know, I can be very convincing." Standing, he tugs me up from the bench and pulls me into his side. "I can *convince* you all night, if you want."

"I look forward to it."

EPILOGUE

OPHELIA — FIVE YEARS LATER

"Mommy, your phone is ringing," Blair hollers from the kitchen where she and Jess are making cookies.

Knowing it will take me a while to get off the couch with a big as I am, I nod. "Okay, can you go grab it for me?" She hops off the stool and runs back toward the bedroom. Jess walks over to help me up. "I envy her agility," I say with a sigh.

He laughs. "She's four. She's a lot more agile than both of us these days. A few more weeks and you'll be mostly back to your old self."

I arch my back and shift my hips. "Six weeks. And I'm not sure I'll ever be back to my old self. This kid is huge and still not done growing. All she does is push on my bladder. Besides, I'm gonna be taking care of a newborn, a preschooler, and a husband recovering from a vasectomy."

"I'll be fine. Plus, Mom will be around a lot during those first couple of weeks. We'll have help."

"Here, Mommy." Blair extends my still ringing phone in my direction.

I take it and don't recognize the number, but swipe my finger across the screen. "Hello?"

"Ophelia?"

My heart lurches and my breath catches. "Lavinia?" Jess perks up beside me, and I press the phone harder to my ear. "Livie, is that you?"

"Yeah. Um, can you come get me? Please?"

I don't think; I just start moving. "Where are you? I'm coming."

"I'm at a gas station in Loudon." The sound changes and she asks someone for the address before coming back on the line. She gives me the address and I'm trying with great difficulty to stay calm.

Somewhere in my mind, it registers that Jess is pulling out his phone and ushering Blair into her coat and shoes and turning off the oven, but I can only focus on Lavinia's words. "Okay, I'm coming. Stay right there. I'll be there in about twenty minutes."

"Please hurry; I can't go back."

"Okay, I'm coming," I repeat. "Lock yourself in the bathroom if you need to. I promise, I'll be right there."

"Alright. Thank you." She disconnects the call and I stare down at my phone in disbelief.

Jess's hand lands on my shoulder and it breaks me out of my trance. "Come on; I already talked to Mom. We'll drop Blair on the way."

Just over twenty minutes later, we're pulling in at the gas station and Jess goes to turn off the engine and I still the movement. "Keep it running. She sounded terrified. I'm not sure what's happened, but we might have to get away fast. Stay here?"

He nods and I haul myself out of the car and make my way into the store and bypass the register and walk straight back to the bathrooms. I enter the women's restroom and peek under the stalls. "Lavinia? It's me, Ophelia."

The door to one stall opens and I'm shocked when I see my sister. She's barefoot and in a long nightgown, her dark hair in a long braid over one shoulder. Her feet and the hem of her gown are caked in mud and she throws herself in my arms, mindful of my belly. She's trembling in obvious terror and I simply hold her for a moment. "You're safe now. No one's gonna hurt you."

She pulls back. "We have to go. Now. Please?"

I nod, my chest aching at the look of panic in her eyes. "Okay. Jess is in the car, he kept it running."

"A man?" Her tone conveys how scared she is and she begins to shake harder.

"It's okay. He's my husband. He's good."

"He's not like Daddy?"

I shake my head. "He's nothing like him. He's wonderful. I promise. He's not gonna hurt you."

After a moment of consideration, she nods and I tug her out of the bathroom. She looks around, obviously worried about someone but I simply pull her along and out to the car. I deposit her in the backseat before climbing in the front. "Go," I tell Jess and he peels out of the parking lot.

She doesn't speak the entire drive home and when we pull into the garage, Jess turns to me. "I'll go start her a bath."

"Okay, and find some sweatpants and a tee shirt for her to wear? I'm not sure any of my stuff will fit her."

"You've got it." He sets off and I gingerly climb out of the car and open Lavinia's door.

"Come on, Livie; we're here."

She blinks, as if coming out of a trance and steps out of the backseat. "This is your house?"

I nod, taking her hand in mine. "Yeah. Mine and Jess and Blair's."

"Who's Blair?"

I smile. "Your niece. She's with Jess's mom right now. You can meet her tomorrow."

She nods as we walk into the house. "And you're gonna have another baby?"

"Yeah. In about six weeks. And then I'll have my body back, thank goodness."

She stops and turns to me. "Are you happy, Ophelia?"

I feel my smile stretch even wider. "Happier than I have any right to be."

"Do you regret leaving?"

"No. I regret I had to leave all of you, but no. My life is good."

"Okay. I'm never going back."

I give her hand a squeeze. "You never have to. You never have to do anything you don't want to do ever again."

"Good."

Jess comes out of the bathroom. "The bath is ready."

I nod and turn back to Lavinia. "Are you hurt? Do you need to be checked out? Jess used to be a nurse. He works at a hospital."

She shakes her head quickly. "No. I'm fine."

But I don't believe her, not with the look of fear that flashed in her eyes when I asked if she wanted to be checked out and something twists in my gut. "Okay. Well, you go relax and get cleaned up. We'll get you some clothes. It'll be pants and I'm sorry about that, but we can go tomorrow and get some things you'll be more comfortable in, okay?"

She nods, her shoulders slumping and I give her hand one final squeeze before dropping it. "We'll get the guest bedroom ready for you. You're safe now, okay?"

"Thank you, Ophelia." She doesn't even spare a glance at

Jess as she walks into the bathroom and closes and locks the door.

I don't even feel the tears until Jess swipes them off my cheeks. "It's okay, Birdie. She's safe now."

I look up at him. "What the fuck happened to her?" I ask in a whisper, not wanting Lavinia to overhear. "She's terrified. What would have made her leave barefoot and in a nightgown?"

He shrugs. "I don't know. Maybe you'll be able to find out."

"I know we haven't talked about this, but I hope it's okay with you if she stays."

His expression softens. "Of course. For as long as she needs. Isn't this what you always hoped for? That she or Ajax or Edgar would reach out and you'd be able to help them? It's one of the reasons we moved into a bigger house. So we'd always have a place for anyone who might need us."

I sigh and nod. "Thank you for still being the best man I know, Jess Tate."

"Nothing to thank me for. Come on, let's make sure the guest room is ready and then you need to get off your feet. Your ankles are stating to swell."

"I'm fine."

"Yeah, and I intend to keep it that way. You've had an exciting evening."

I snort a laugh. "That's the understatement of the century. If I weren't pregnant, I'd be dragging out the jar of moonshine right about now."

He tilts his head in the direction of the bathroom door. "Might not be a bad idea for her to have a drink. Something to help her sleep?"

I shake my head. "She won't drink it, I don't think. Not yet. She's gonna have to deconstruct. It's gonna take time. Probably years. She was in it longer than I was."

"Well, she's taken the first step. She'll get there. Just like you did. At least she's gonna have you to help guide her."

I nod and look over at the bathroom door and vow to myself that Lavinia won't ever have to feel the terror she does right now, ever again. And someday, I hope she can be as happy as I am.

ALSO BY RACHAEL OGLE

Until Duet

Until August (Until Book 1)

Until Forever (Until Book 2)

Until August and onto Forever (Until Books 1 & 2)

Summer Lovin' Series

Fake it Till You Fall (Summer Lovin' Book 1)

Falling into Forever (Summer Lovin' Book 2)

Fake it to Forever (Summer Lovin' Books 1 & 2)

Knox County Series

My Ada Mae (Knox County Book 1)

Not Your Girl (Knox County Book 2)

ABOUT THE AUTHOR

For as long as she can remember, Rachael has been a voracious reader. At the age of eleven, she discovered her grandmother's stash of clench-cover romance novels and she was forever changed. A lover of many, many fictional men and one very non-fictional one, she strives to write real and emotional characters who always get their happily ever after. Rachael lives in East Tennessee with her husband and two sons on their family farm. When she's not tackling her endless TBR, she can be found drinking all the coffee in existence.